REBORN

LELA ROBICHAUX

REBORN

To my family who have supported me through this journey; especially my mother, whose presence is always with me and encouraging me to reach for my dreams.

ONE

Meylaran Moonshadow crept toward the darkened home, eyes adjusting to the inky surroundings. Her elven sight allowed her eyes to shift so the darkness became much like twilight. Creeping silently, she carefully made her way toward the door. A door she was sure would be locked, especially in Seaside where thieves were as common as waves on the ocean. She crouched in front of the door, closed her eyes and imagined Garrin mirroring her movements at the front of the home.

Taking a steadying breath, she ran her hand over the rough wood and came to the cold metal of the lock. From her left boot, she pulled a small pouch. Her deft fingers had it open within seconds and she was selecting the slender tool she would need to conquer this obstacle. Quiet as a whisper, she slipped it into the lock and began to move the rod until she felt the hook at the end catch. *Careful now*. She jerked it to her right and heard the distinctive "snick" of the mechanism. A half-hearted grin that only turned up one side of her mouth spread across her mysterious face. She brushed a stray lock of her auburn hair behind a slightly pointed ear. Only half her heritage was elven but it lent her a beauty that was uncommon in the human race. Mingled with her mother's human inheritance, it gave her an unusual and exotic appearance.

The thudding of her heart and the grip of her insides calmed. She would never love this as much as Garrin. She didn't enjoy this part of her chosen profession. *Well, it puts food in my stomach and a roof over my head*, she thought and turned the handle, pushing the door inward. Moving in a crouch she entered the house, stopping just inside for her eyesight to adjust once again to the changing darkness.

She let her other senses reach out to her surroundings. She heard the skittering of tiny feet rush from one end of the room to the other. Unmistakably a rodent searching for its next meal. She inhaled through her nose and was assailed by a mixture of smells - different herbs, oil, flour, the clean smell of soap and a whiff of fresh water. *Kitchen.* As she moved her eyes around the room, shapes formed and became recognizable. There was a table to her left and a counter than ran the length of the wall on the right.

Mey's thoughts again turned to Garrin. He would be in the front of the house. The plan was for each to enter at a different point and make their way toward one another in the center as they searched for the mask. All they had was a description. She had no idea why the mask was so important, but the price was right and it would keep her and Garrin fed and housed for the next month. When the mage approached them with the prospect of locating and obtaining the magical mask, the look in Garrin's eye had told her this was most certainly their next project.

She almost laughed aloud as she thought of how much Garrin enjoyed these expeditions. He was like a child anticipating gifts at a lifeday celebration. If he had his way, they would support themselves on nothing but sneaking into people's homes and happening upon their most luxurious belongings.

With a shake of her head, she moved further into the room. The cupboards and shelves that lined the wall to her right looked like a good place to begin. She searched very quickly and very thoroughly. All the obvious places yielded nothing. She moved on to the less obvious; looking in jars filled with flour, sugar and dried herbs. A muffled thud froze her instantly. Her heart hammered as she frantically squinted into the darkness.

Damn, Garrin, could you be any clumsier?

Slowly replacing the jar on a low shelf, Mey moved toward the doorway leading into the next room.

She recognized the shape of a large table, chairs pushed closely around it. The walls were covered with tapestries and paintings. Except for the front wall. This entire wall was lined with rows of shelves holding every kind of book she could have imagined. Her eyes widened slightly. Curiosity threatened to overwhelm her but she reigned herself in and deliberately started searching the opposite wall where the largest painting, an old woman in black, hung.

Checking behind all the paintings, under all the chairs and beneath the table, she found naught. Nothing but papers hidden in the secret drawers and cubbies the owner probably thought were cleverly concealed. She paused before the bookshelves, breathing in the musty smell of the books.

Sharp memories of her father stabbed at her; reading to her at night while she fought sleep, longing to hear his voice make the music of the words come alive and dance in her mind. Scowling at the tear rising to sting her eye, she forced the memory back and focused on the job at hand.

A sudden movement in her peripheral vision disturbed her from her reverie. Just a shadow. *Jumpy tonight, eh, Moonshadow?* She reprimanded herself silently.

Garrin was being awfully inept tonight; he wasn't keeping it very subtle. She sighed softly, returning her attention to the bookshelf. Her fingers played lightly over the spines of the books, feeling the raised lettering and leather bindings covering each one. She scanned the titles: *Life on Cantor: An Adventurer's Guide, The Power of Herbs, Disguises for Every Occasion.* She paused. What would a flour merchant need with disguises? Perhaps it was just a hobby, but the book stood out and not just because of its title. It was the largest book on this shelf. She pulled it from its spot.

The cover was plain, nothing ornate. But when she opened it, excitement surged from her fingertips all the way through her body like a sudden bolt of lightning. The pages had been cut away and made hollow. Inside sat a small golden mask; or rather, golden-*plated.* The mask itself was made from cloth, covered with sheets of thinly hammered gold, brightly painted etchings lining the edge. They could have been words, but none that Mey had ever seen. A faintly familiar and annoying tug at her mind quickly let her know this item had magical properties.

This was what they had come for. Her stomach leapt. She quickly took the mask and replaced the book exactly where she had found it. She placed the mask into a small wooden box given to them by the mage and slid it into her tunic. She made her way back through the kitchen to the door she had entered. She slipped out quietly, took the lock-pick from her boot and made sure the lock was secure once again. Everything as it was. She made her way around the side of the home, forcing herself to take slow, steady steps.

Keeping her eyes on her feet, she ran right into something very solid. Biting her lip to hold back the scream that would have escaped otherwise, she looked up. Realizing immediately who it was, her racing heart returned to normal and anger quickly took over.

"Damnit, Garrin!" she whispered as she slapped him lightly. "What are you doing? You've been awfully clumsy tonight!"

"What? How am I clumsy? *I* was looking where I was going!"

She scowled at him, green eyes sparkling. "You know what I mean. All that noise inside and then letting me see you moving about. What were you trying to do, wake the dead? I've got the mask, by the way," she added, pulling it from her tunic to show him.

Elation overtook him and he reached for the thin box. "Wait." A look of confusion passed over his features. "I never made it inside. The lock – I couldn't spring it…" He let the sentence trail off as he grasped the box. Sudden understanding crossed his face and his eyes widened as he seemed to focus on something behind her.

Mey turned, and not a moment too soon. Slinking up from behind were two men. As soon as they realized they'd been spotted, they rushed at Mey and Garrin. With only a split second to make a decision, Garrin shoved the box into his own tunic and grabbed Mey's arm. He pulled her out of the way just as the men jumped at the spot where they had previously been standing. Two more dark and looming figures appeared around the corner of the house where Garrin had been.

With two simple words, "Artisan's Corner," Garrin's plan was made clear. They were splitting up. Mey nodded once and took off without hesitation. She could hear Garrin's heavy footfalls heading the opposite direction. She looked back after a few seconds and saw two of the men following her. She quickly assessed the situation. The others must have taken after Garrin. She crossed behind a row of houses, trying to stay in the shadows as she ran.

She could still hear her pursuers, but mostly she could *feel* them, closing the gap she had put between them with her initial sprint.

She began to silently curse herself for not seeing this coming. The item the mage wanted was valuable. Any magical artifact would fetch a pretty copper as well as unwanted attention. Why had they not taken more care to ensure they were not followed? The tug of power within the mask wasn't very strong, but it was there and Mey knew she couldn't always trust her inherited instincts. They had been wrong before. The seeds of wonder at what it was used for and why the mage wanted it sprouted.

She came out of the last row of homes into the market. There was more open space here; but many more shadows to play with. The larger, permanent carts were covered for the night. Surrounded on each side by buildings that housed the loftier shops, the market formed a square within the middle of the open courtyard. She found the cart where the baker sold his cakes and breads. Slipping behind the cart; she caught her breath while she scanned the open area. In about three heartbeats, two men emerged from the same alley she had just left. She quieted her breathing and tried to get a better view of them. No one she recognized, that was for sure. They quickly looked around and then headed for the street that would lead them straight to the docks. Mey waited at least ten minutes before she moved. She slowly uncurled from the crouch in which she had been frozen, slid around the cart and out into the opening. Staying low, she sprinted across the clearing to the street the men had taken. She listened for several seconds before following.

Briefly, she wondered about Garrin and how he had fared with the men who were after him, but the thought came and went quickly. She had no need to worry for him; Garrin could take care of himself better than most. She made her way to the dockside where a number of taverns lined the walk. Heading right for the loudest, rowdiest, and roughest looking building along the row, she kept alert to her surroundings. She entered the Artisan's Corner inconspicuously and made her way to a back table where she could fit herself into the shadows. She let her eyes scan the room. Garrin was not there yet. She settled back into the chair to wait.

****

Mey looked up from her drink for the fifth time as the door of the tavern opened again. She smiled when she saw Garrin enter. He gazed around the room quickly, spotted her and headed her direction.

"You still have it?" she asked, anxious to know if the object they had obtained for their benefactor was safe.

Garrin pulled the small, flat box from inside his tunic. His grin was as big as hers and took up his whole face, causing small wrinkle lines to show around his brown eyes. "I think I lost those grubby dock-crawlers that were following us. When we leave here, you should carry the mask just in case; throw them off if they decide to come after us again."

Mey opened the box and examined the mask as Garrin tried to gain the serving girl's attention to order himself a drink. "I wonder what's so special about this, besides it being worth more than a handful of coin. That mage sure was bent on having it." Laying the mask gently inside the crude case once again, the two thieves leaned over it blocking out prying eyes.

"Who knows? Mages have strange ways. They find value in other people's every-day junk," Garrin said offhandedly. He had no curiosity about the things he was commissioned to retrieve. He just wanted to get paid. Mey, on the other hand, felt a power within the piece and wanted to know more: what it did, why it was created, and to whom had it belonged along the way. She got that curious nature from her father.

Her father, being an elf, had an unending curiosity – especially about magical power. Elves had an innate ability to detect and discern properties of magic. Of course, her own ability wasn't as strong; she was only a half-breed, her elven blood diluted by her mother's human contribution.

She quickly put the mask away as the bar maid approached. As always, Garrin asked for mead and settled back in his chair to pass the time before they continued on to meet their employer. He threw one leg up on the chair next to him to deter uninvited guests and began peeling off his black leather gloves.

"Sounds like Big Jo's looking for a wager over there." Garrin nodded toward the big man near the front of the establishment. Jo's booming voice carried over the entire room, trying to find a taker for a game of throwing daggers. A light smile touched Mey's lips.

"That would just be cruel, now, Garrin. I've set the record straight so many times with him. I can, and have, beat him while blindfolded. It would be plain mean to take his money like that."

Garrin laughed out loud, filling the room with his light-hearted spirit. Many eyes turned toward them, including Big Jo's. The hulking tower of a man glowered at them but quickly turned away. Obviously, he did not care to be humiliated again.

Mey and Garrin chuckled together, each remembering times she had shamelessly outdone herself to beat the bigger man in throwing daggers. Garrin suddenly sprang from his chair and called out, "Jo, we'll take your wager!" He winked at Mey and whispered so only she could hear. "It's just the right amount of time we need to shake our friends. A quick game and then we leave," he assured her before she could protest.

Shrugging, Mey lifted herself from her chair and stood next to Garrin, the smile never leaving her face. Her hands moved in what looked like a nervous attempt to loosen her joints. In actuality, she was using the hand-language Garrin had taught her years ago to tell him just what she thought of Big Jo and his dagger-throwing contest. Garrin laughed out loud again when he caught what she was saying.

"This had better be worth my time, Jo," Mey said as she strolled over to where the big man stood. "Have you been practicing?"

"You just throw daggers, lady." Jo was a lumbering hulk of a man with a stench to match. "We hit the target, there," he said, pointing to the circles marked on the far wall. "Best, three out of four."

"Sure. What's the wager?"

"Ten gold coins."

With a glance back at Garrin, Mey sighed and pulled a dagger from the belt at her waist. She knew that ten gold was probably all the money Jo had. She felt the heft of the dagger in her hand. The balance was a bit off, but she knew this dagger well. Shifting her weight to compensate, she flung the dagger forward with only the slightest flick of her wrist. The movement was so fast that had you not been watching, you would have missed it all together. The dagger hit dead center of the inner ring of circles. Mey bowed at the waist as she backed away from the line marked on the floor.

Jo grimaced slightly as he moved in to place. He drew a deep breath and let the dagger in his hand fly. His own throw landed one ring outside of center. Mey lifted an eyebrow as she shot another glance in Garrin's direction. Her fingers made a series of movements. Garrin had long ago come up with this way to communicate between only the two of them.

So he has been practicing! her fingers flashed. Garrin chuckled.

The next series of throws went to Mey's favor as well. No one had ever beaten her before besides Garrin and she had surpassed him years ago. As the third round came about, Garrin stepped forward.

"Why don't we up the stakes, Jo? You've come very close on the first two throws. I think the last set should be two daggers thrown." Garrin loved to show off Mey's talent to its fullest; he was like a proud father. Mey rolled her eyes but didn't object. That would be taking the wind out of Garrin's sails and she couldn't do that.

Jo's eyes flicked between the two of them, suspicion evident on his small features. Sweat broke out in tiny beads across his forehead and trickled down his temple. He nodded somewhat reluctantly.

Mey stepped up to the line once more. She focused on the two separate circles drawn on the wall ahead of her. She let out a long, slow breath as she judged the distance between the two and then her own distance away from them. She slipped two daggers from her bandolier and held them in her right hand. Moving the hilts carefully between her fingers, she calculated for the slight difference of heaviness in the two weapons. As quick as a snake, she snapped her wrist and the two daggers flew from her light grasp and thudded heavily into the wall ahead. All eyes turned to the wall, where the two daggers stuck, one in each circle, dead center.

Jo's face had turned red as a beet, hands clenched by his side. Mey just shook her head; it ended much the same each time. Garrin sauntered over to Jo and held his hand out in expectation. Jo reached into his pouch and handed over a handful of coins. Mey was surprised that he actually had the coin and briefly wondered where it had come from. She shrugged it off; it wasn't her business what people did to survive around here.

She moved closer to Garrin. "I think we need to make our exit. The mage awaits us and we're losing moonlight."

"Sure, kid." He flipped a coin toward Big Jo. "I just can't leave you empty handed," he said with a grin.

Mey rolled her eyes. He was so dramatic sometimes, but she still smiled at how he called her 'kid'. She was about thirty years his elder. With the elven blood that ran in her veins, she would outlive him by about eighty years. A pang of sadness at this thought gripped her chest. She pulled on his arm to get him moving.

As they exited, Garrin managed to slip the waitress three of the gold coins they had just acquired. Once outside, he was all business, bringing himself back to the job at hand and forgetting all that had transpired inside the tavern. His eyes were scanning their surroundings.

"I think we should split up again."

Mey nodded. "I was thinking the same." She switched to hand signals. *Anyone watching would expect you to have it.*

Garrin signaled back. *You head toward the docks, I'll move through town for a bit. If I'm not there in twenty minutes, go ahead and collect.* He gave her his most genuine smile and winked. "Meet me back here if you finish up before I do." He turned and slipped around the building. She blinked only once and then she could no longer see him.

Sighing, she turned to make her way toward the dockside. An inkling of fear crept up from the depths of her insides. She swallowed hard and pushed it back down. The feeling was gone before she had a chance to wonder at where it had come from.

TWO

The wait was excruciating but wait she did. She moved along the dock until she found the designated spot: third post from the intake building, then twenty paces out.

"I'll take my wares." The words startled her.

Not letting the mage know he had startled her, she lifted an eyebrow and crossed her arms in front of her chest. "I'll take my money."

Mage and thief stared at one another for a moment, each challenging the other. A smile slowly cracked the stone features of the mage. "Of course." He reached within his tunic and pulled out a pouch. It jingled as he handed it over. Mey took it as she held out the box containing the mask with her other hand. As soon as his fingers brushed hers, she felt a sensation of falling. The familiar surroundings of salty air and lapping waves seemed to melt away, revealing someplace not quite as comfortable; an alleyway. The litter and stink of rotting food was as real as the beating of her heart. She looked around, frantically scanning the surroundings. There were people; lots of them. They passed and crowded her, but never looked at or acknowledged her presence, as if she didn't even exist. A soft, whispering voice broke into her mind. "Your friend looks to be in some trouble."

Her head snapped around and she scanned the crowd. In the middle of the fray, she saw Garrin's face. Strong will and determination showed in his set jaw and hardened eyes. He held his sword in a defensive stance. *Too many*, she thought. *There are too many of them!* She tried to move forward, to reach her friend and offer some aid. She was held fast. She fought to raise her leg but it was as if someone were holding her feet firmly in place. "NO!" she screamed, but nothing sounded in the mass of people around her.

A quiet voice sounded in her mind. "You cannot do anything. What you are witnessing has already taken place. There is no preventing what has already passed."

Her eyes widened as she took in what was transpiring. They were going to kill him! She fought against the vision with every fiber of her being. *A trick!* she told herself. *A lie! This isn't real!* "Garrin…Garrin, can you hear me?" But the scene played on. Massive men drew closer to the slight figure, now backed against the wall. Fierce eyes darted from one to the next, defying them, daring them to try something. Garrin shifted from foot to foot, balancing himself and measuring the odds. As quick as lightning, he sprung upward, grasping a low eave and heaving himself over to jump clear of the men. Mey's heart leapt with him.

Time seemed to slow as she watched the men jab, slash and reach for Garrin as he passed over them. As he landed, one of the men turned and Garrin's eyes went wide. A range of emotions passed over his features: pain, fear, regret, pride, anger. Mey let out an anguished cry; the sound breaking the rapt silence between the mage and herself. Screaming, she turned toward the voice in her ear and forced all of her hatred and anger at the mage. He flew back with the force of the blow, surprise evident on his face. She closed her eyes, and the sensation of falling returned. Everything seemed to swim together.

When she opened her eyes, they were on the dock once again. She heard a muffled grunt as the mage struggled to his knees and finally to his feet. His hands were covering his head and he shook it frantically to clear it.

Mey was vaguely aware of his footsteps cautiously approaching. She felt him lean in to her and heard the fierce whisper of his voice. "Where did you learn to do *that*?"

Ignoring his question, she asked her own. "Why? Why show me? To what purpose?"

"I don't choose the vision."

"It's not real," she said through clenched teeth, ignoring his cryptic response.

"Yes, it is real." He stepped in front of her. "Now, how did you do that? How did you throw me out of my own spell? How?" She turned her green eyes toward him then. He shuddered.

"I don't know!" She spat the words at him. "And even if I did, I would die with that knowledge rather than reveal it to you!"

He dropped his hand and as he looked into her eyes, a spark flared there. The tiniest bit of light, but it was there! He looked closer at her face. Beautiful, haunting, frightening. He took a step back. "The alleyway - behind the Twisted Twig."

Mey blinked. The spark disappeared, almost as if it were never there. She stared at the mage for only a moment longer, and then she was gone. He followed her movement with his eyes, and wondered to himself. He marveled at the feeling that gripped his heart. *She's the one*. It frightened him.

****

Mey ran through the streets, heedless of anyone or anything. The only thing going through her mind was Garrin. Was it true? He was the closest thing to family she had. Emotions hung on the fringes of her heart, threatening to overtake her at any moment. She fought them and pushed them away. After all, she wasn't certain yet.

She slowed as she approached the entry to the alleyway. There she stopped and listened. Not a sound; not even the usual sounds of rodents and animals prowling the trash at the back of the shops. Peering in as far as she could, Mey strained to see something, anything. Was that something on the ground? She blinked and tried to focus. Fear gripped her stomach and twisted it so tight she nearly lost her footing. Hesitantly she entered the shadows, keeping enough presence of mind to blend herself into her surroundings, keeping as quiet as possible.

Tears started to form in her eyes as she approached the dark stain. Her heart was telling her it wasn't Garrin's blood, but her mind was insisting on accepting the reality of the mage's vision. She looked down. There were rust-colored spots on a canvas that was draped off to the far side of the building. She choked back a sob that threatened to give her away to anything or anyone that might be nearby. With shaking hands, she reached down to move the cloth aside. As the cloth slid slowly away, she closed her eyes, readying herself for what she would reveal. She opened her eyes and squared her stance, pulling strength from the memory of his voice. She looked down. Nothing but trash. A gasp escaped her, as if all the wind had been knocked from her lungs.

Quietly, she knelt and reached out. She touched the dark stain on the cobbled ground and mouthed his name, "Garrin." She let the tears come. She couldn't deny what was right there in front of her face. They must have dragged him off, planning to dump his body unceremoniously in a place no one would ever find. He didn't deserve that, not Garrin – the brother she never had. She let her wounded heart open and spill forth the poisonous emotions that had been held at bay. She bowed her head and sobbed silently for a very long time. All the questions that would go unanswered ran through her mind, along with all the promises and all the dreams that had gone unnoticed by the fates. Her heart longed for him to embrace her with his strong, comforting arms. That she would never again feel his comforting embrace cut the wound deeper.

Mey stood, turned and walked from the alley, not once looking back. She walked away from the only life she was comfortable with, striding slowly into the unknown future. Losing Garrin was like losing her father all over again. Of course, she wasn't entirely sure if her father was truly lost. She stopped before stepping into the street beyond. She made a silent vow then and there to recover at least part of all she had lost in her lifetime. If she couldn't find her father, she would at least piece together his legacy. The only thing in this world that was left to her to claim.

****

Mey thought about how Garrin's body *should* be burned on a pyre outside the city. Some of the races still believed in putting people in the earth after death. She always honored her elven heritage in the belief that once dead, the body belonged not only to the earth, but to the sky, the sun, the wind, and the water. Burning the body released the soul so that it might fly to every end of the world and become part of all that exists. Garrin wouldn't have minded. He'd always said that after he was dead, he wouldn't care.

She felt lost with him gone. They had been together for so long now that she couldn't really remember a time without him. But there *had* been a time without him. A very long time; after all she was eighty years old. Nearly twenty years with Garrin was a drop in the bucket when put in terms of elven life. She did not age as slowly as full elves, but she aged slower than humans. She always knew she would outlive Garrin, but this was too soon.

The days swam by endlessly and the nights only brought loneliness. It seemed an eternity had passed in the few days after losing Garrin. Mey stayed in a small room above a tavern that looked as though it would tumble to the ground with one good gust of wind. A place Garrin had proffered. She spent most of her time in the large open room downstairs that served as the tavern's common room. She watched the rabble that drifted in and out, saw the seedy dealings pass between them, heard the contracts made on some poor soul's life and more than once was approached by the dirty, crude and foul-smelling patron who thought her an easy target for a night's romp. For the most part, she sent them on their way with harsh words and threats of a short life if the inquiry were to go any further.

There was an unlucky one, however. He had looked a lot like one of the men that had followed her and Garrin that night. Suddenly, revenge seemed very sweet. She played into his hands, letting him think he was going to enjoy a night of special attention. She caressed his stinking face and kissed his foul mouth without ever once pulling away; leading him the whole time to believe she was only there for one purpose.

She took him up to her room. He was all too eager and full of the strong spirits that this place served. They entered the room and she was quick to lock the door behind them. She turned and smiled at him. If he could have guessed what was behind the smile, he would have run as fast as he could and very far away.

****

A couple of weeks later, as she sat, sipping, but not really tasting, the wine in front of her past events of her childhood plagued her. Time went on and eventually she found herself thinking of the mage. An image of him burned into her memory; the eyes, crystal blue, bluer than any she had ever before seen, haunted her. She saw truth in those eyes. A truth Mey wasn't so sure she was ready for.

Lost in her reverie, a voice, vaguely familiar, tore her from her thoughts and she shuddered. "The elf, Moonshadow. Where is she?" She looked to her right, where the voice seemed to have come from and instinctively hunched further back in the shadows. No one was there. In fact, no one was within more than ten or so strides from where she sat. She listened more intently and focused on the voice. "I have business to discuss with her. I know she's here. Tell me where I can find her."

Puzzlement clouded Mey's face. She had no business with anyone. In fact, the only job she had taken since Garrin's death two weeks earlier was petty thievery. Lifting a purse here and there, acquiring a wanted item for someone who claimed it was his to begin with; just enough to get her by. The last of those had been days ago. She had spoken to no one else of any business.

A strange sensation crept into Mey's head. Twisting and writhing its way deeper into her mind. She pushed at it with a force that seemed to rise within her.

The voice resounded in her mind as she tried to determine how she knew it and from which direction it had come. She scanned the room with keen eyes, looking for its source. Then she saw him. Her eyes narrowed and anger began to bubble deep within. She let the energy of that anger fill her. As if she had tapped him on the shoulder, the mage turned, with some confusion, and looked directly at her. The smile that spread across his face was as repulsive as it was intriguing. "Ah, I have found you." As she locked onto his gaze, she realized this time the voice was in her mind. She let out a gasp of surprise. Only one other had communicated with her this way, and he was miles away, in Orphana, the elven homeland in the south. The mage's smile twisted further upward with the indication that he knew the thoughts in her mind.

He began walking toward her, slowly, and with purpose. Mey instinctively placed a hand on the hilt of a dagger. She felt trapped, like an animal snared. Her mind fought desperately to free itself.

As suddenly as it started, she felt him let go. When she looked up, he was sitting in front of her.

He peered intently into her eyes, his face alight with a mix of both surprise and curiosity. "Interesting," he murmured. "You have once again managed to break the bond between myself and my spell. And the light was brighter this time."

"What light? What do you want from me? You got your precious mask," she said. "Why do you keep following me?"

He looked at her, as if only just noticing where he was. "Oh, yes. I sought you out because I need your help."

"I want nothing more to do with you. Leave me alone!" Mey started to stand, but quicker than the eye could trace, his hand snaked out and held her arm fast. She froze. The touch set every nerve ending in her body on fire. She narrowed her eyes and glared at him. "Remove your hand."

He held her a moment longer, searching her face. Slowly, he released his grip and let go of her arm. "Let us start again. Please…sit. I will explain."

Mey straightened and looked at him warily. She spoke quietly. "I don't know what power this is that you possess. I don't trust it. A very dear friend of mine is dead because of a job *you* commissioned. I will promise only to *listen* to your proposal." She sat back down in the chair across from him and gestured for him to continue.

He was silent for a moment. "My name is Thom Uray. I was sent from the Mage's Circle to locate the person who can collect the Heartstone of the Idylic; the essence of dragonkind that the world is so desperately missing. It is rumored that creation itself is caught in the facets of its surface. Since time began, the Idylic was kept with the creatures of dragonkind. These creatures were entrusted, by the creators, with the safe-keeping and well-being of the world. Throughout history, one has been designated to sit and keep watch--"

"I know the history of the world," Mey interrupted. "Do you have a point or am I subject to continue the studies I left behind as a child?"

"Very well. When the last Keeper was forced from this world, she shattered the Idylic and scattered its pieces to the far corners. Through the years, the Mage's Circle has dedicated itself to preserving the history of dragons. The prophecy says that one day, one of their own lineage will be recruited to find the lost Heartstone and bring them back together. This chosen one has the power of the dragons."

"So what do you need my help with? I am no mage. And I have never been privy to anything the Mage's Circle has done before." Bitter sarcasm dripped from her words like acid.

"Before the Keeper left our world, she forced the only true dragon left here to make a choice. It is said that this dragon had fallen in love with an elf. She was given the choice to be with the man she loved and become tied to this world in mortal form or to join her kindred and leave this world forever. The dragon chose a life with her elven love. The power of her ancestors has lived on in her line."

"Mage, you have five more seconds to get around to what this has to do with me. You have done nothing but rant of the torn Idylic and the choices of a race that died out centuries ago. If this was entrusted to the Mage's Circle, what use is this to me?" Mey's eyes held the warning that if a point was not reached soon, the mage may very well meet the creators he spoke of.

The mage smiled as he continued. "No one has encountered dragonkind for hundreds of years. Not until, on a dock, several nights ago, a half-elven thief used the power of her ancestors to break a mage's spell."

Mey's eyes widened with every word he spoke. The realization that he was speaking of her took a moment to register. When it fully did, the ridiculousness of his statement struck her. She began to chuckle. The laughter hit her with such force, she couldn't stop. It felt good. All the pain, the frustrations, the lack of sleep in the past few weeks, came out in that laugh. She let it go, let it cleanse her spirit of all the negative presences. Tears sprung to her eyes and between gasps, she managed to speak. "You can't possibly…you think I…"

The stricken look on the mage's face made her laugh harder. *He actually believes this!* she thought in wonder. People were beginning to turn and look their way.

"Please," he hissed, "you are attracting unwanted attention!"

But she couldn't stop. She hadn't felt this much like herself in days. She continued to laugh, not even attempting to stop it. Anger boiled to the surface of the mage's eyes. They flared and color blossomed in his cheeks. He stood, shoving the chair back without heed to anyone behind him.

"I am glad you find this all so amusing," he said and stood to make his way toward the door.

Mey quickly tried to compose herself, wiping the tears away from her face and taking a couple of deep breaths. *Damn!* He was gone so quickly. She rushed out after him and caught sight of him a few buildings down. "Wait!" she called and started after him. The mage continued to walk on.

She caught up to him and reached out to grab his arm. He stopped, but did not turn. Mey took a second to catch her breath, then addressed him. "I'm sorry. It is hard for me to comprehend. I cannot believe anything special belongs exclusively to me. I don't mean to offend."

The mage was silent. Slowly, he turned and regarded her thoughtfully. "The Mage's Circle will pay generously. More generously than you've known, I'm sure." There was no mistaking the sarcasm in his words.

"What is required of me?"

"Travel across Cantor, through the Barren-Lands and into the Faery Isles. That is where the Circle believes the Heartstone has been located. Happenings there indicate as much. I will travel with you, along with others we will be required to recruit. A journey of several months, at least."

Mey chewed her lip. Nothing was holding her here, after all. Not anymore. She looked around her at the ramshackle buildings; her home for the better part of her life. *Odd. It doesn't even feel the same*. She thought of Garrin; imagined the excitement she would have seen in his face at the prospect of getting away from this place. A smile played at her lips. She thought of her father. The last image of him fading a little more as time passed. Finally, she looked at the mage. He was resolute in this matter. It obviously meant something to him and as much as she hated to admit it, she needed the money. She made up her mind.

"I accept."

"Very well," he said, a smile playing at the corners of his mouth. "We start preparations in a day's time. We will be ready to leave in a week."

She held out her hand to seal the deal; he hesitated, then took it.

THREE

The day before they were to leave, Mey and Thom sat idly, sipping spiced wine. They had spent the days searching for seasoned adventurers to travel with them. The nights were spent in debates over the magics Thom purported her to possess. He was very knowledgeable of the old dragons and told her stories that she found were much like the ones her father used to tell her when he tucked her into bed at night. They disagreed on much, but she liked him. He was genuine and struck her as honest. She trusted her gut feeling on people; she was usually right about these things.

They had gathered their traveling gear; Mey "acquiring" much of hers by her own means. They had horses, packs laden with survival tools and food, waterskins, brimming full. What they did not have were acceptable traveling companions.

The notice Thom had posted in various locales within the city had brought every low-life and retired adventurer out of hiding, hoping to obtain a semblance of wealth and notoriety; neither of which they were promising. The story was they wanted experienced traveling companions to accompany them on a journey east of the Barren Lands. Mey had argued that no one in their right minds would cross the Barren Lands. Thom had confidence in the Mage's Circle, who assured him prospects could be found in Seaside.

So they sat, Mey smug in her assumptions, Thom downcast and brooding, but not relenting faith.

"Well, we have one willing to meet us halfway," Mey pointed out. She had contacted Oboderen, her uncle and her father's only brother. He had literally jumped at the chance to see her again and to get out of Orphana where he had spent the last winter with his cousins. They had not spoken since Mey and her father had last visited the southern lands, over twenty years hence. She had been a babe really, considered young to the elven people.

Thom cut into her thoughts, "Yes, a week's journey *alone* to meet up with him. I was hoping for an escort from the beginning. You have never traveled and my own travels have been limited to the roads of magic." He finished off the glass in front of him and hailed the girl for another.

"I traveled once with my father," Mey protested. But added, "I'll concede that it has been many years and I was young." She stared off, losing herself again in thoughts of her father and the wonderful time they had on that single journey so long ago.

Thom looked at her. Sorrow and longing sparkled in the silver flecks of her eyes, making them appear to dance. She was beautiful.

What am I doing? Thom wondered. *This woman is in my charge!* He lashed himself silently and forced himself to look away. As soon as he did, he was instantly sorry in having done so.

Making its way toward them through the crowded room, with enough noise to grab even the creator's attention, was the filthiest dwarf he had ever seen. The dwarf stumbled toward them, singing loudly (and off-key) of glorious battles, dragons and ale. He stopped about midway to their table and looked around as if unaware of what he was doing. "Who is seeking a traveling companion to the Barren Lands?" he growled loudly to no one in particular.

He leaned in closely to the nearest table, peering at each person in turn. The patrons quickly pointed in their direction. The dwarf turned his grimy face and fixed his drunken stare on the half-elf and mage. He promptly fell over his own feet trying to reach them. Despite his obviously inebriated state, the dwarf was up again quickly and heading to them. Thom let a slight sigh escape him, and then straightened himself to greet the potential travel-mate. Mey did her best not to cover her nose at the offending smell that preceded the dwarf.

The dwarf positioned himself before the two and bowed unsteadily. “Durlag Rockcrusher, at yer service.” He then stood, swaying, obviously expecting something.

Mey and Thom glanced at one another, and then turned their attention to their prospective companion. Thom spoke first. “I am Thom, of the Mage’s Circle in Val. My companion, Meylaran Moonshadow.”

“Durlag Rockcrusher,” the dwarf repeated, then waited expectantly. After the brief silence that followed, he continued, “Me father helped to banish Arlien.” Again silence followed. Mey and Thom glanced at one another. When it was obvious that no recognition was forthcoming, the dwarf raised his voice. “The dragon what kept the dwarven clan Rockcrusher captive! ARLIEN!”

Taking a hint from the dwarf’s irritation, the two bobbed their heads and mumbled what would pass for delayed recognition and awe.

“Now,” continued Durlag, a smile returning to his face, “I hear you seek companions to travel the wild lands.”

The uneasy tension passing between the three was evident. To Mey’s thinking, a drunken dwarf wouldn’t be the best choice in traveling companions, but they also had no other prospects. Seeing their decision plainly before them but not willing to commit for them both, Thom spoke up first. “Uh, if you will excuse us, good dwarf, my companion and I must discuss an urgent matter alone. Please, seat yourself. We will only need a moment.”

The dwarf grunted his reply and dumped himself unceremoniously into a chair. He pulled out a flask and took a long draw from it. It was the most unusual thing Mey had seen; by way of drinking vessels, that is. It was a beautiful blue hue with swirls of white running though it – pearl, perhaps. There was intricate silver worked around the edges and on the stopper. The smell however, could have knocked down a horse. Mey caught herself thinking about what she could do with the coin something like that would fetch as Thom led her a few steps away.

“We could really use someone who knows the country,” he was saying to her. “He seems to have seen his share of fighting, as well. We need his experience.”

She glanced at the mage, trying to read the thoughts on his face. He was absently rubbing his temples. His face was a blank, as usual. She couldn't catch even a glimpse of what was rolling around behind the mask. "Fine," she said, "but I'm not about to look after his filthy backside while I'm trying to keep myself alive. If you haven't noticed, our *friend* there has a bit of an issue with keeping himself clear-headed." She wrinkled her nose as she glanced toward the dwarf, who was scratching himself in inappropriate places. The dwarf let out a belch that would knock down even the stoutest of men.

Thom's face had gone slack and his eyes took on that glazed, far-away look that told Mey he was deeply entranced in communion with his brothers of the Mage's Circle. She sighed as she waited. He suddenly looked over at her and smiled his big, lop-sided grin. "We will take the dwarf. He will be very valuable to us." Mey cocked an eyebrow to show her skepticism, but she found herself smiling back at the mage. There was a charm to this one she would definitely have to watch out for, she thought to herself.

They turned back to Durlag and Thom engaged the dwarf in conversation about his background. Mey was barely listening. She was vaguely aware that he was regaling the mage of his pilgrimages across Cantor. She was thinking of how distracting his stench was as he launched into the story of how his father had joined the group that had chased the last dragon from the world. An electric shock seemed to jolt through her nerve endings and little hairs rose on the back of her neck when he said the dragon's name: "Tanahil." She abruptly stood and the other two looked up at her, slight surprise on their faces at her sudden movement.

"I need some air," she said curtly and before anything else could be said, she moved off toward the door and outside into the afternoon sun. She scanned the street around her. There were merchants across the way, some selling sweet treats and wine supposedly from the far lands of the elves. Next to that was a shop selling all assortments of trinkets. She moved to scan the display of the merchant's items arranged on a small wooden table. A glint caught her eye. Looking over, she saw a small assortment of daggers, throwing stars and other dangerous hand-held equipment.

With a small smile, she moved over to this display. *Now this is more like it.*

There was an array of small, sharp daggers as well as some that were a bit longer; made for hunting. She let her fingers brush lightly over the weapons. Her smile deepened, and her thoughts turned to the lessons Garrin had insisted she have every morning. He was very good with daggers, but as the years had passed, she became better. He had taught her all he knew: throwing, fighting with a single dagger, fighting with two daggers and eventually fighting with dagger and sword. She much preferred the throwing. She had mastered throwing several with one hand and eventually throwing from both hands. The back-alley and tavern contests became a bore to her; she could beat them all and usually walked away with a purse full of gold and silver.

She picked up one of the more ornate weapons. Usually this type was not good for fighting. The handle was carved bone and had stones inlaid in the shape of a dragon. She held it closer to her eyes, the sparkling stones mesmerizing. The blade was perfectly worked; steel shining almost blue in the sunlight. She weighted it in her hand to test its grip and balance. It seemed made for her.

"That's the finest blade you'll find anywhere in these lands, my lady." The merchant had ambled over when he noticed her interest. She looked at him. His sparse white hair did not do much to cover his pink head and his beard hung almost to his waist. He was smiling at her, showing the gaps between teeth that were slowly rotting and falling from his mouth as the years passed. The smile across his face did not quite reach his eyes, she noted. She looked him over curiously.

"I've seen fine weapons. This one seems hardly fit for anything but cutting the meat at your dinner table. This gem-work would cut your hands to ribbons before you laid your first strike to an enemy." She was going to set it back, but found herself loathe to put it down. When she moved to replace it on the table, something pulled at her, willing her to draw it closer and not let go.

"But it's very valuable, that." The old man dropped his voice to almost a whisper. "It's made of dragonbone. The handle was carved by one of the last elves to commune with the dragons. It's said she gave the bone to him after she was wounded in battle with a foe. Fine work, it is. Plainly work of the elves. They say only dragonkin can wield such a weapon."

She was turning the blade in her hand, examining the craftsmanship. "How much?"

"Fifty gold will have it yours, my lady."

She couldn't help but think that this price was a bit high, but she found herself saying, "Done," and handing over the coin. She drifted away; a bit confused at why she had just paid twice for this dagger than what it was actually worth.

As she moved away from the merchants and back toward the inn where she had left the mage and dwarf to work out the arrangements of travel, she caught movement out of the corner of her eye.

She looked over her shoulder and moved back a step to the alley entrance she had just passed. She was certain she had seen a shadow move as she passed. Peering down the alleyway, she saw nothing. The doors to the row of small rooms were all securely shut. Yet, she was sure she had seen something. She took a step closer in, putting herself at the entrance between the two buildings. There! Again, at the end of the narrow street, she saw the fluttering of movement. *Probably some animal scrounging for scraps*. But the thought did nothing to quell her growing anxiety. She felt her middle tightening and knotting. A flash of memory came to her of Garrin surrounded by filthy sell-swords, leering in at him. She could smell their stench as plain as if she were there.

Tears stung her eyes and she tightened her jaw on the emotion that threatened to spill over. At that moment, the shadow she had seen seemed to emerge from the solid wall at the back of the alley. Mey's disbelief was instantaneous. The shape was a man, but only shadow. Hazy light surround the form as it moved closer to her. A low buzzing emanated from it, wormed its way into her ears and further into her head where it began to squirm and writhe. She closed her eyes, trying to block out the scene and sound around her. Instincts told her this was magic at work and blades were mostly useless against sorcery. She wished she wasn't alone. She wished Thom were there. He would know what to do.

With her thoughts lingering on the mage, she slipped the new, bone-handled dagger into her left hand and filled the right with a fine and comfortable blade she had carried since childhood. She automatically crouched low and slithered back, close to the wall behind her. If she kept something at her back, no one could sneak up on her to take that advantage. The buzzing noise was getting louder and louder. The sting of the noise touched her eyes and they began to water. Blinking back uncontrolled tears, she tried to focus on the shapes in front of her while shifting the weight of her weapons in her hands.

The shadows became separate from everything around them and took on individual forms. There were two distinct figures that were very man-like. The forms began to come closer and closer. Unchecked tears ran down her cheeks and her mind was screaming that this magical attack was unfair! She went through the motions of pulling her arm back and letting the dagger fly straight into the face of the nearest form. The dagger passed harmlessly through the shape and clattered to the ground behind it. It felt as though the only part of her that actually moved were her eyes as she scanned her surroundings. The noise of a thousand buzzing insects crawled through her mind and froze her limbs in place.

Her mind kept returning to the mage. If Thom were here, he could defeat this magic in an instant! Where was he? Images of her death at the hands of these creatures played round and round her mind and intertwined with images of him. Just as she felt the hot breath of the creatures before her, a brilliant light burst through and filled her with warm sensations that chased all other thoughts away. The light grew so bright, her next thought was that it must surely burn her; nothing but the sun could emit such brilliance. And, as quickly as it had appeared, it was all gone. Darkness rushed in from the edges of her vision and took over her entire world. She sighed and felt herself falling. There were no more thoughts or feelings. Only a weightless blackness with a silence so profound she really believed she must have been struck deaf.

FOUR

Mey opened her eyes with some trouble. Her head felt heavy and had begun to immediately ache with a dull pounding that reminded her of having too much wine the night before. As she tried to take in her surroundings, she saw a figure in the doorway. It was fuzzy and it took a moment to bring it into focus.

She tried to sit up but found that it made her dizzy and a little sick to her stomach. She groaned and fell back onto the bed instead. Thom was at her side almost in the same instant.

"Water." The words felt thick and garbled in her mouth.

A cup was held to her lips and she drank greedily. The water was cool and it put out the fire that burned all through her body. She felt satisfied at once and her head began to clear. She indicated she wanted more and the cup was once again brought to her lips. She drank her fill and pushed the cup away gently.

"What happened?" she managed to say before her throat closed and a cough overtook her. She looked over at Thom who was refilling the cup with fresh water in case she would want more. His hands were shaking slightly and he spilled a few drops. He looked at her and his eyes seemed to hold a fear she had not seen there since they had met. "Thom? What happened to the shadows? The last I remember was a bright light. Then…nothing."

He nodded, cleared his throat and said, "I got there just in time. The shadows you encountered are part of a Shadow Guard. They were sent to stop you from beginning this journey. I don't know who is behind their presence here, but I am sure you were their intended target and no one else."

Mey had sensed that was the intent the moment she encountered them. "But, the light? Where did the light come from?"

"That was me," he continued. "You needed my help. What else was I to do? One moment I was sitting, talking with our new companion and the next an image of you being overtaken by Shadow Guard was all that filled my mind. And I heard you, calling my name; calling for help." He looked right at her. He seemed uncertain as to what to say next.

Her shock was evident. "But I only thought that…I thought about how your magic would be beneficial in that situation and I thought of how much I wanted you to be there…" her voice trailed off as she realized what must have happened between them. "I called you and you heard me."

He nodded. Silence hung in the room, thick and uncomfortable. Mey swung her legs around and over the side of the bed. Her first instinct was to run; get out of this room and away from Thom. She wasn't really sure she was ready to feel what she was feeling. Garrin had been the only person in her life she could trust for so long, it was strange to her that someone could ever take that place again. She planted her feet on the ground and tried to stand, immediately realizing that was the wrong idea.

Thom was there, catching her. Her head swam and the dizziness almost took her into complete darkness again. She let him lead her back down to the bed to sit. His touch was so comfortable. There were so many other confusing feelings that bombarded her, so she decided to push it all away. She instinctively jerked away from Thom as she sat on the bed.

"Thanks," she mumbled. "Guess I took that a bit too fast."

"Just sit for a few moments longer. You should be fine; you weren't severely injured, just hit your head when you fell." His face was red and he seemed to be trying to avoid any eye contact with her.

Mey shrugged. "Durlag!" The thought of the dwarf came to her and just as she said his name, he was coming through the door.

"Lass! That was some tumble you took!" He ambled over to her. "You sure know how to take a fall! Why, I remember once, when I was just a wee dwarf…" his voice ran on and on in the background of her thoughts.

She watched Thom as he stoked a small fire in the corner of the room. It was then she realized they were in her room back at the inn. What was supposed to be hers and Garrin's room. He must have brought her back here after she fell.

What had happened between them, though? He had obviously seen her thoughts as she faced the Shadow Guard. She was curious about the link between her and this wizard. Why was it there? It must have begun at that first meeting, on the dock. When he touched her and threw her into his spell to show her what had happened to Garrin.

He pulled a chair over to the fire and sat there, staring in and looking just as lost in his thoughts as she was in her own. What was he thinking? Was he thinking about her? Almost as soon as she thought that, he looked up at her. It startled her and must have shown on her face because he chuckled.

"I wasn't reading your thoughts. I only felt your stare."

"Oh," she said quietly. "I…I'm just very confused at how I could call you with my mind."

Durlag had fallen silent and she didn't exactly remember when his story had stopped. He seemed content to just pull another chair toward the fire and seat himself. He took long draws from the flask he kept on his belt.

"I don't know, either. I think that maybe the Mage's Circle could have some answers. I will contact them tonight and present it to them."

"We should still leave in the morning. Oboderen will be expecting us in three days at Andari Point."

He nodded, again lost in his thoughts. Probably anticipating his conversation with the other mages.

Her limbs felt as though they needed a good stretch. She stood slowly, aware of every muscle, every movement. She raised her arms and stretched herself, reaching for the ceiling. She rolled her shoulders, moved her head cautiously from side to side. It seemed to help work out some of the kinks that were causing her pain. She walked to the window.

"Tell me a little more about these Shadow Guards. How are they defeated?"

"Being creatures of darkness, of course light will counteract them. Pointed weapons, such as sword, daggers or arrows will have no effect; unless they have been touched with magic." He was deeply lost in thought, not quite completely there with them.

"Where do they come from?"

"They originated from the dark magic practiced when the Mage's Circle first split. There were a few mages who did not agree with the philosophy of the larger whole. They broke off into their own faction and practiced magic without boundaries. From that magic spawned new creatures."

"Creatures of darkness," came the soft voice. Mey turned her attention to Durlag. The sadness in his eyes was so profound it seemed she could almost *feel* it. "Yes, I know a thing or two about these creatures of darkness."

Thom and Mey waited; instinctively knowing not to interrupt. Something in Durlag's face told Mey that what he was about to reveal deserved a modicum of respect.

"It weren't shadows that got Gord, though. Fire, it was. It crawled up from the floor of the cave. The farther we made our way in, the hotter that blasted hole seemed to get. The pungent smell of sulfur was everywhere. We thought to find gemstones in that cave. That's what all the old-timers said were in there.

"Gord just stopped, all at once it seemed. 'Gord?' I asked him. When he turned around, sweat was pourin' down his face. It was hot in that blasted cave, but not *that* hot. As I stood there, with my durned mouth hangin' open, he just got redder n' redder. He was afraid. Then, from nowhere, there was fire. Shootin' up from the ground, it folded itself all around Gord." Durlag's voice dropped. "He screamed. I can hear that scream still. There's no sound like the scream from a man dyin' by burnin' alive…"

A shudder passed through him and he shook it off without seeming aware of it. He looked up at Mey and Thom. "There was eyes in that fire. A darkness within the flames. Then those eyes seemed to focus their attention on Gord. At least the screamin' stopped. But what happened next, I've never told another soul. Those eyes took something out of Gord. I could see it lookin' all cloudy like a mist."

"What happened then?" Mey asked.

"I ran, lass. I ran farther and faster than I ever run in my life." The touch of bitterness in his voice was plain. It obviously pained him to admit that weakness.

"A Flame Soul." Thom was looking at Durlag, a hint of wonder revealed on his face. "I have only seen renderings of these creatures in books. The fire needs souls to feed its dark existence."

"So," Mey said after a time, breaking the heavy silence and desperate to end all this talk of evil creatures spawned from darkness. "We leave tomorrow at day break, as planned?"

Thom cleared his throat. "Right." Mey watched him as he moved about the room collecting his various papers, bottles, and pouches. He seemed as though he was trying very hard not to look at her as he completed his tasks.

Durlag excused himself to wrap up whatever ends he had before their journey in the morning. The room was empty but for the two of them. The fire was warm and the sounds from it comforted her. The sudden voice across the room startled her.

"Rest well. You should be ready for travel in the morning. Just keep yourself still and get your rest tonight."

"Thom…" she wanted to say how much she appreciated his coming to her aid. How she felt she could trust him and how this was such a foreign feeling to her, but the only thing that came out was a quiet, "Thank you."

He inclined his head slightly as he backed out of the door.

She fell heavily back onto the pillows. Why couldn't she just say it? She was uncomfortable with these feelings. She had never been close with anyone except a handful of people in her lifetime. The only two that even came close were Garrin and her uncle. But Garrin was the big brother she never had and her uncle lived in the elven lands so she hadn't had much contact with him except through the mind-link they shared.

They were the only people in this world she felt she could trust. But now, this mage had saved her life. He was confident with her skills and her abilities. He held her secret and was the only person who could let her in on her true heritage. She felt a deep trust for Thom and that was startling to her since she had only just met him. There seemed to be a bond between them that had formed with the magic that was part of them both.

She sighed, trying to push all the worrisome issues out of her mind. She was good at avoiding things that made her uncomfortable. She wasn't overly tired so she focused on trying to contact Oboderen. Since she was small, they had a link that allowed them to communicate silently. The further the distance, however, the less it seemed to cooperate. If he was on the road out of Orphana, it should be easier. The closer he was to the elves, the less chance of success. All elves could communicate this way but it was harder for Mey, probably because she was a half-blood. The only one she had ever had any success communicating with was her uncle.

She closed her eyes and slowed her breathing. She chanted his name under her breath, "Oboderen." The name was easier for her now. When she was a child and her father had taken her into the elf land to meet her relations there, she had stumbled over the name, Oboderen Moondance. He had laughed heartily at her attempt and accepted the nickname that had come out of her try. "Bob" was her favorite elven relative. He was always cheerful and ready to help when he could. He was genuine in his feelings for her. The others seemed only to tolerate her because of her father. There always seemed a hidden disdain just below the surface. She knew that because she was half-blood she would never fully be accepted. Bob was different.

When she had been able to contact him about this journey, it surprised them both. Their link was tentative and she had limited time to convey everything to him. She wasn't able to tell him about the dragon heritage the mage believed was hers. Or the exact nature of the journey. She had only told him that she needed him and that the journey was necessary. He agreed without hesitation and conveyed to her a meeting point and how long it would take him to reach it. That was all they had discussed. She was anxious to see him and talk to him about her father. She was sure he could yield some clues as to where to start looking for him.

A cold sensation seemed to blanket her and she recognized Bob's mind when it touched hers. *I will reach Andari Point tomorrow night*, the thought came to her.

A minor setback here. We will reach the Point in three days. Three of us. Myself, the mage and a dwarf. She was almost giddy with excitement to see him again after so many years. *Safe journey, Uncle. I will see you soon.*

Safe journey. I look forward to it. He broke the link. It was a strain on them both and if he was traveling alone, he needed all his attention to keep himself safe.

Mey lay back on her bed and sighed. She closed her eyes and wanted nothing more than for sleep to overtake her. As she drifted off, an image formed behind her eyes. Two figures shimmered there, hazy but recognizable. Garrin was there: as he was there every night she closed her eyes. But this time, another figure was beside him. The figured floated closer and she recognized him. Thom was there, beside Garrin to guide her sleep and keep her protected. As she drifted off into the darkness, a small, contented smile lingered on her lips.

****

Thom stared at the window without seeing what was on the other side. He concentrated more on the silent words running through his mind. The spell that would bring the Mage's Circle to him. The room changed around him, melting into a different scene. The rough wooden walls fell away to reveal polished stone. The floor transformed to the smooth, faceted rock that ran throughout the massive buildings that housed the mages of Cantor.

One by one, people appeared all around with Thom sitting cross-legged in the middle. He knew his eyes were closed but he saw this scene with the clarity of a waking dream. The eldest, with stark white hair and few teeth left to him, spoke. "You have another report so soon?"

"Yes. Shadow Guard are already converging to dissuade our journey. Someone knows our intent and is actively working to sway us."

Another spoke, her high-pitched voice ringing in Thom's mind like tinkling bells. "We have had word that some factions of priests are not happy with our ideas to bring the Idylic together so that the path is open once more to our world. They are afraid the dragons will bring all manner of dark beings with them to punish us for our follies."

"They would be right to do so if they chose," a deeper, more distinctly male voice echoed. "Who were we to decide the fate of an entire race?"

Thom spoke again. "But would the priests call Shadow Guard? These creatures are of darkness and ill magic."

"Not the priests," the old man told him. "Someone the priests have turned to. Someone they trust to help them in their cause. But for Shadow Guard to be involved, it must be a rogue mage. Divine magic cannot call forth the shadows. We will work on pinpointing this mage."

"Fine. I will concentrate all my efforts on getting Mey safely across the Barren Lands. We meet her uncle at Andari Point in three days, which adds another to our small band. We will keep her safe."

Maybe the old mage noted something in his voice, but his tone turned sterner. "Thom, you are charged to her safe-keeping and that is your *only* task."

"Of course." Thom hoped that the magical connection did not reveal the fluttering of his heart as he said this. The truth was he was already beginning to see her as more than just a 'task.'

"She is dragon-kin. She must be the one to call them back, Thom." There was sadness in the old man's eyes that Thom couldn't ignore.

Again Thom acquiesced and made a hasty excuse to retreat from the spell and the scrutinizing minds of the other mages. As the room came into focus, he breathed more deeply and steadily. His eyes came back to focus on the window in front of him. The large crystal gemstone that was laid in front of him glowed faintly then flickered out. He hastily wrapped it in the worn leather cloth and put it away in one of the many pouches around his belt.

He rose and walked toward the window. The words, *'she is only a task'* sounded again and again through his thoughts. He sighed deeply. She wasn't only a task. She had ceased to be that since the day he laid eyes on her. The spark within her eyes drew him in deeper each time he saw it.

Dragons were known to pull a person in as their protector and hold them helplessly spell-bound. But how could she be doing this? She didn't know anything about her heritage or about dragons! Could her dragon blood be doing this all without her knowledge? She certainly seemed to be displaying other traits known to exist in the dragon line. She had called to him; summoned him when she needed help.

Was this just a mechanism to call a protector or did they have a deeper connection? She did have elven blood running through her veins, after all. She was not purely selfish, as the mages had learned most all dragons were. They had existed only to balance the nature of the world. Everything had rested on their shoulders and from that, over the years, they had grown smug and detached.

Thom searched the night sky for nothing in particular. The stars comforted him. Most of his studies in magic centered around the stars and the magic held within the vastness of the sky above them. He turned to this familiar vision now when he felt vulnerable and even a bit afraid. He was only supposed to have found the girl that was the last of the dragon line here on Cantor, help her to retrieve the Heartstone of the Idylic, and then lead her to the place where the statue stood so that it could be rejoined and she could call forth the dragons to return to this world.

It was clearly much more. He couldn't deny that he found Mey very beautiful; he didn't think anyone could deny that fact. Beyond the beauty, however, she was clever, shrewd, fiercely independent, and one of a kind. He found those qualities attractive as well. He would have to push all of this to the back of his mind and keep his task the first priority. If he did not safely deliver her along with the Heartstone, the entire world could cease to exist. That was far more important than his desire for a woman.

He turned away from the window and prepared for sleep. Tomorrow they would start the first leg of their long journey. He needed to be ready. The Shadow Guard were only the first of many trials they would undoubtedly face. He thought of who the priests might have turned to when they learned of what the mages had planned to do. Only a handful of names came to mind. Not many mages practiced the dark side of magic. And fewer still could actually put it into play. One of those names had a very close tie to their quest and he felt uneasiness grip his heart, making it flutter.

As he drifted to sleep, his mind brought up an image of Mey. Beside her, he saw another image come into focus. He could only hope this one was not following them on their journey. He couldn't bear to think of the devastation that he might present if Thom was right.

FIVE

As dawn broke through the lingering haze of night, Mey was prepared to leave the city and begin the trek east. The prospect of seeing her uncle had her excited to leave this gods-forsaken city made her feel like she was flying. As she walked down the street, avoiding the filth that collected in the gutters and ran toward a central point of the town, her hand moved to lightly touch the new dagger at her waist.

She wasn't sorry to see all of this go. This town had been her home for many years; its attraction had been the severe underemployment of sheriffs or enforcement of law. She and Garrin met here and had had to lie low for a while soon after. She was clumsy and had botched a very important job for some very powerful people. Garrin had stepped in to protect her. A small sigh escaped her. There were no more tears, only wistful memories. Frustration played into her mood as well. Everyone seemed to be *saving* her. Everyone she had come into contact with – her father, Garrin, and now Thom – had played the role of protector in her life. That didn't sit comfortably with Mey. In fact, it infuriated her. Trying harder to take care of herself would have to be a priority. And proving that she didn't need to rely on anyone else to survive was a must.

She approached the small, dilapidated building that was calling itself a stable. The snoring tipped her off that the dwarf was here before she even saw him. Mey rolled her eyes as she rounded the corner and saw Durlag sprawled over his gear, his flask gripped tightly to his chest. He must have slept there all night. She gently poked a toe in his ribs. He snorted once, rumbled something unintelligible and rolled himself over. Mey was about to suggest leaving him where he lay, when he sat bolt upright and turned wide eyes toward her.

And just like that, he was ready to leave.

She shook her head in amazement. This dwarf was a marvel to her. He stayed drunk most of the time, was filthy, and smelled to the high heavens. But his reaction time was the like of that she had never seen before. Her smirk must have told him more than intended.

"These old bones are accustomed to traveling life, lass." He rubbed the long whiskers that sprouted from his chin and stretched his arms and legs as far as they would go. He creaked with the movement, but sighed in contentment once he was done.

Mey found herself smiling at his ridiculous appearance.

"You seen that mage this mornin', girl?"

Her eyes quickly scanned the street and the landscape behind it. "No, I haven't. I would have thought he would be the first here as anxious as he was about leaving those Shadow Guard behind."

Mey busied herself; checking her pack and bed roll to make sure everything was secure. Moving on to her weapons, she made sure each dagger was secure on the bandolier lying across her chest, in her boots, up her sleeves and in the belt at her waist.

By the time she'd done all this, Thom was approaching, leading two very tired-looking horses. He had equipment packed and slung over the back of one and the other was burdened with a well-worn saddle that had seen better days. Several pouches hung from his belt, more than were there before. He must have spent his morning procuring components, which meant mostly stones that would aid him in his spell-casting. She was learning way more about mages than she ever cared to.

"Glad you decided to join us this morning," she mumbled to him as he stopped to adjust the saddle on the horse. "What good will we get from these nags? They don't look like they will last out the hour, let alone a three day journey."

"See, lass, that's where yer wrong," Durlag put in. "Horses like these are fine for journeys. All they need is some love and care. They'll do fine." He stepped up between the two horses and laid a hand on each. The horses nuzzled his hands and stepped in closer to him as he began to talk quietly to them both.

Mey looked at Thom, who seemed to have the same dumbfounded look on his face. Both smiled and chuckled, as if to say, "Who knew?" At least it was clear who was taking care of the horses on this trip.

Her eyes roamed the small street, stopping on each building briefly. This place was small, but not so small that you felt smothered. Just big enough to get lost in if you needed to. She had wandered into this town twenty years ago. In her sixtieth year, a babe for a half-elf, she had already lived on her own for about ten years. Her father had gone missing and it was a time when she had no idea who she was or what she was going to do with her life. Dipping her fingers into petty thievery to stay alive was already familiar territory; picking a pocket here and there to pay for food or lodgings. For the most part, weapons were familiar to her; she'd a dagger or two and the sword her father had gifted her on her thirtieth nameday by the time she made her way to this seaport town.

This was where Garrin entered her life. It still pained her to think of him, but she also found some strength in his memory. Their first meeting on the dock was etched in her mind and it was not likely she would forget it. Her thoughts took her back there as she rubbed a gold coin between her thumb and forefinger.

She'd been so hungry and it had been days since she had eaten anything decent. She had been sitting outside the Dockside Tavern. The proprietor, not being a very original man, but a nice one, would let her stay most of the day in the shade of his awning, singing a song, doing a few card tricks or whatever else she could come up with to earn coins.

She had seen him enter, young, presumably careless and a purse full of coins. Lifting purses was no big deal since she'd done it before. She had gotten good at it and for the most part, a person wouldn't even notice it missing until she was long gone. She waited for him to leave the tavern. He was there a long time, but Mey had definitely thought it was worth the wait. The coin in his purse would feed her for many weeks. He finally exited, now with a pronounced lilt in his step, she was sure this would be an easy mark.

She tensed as he passed her. Mey's palm was so sweaty she almost dropped the dagger she held. Like lightning, her hand came out; the dagger at the strings of the purse. With the strings cut, the purse was falling and she reached up with her other hand to catch it, poised to run the second it hit her hand. But it never did. It took her a moment to realize that another hand had caught it. Looking up, she stared right into Garrin's smiling face. She was quick, but he was quicker. As Mey had turned to run, he caught her by the scruff of her clothes and pulled her to him. "Walk," he whispered in her ear. The tone of his voice left her no doubt that pain would follow if she did not obey. "Like we are old friends just come from drinking our afternoon away at the tavern."

With him gripping her tightly, she had no choice but to follow his lead and they both laughed out loud as they stumbled away from the front of the tavern.

As they walked, he maintained a firm grip on her arm. Mey knew that running was not an option. She could never break that grip. She slipped a dagger into her palm from its hiding place within the arm of her tunic. She would hurt him if she had to. The crowd of people was thinning when he abruptly stopped.

He spun her toward him, twisting her arm in his iron grip. She squared her shoulders and looked right at him. She was not ashamed of what she had to do. His eyes were steel gray. It reminded her of metal; liquid metal. His dark hair curled about his face framing his hard features. But as she stared at him, something in those eyes softened just a bit as he took in her ragged appearance.

Reaching into the pouch, he pulled out a coin and pressed it into her palm. "No need to steal from me. If you want to learn, it's yours."

Immediately Mey was suspicious. "Learn what? I don't sleep with men for money."

His laugh was louder than anything she had ever heard. It turned heads, but it was full of honesty. His smile was broad. "I like you. You are straight and to the point." The laugh fading, he bent closer to her. "Not that. You're too skinny for my taste. I am talking about learning to properly cut a purse, pick a lock. You have a fast hand and a look that can easily be disguised. Do you want to learn?"

She could not say she wasn't intrigued. He seemed so enthusiastic that it caught her up and she found herself really *wanting* what he was promising.

With resolve, Mey nodded once. "I want to learn."

****

Fate had sealed the deal with Garrin and brought her here, to a dirt path leading out of town and into an unknown future. She sighed and returned the coin to her pocket as they started walking toward the treetops south of the town. Seaside was fading behind her.

The prospect of finding clues of her father's fate on this journey lingered heavy in the back of her mind as well. Knowing he was out there somewhere left her with a nagging pull to seek him out; to find the trail he left and follow it.

They had walked for half the day, each keeping to themselves, when Thom's voice broke the companionable silence. "I didn't know you carried a sword." When she looked over at him, his gaze was fixed at her hip, where the old sword hung.

"Not normally. It was Garrin's. And, I guess we can use any help we can get, right?" Looking at his skeptical expression, she chuckled. "I know how to use it, if that's what you're afraid of. I'm not the best, but I can manage."

"Did Garrin teach you?"

"Some. My father insisted I have a tutor when I was very young. He always believed that, as a woman, I would have need to protect myself."

Stopping abruptly, Mey motioned for Thom to do the same. He was looking at her curiously, perhaps wondering what she was doing. Durlag, trailing with the horses, joined them.

"Is this camp for the night?" Durlag asked. "We've not been gone long, but I'm for setting up and relaxing for the rest o' the day."

"No," Mey said, shortly. "Don't you smell that?"

"Smell what? All I can smell is these here horses and the fine aroma in this here flask," he emphasized this by taking a long drink from it.

Mey made a full turn, eyes searching the surrounding trees. "Something's out there." When her eyes again came to Thom, she stopped. Taking in a long breath through her nose, and letting it slowly out, her eyes narrowed. With her voice barely above a whisper, she told them, "Goblins."

Thom's heart skipped a beat. The light was there, in her eyes, where it hadn't been only seconds before. It was hauntingly beautiful while hinting at danger. "We keep moving. Steady pace as far as they will let us. We need to find a clearing if there is to be fighting. All these trees will not agree with any magic I would unleash here."

Mey nodded, turned and immediately started walking again. Thom watched as her pace quickened. One hand fingered the hilt of the sword hanging from her hip. In the other, there was a dagger.

He noticed Durlag loosen his hold on the reins and, with a swift movement, unstrapped the big axe across his back and held it over his shoulder. He faced straight ahead, but his eyes searched all around as they moved.

The trio walked in silence, each one tensed and ready for the slightest advance of the creatures following them. Every few moments, a rustling in the treetops or the sound of a breaking twig underfoot, reminded them that they were not alone here.

****

Up ahead, the road broke out of the trees; Mey could see it not thirty or so paces forward. At that moment, she ducked and rolled as a spear narrowly missed taking off her left ear. Coming up in a crouch, a dagger in each hand, her eyes strained to catch a glimpse of the attacker.

She sensed the movement of her companions, and knew that Durlag had come forward and Thom had retreated behind them. Thom wore no armor and bore no weapons besides his magic, so it was the best place for him.

Glancing to her side, she saw that Durlag heaved the great axe before him with both hands. He handled it as if it was a feather and it was strangely graceful to watch. He squared his shoulders and planted his feet, allowing his attackers to come to him. A smile played at his lips.

"If'n yer comin', you stinking dogs, COME ON!" Durlag yelled out. As if on cue, a half dozen bug-eyed faces appeared randomly from behind tree trunks and among branches. The yellow eyes glowed from the shadows in the woods. Behind her, Mey heard a small sound escape Thom.

Instincts took over. She focused on a face close to her and the daggers shot from her hands, soared straight at the slavering mouth and yellow eyes of the goblin. They hit with force and the creature flew back into the trees and landed right between a couple of its friends, daggers protruding from its open mouth and forehead. A beat of silence and then screeching from the small, thin, greenish-grey creatures followed.

Another pair of daggers had replaced the ones just used in Mey's hands. The creatures all advanced in a run. Mey had time to let loose another volley. She saw four small streaks of magical light darting toward one of the creatures as she pulled the sword from its place at her hip and readied herself. The crackling projectiles of energy hit a goblin to her left and she could hear the searing noise they made and smell the burning flesh as the creature went down with a scream. Chancing a quick glance over her shoulder, Thom had one hand outstretched and another fumbling within the pouches at his belt. She grinned at him in approval and he merely shrugged as if to say, "It was nothing."

She turned her attention back to the rapidly advancing goblins. Their bodies were covered by small cloths that hung limply about the waist. They all carried medium-length spears, with an extra strapped to their backs. It was going to be hard to get close enough to them to use the sword, but she had no time to find a vantage point for throwing daggers.

From the corner of her eye, she saw Durlag move forward with a speed and grace that surprised her. He swung the great axe over his head in a powerful arc that came down to cleave the spear of the nearest goblin in two. In the next quick motion, reversing his grip and spinning bodily, the axe came around to take the goblin's head off. As the lifeless body fell to the ground, her fears on having to cover his backside were laid to rest.

A primal scream took her attention away from the dwarf and back to her own situation. Two of the foul smelling creatures were coming toward her, spears poised for a throw. One let loose with the weapon and it soared dangerously close as she jumped to the side. Mey saw the opening and took it. She ran swiftly at the empty-handed goblin. She brought the sword around and down on its shoulder as it reached for the spear strapped to its back.

A blood-curdling yowl cut the air, and she barely had time to duck as another spear came at her head from behind. She rolled to the right and sprang back up, bringing a dagger to bear backhanded at the second attacker.

The steel met little resistance on the soft skin of the goblin and she buried it to its hilt in the creature's neck. It fell with a thud. She felt a stab of stinging pain in her left leg and spun, drawing another dagger from the bandolier across her chest. Anger flooded her as she realized the first goblin had gotten to his spear and had jabbed her weakly in an attempt to save his friend.

A guttural growl escaped her lips and shock at her own savage response almost did her in. She heard Thom chanting behind her and a strong gust of enchanted wind knocked the beast to the ground. Mey recovered enough and in time to bring the sword down over her head into the goblin's chest.

She realized someone was calling her name. Slowly, everything came into focus. Turning at the sound, she saw Thom. He took a step back when her eyes met his. He hesitated, but then he continued forward.

"Mey, it's over. They're all dead," he said.

Looking around her at the bodies of the goblins, she realized what he was saying. The fight was over. Durlag sat by the horses, flask at his lips. He was talking to the animals between sips, soothing their fear. The smell of blood hit her nostrils and she reeled from the impact. The overwhelming urge to pick up the body and rip through it with her teeth almost made her sick.

She spun away or she would have lost the contents of her stomach. The savage feelings subsided as she gained control of her senses. Big gulps of air helped. What was happening to her?

Thom broke the silence that had crept up in the aftermath of the battle. "We need to build a fire. Burn these bodies. We'll have every beast living in these woods after us if we leave them." He looked over at the dwarf enjoying his after-battle drink. "Durlag, we'll need firewood. Would you mind?"

The dwarf grimaced as he stood, belying every move he had made while engaged with the goblins. "Sure, lad," he managed to get out before he tripped and stumbled. "Firewood." Repeating this word to himself as he moved on, he made his way into the woods.

"You're hurt," Thom said to her as he turned his attention to her.

"It's nothing," she gasped. "Just a scratch, really. I'll clean and bandage it." She sat heavily and was grateful she made it to a seated position before she fell flat on her face.

****

Cool hands were on her face, turning it upward. Lifting her eyes, she saw Thom. "What just happened to me?" Tears pricked the corners of her eyes but she was refusing to let them fall. The last thing she wanted was for him to feel sorry for her.

Thom reached to push the damp hair from her face just as she pushed herself up and he ended up poking her eye. As she instinctively covered her face, he mumbled an awkward apology, clearly embarrassed. Then he said, "It's just getting stronger. The dragon blood inside you yearns to be free and to be what it was meant to be. Your elven side fights against it." He was trying to be reassuring, but he certainly wasn't very convincing sulking in his embarrassment.

"Why me? Why now?" The words were meant for her alone, however, they were out of her mouth before she could stop them.

"I can't answer all your questions, Mey, but I *can* tell you what I know. Let's get this mess cleaned up, get a camp started and tonight we'll discuss this further." Thom busied himself with unburdening the horses of their loads and finding a spot for the animals to graze. Mey watched him until he turned to her. "Are you going to help or just daydream?"

She found herself smiling at him. "I'm on it." She went toward the closest body with the intent of lessoning its load into the afterworld.

SIX

After having created a makeshift pyre for the goblins and bandaging Mey's leg, the three of them sat around a small campfire. Durlag cradled his flask as if it were a precious child. Mey and Thom moved themselves to a position at the edge of the firelight, watching the night for any signs of more 'visitors.'

Thom was bringing her up to speed on the nature of dragons as he had read it through the histories. "Will the dragon blood overtake the elven?" Mey asked him.

"I don't know the answer to that. No one has ever encountered a half-breed before. You are the only one. The Mage's Circle knows that Tanahil chose to stay in mortal form with her elven lover and they married. There was only one child. Tanahil died in childbirth. The child was raised away from the elves for fear of retribution."

"Yes, it is frowned upon to seek love outside the race. They view it as contamination," Mey remarked. The pain she felt surely must have shown on her face before she could hide it. "My father never spoke of my mother." There was a long silence. "So, Tanahil was my mother." It was more a statement than a question.

"She was," Thom answered. "Elves are a very long-lived race and dragons are practically immortal. The histories tell us that your mother and father lived many long, happy years together. They spent four hundred years mending the land and the people of Cantor after the devastation of the last Dragon Wars. And then they were blessed with a life of their own. You were born to them."

Mey let her thoughts roam back through the years and then finally said, "In early years, I remember my father being distant. He was detached from the world around him. Losing my mother must have been devastating to him. Of course I asked of her, to which his only reply was that she had died. I never questioned his answer. Around my twentieth year, I remember him spending more time with me. That is when we traveled to the elven homeland."

Neither spoke as they sat, watching the flames of the campfire lick up toward a sky dotted with small points of light. Durlag's snore was oddly comforting in the silence.

"I'll take the watch from here," Mey offered as she stood. Thom inclined his head and rose.

"Mey, the Shadow Guard that attacked and these goblins today; they are all part of the plan to stop us. You need to realize that the further we go, the more danger this journey presents."

"Right," she answered. "Once we meet Bob at the Point, we can discuss all this a bit more. There's a lot I need to know, about dragons, about this Idylic and about myself." Walking a few paces, she stopped and then turned back to him. "Thanks, Thom. You've saved my life twice now. I owe you."

"You owe me nothing, Mey," he said. "Good night."

****

The next morning found them back on the road to Andari Point. The air was chill in the morning but warmed steadily as the sun passed through the sky. The small group remained watchful but the days and nights were uneventful.

They reached Andari Point on the evening of the third day. Dusk was settling over the hills and the trees cast shadows about the clearing. One particular rock jutted over a crevice carved deep into the side of the hill. A lone figure stood at the edge, looking over the hills beyond.

The tall, slender figure turned as the group came up behind him. The handsome features of this elf were marred by a long, thick, reddened scar that started at his temple and twisted its way down past the eye and along the jaw bone, ending somewhere beyond the collar of his shirt. A warm smile spread across his face as his clear, green eyes came to rest on Mey. He held his arms out to her.

"Uncle!" Mey called as she took off to greet him. She ran to him but stopped just short of barreling into him and taking them both right over the edge. Reaching out she took his hands and bowed low to him; a traditional greeting for an elder among the elves.

"Forget that nonsense," the elf scolded her playfully. He pulled her up and enveloped her in a smothering hug. Mey buried her face into his strong chest and breathed in his wonderful, woodsy smell. No matter how long they had been apart, this smell lingered with her. Emotions were overtaking her and she pulled back from him.

"Uncle, there is so much we need to discuss." The small hesitation in his eyes caused her to look over her shoulder. Her companions stood there, doing what they could to let the two have their moment. "Oh, I am sorry," she said. "These are my friends. Thom Uray, of the Mage's Circle and Durlag Rockcrusher, of the Clan Rockcrusher." She motioned to each in turn.

Bob bowed low from his waist. "An honor," he said.
He was sizing them up, she knew. She took his hand to lead him over to her friends.

"They have proven to be good warriors and have each saved my life at least once." This bit of information would mean more to Bob than anything else she could say. Bob was different from other elves. He did not have the haughtiness that most carried about the other races. Respect ran deep in him for all creatures.

Very much the loving uncle, the time they spent together so long ago had stayed with her. Her father had not gone into detail about her family, but he had hinted that she should mind herself from going about and hugging elves. Elves were more dignified than that and he was sorry he had let her get away with acting in such a manner for so long. Bob let her hug him as much as she had wanted.

"Mey," Thom began, "Durlag and I will set up camp. You and your uncle should talk." He gave a meaningful glance at Durlag, who did not yet know the true nature of their journey, and started unpacking the horses.

Moving back to the edge of the large, flat rock the two of them settled themselves. There were so many questions Mey had for her uncle. Certainly he knew more about her mother than anyone else could tell her at this point. She wanted so desperately to know what her mother was like; a feeling that had only recently come up. In all her eighty years, there had not been much curiosity about her mother. Her father had always been enough. Of course, without a mother, there were lessons she had to learn the hard way; lessons that mothers usually taught daughters. And the biggest lesson of all, her heritage, would forever be lost with her mother, leaving her to rely on the memories of others.

****

Bob proved to be a good addition to their small party. He fit in quite nicely. At just over five-hundred years old, he had known the world before the dragons had been forced to depart.

Elves grow physically at about the same rate as a human, reaching full growth in about their twentieth year. Their minds, on the other hand, do not fully mature until about a hundred years. During these first hundred years of life, elves are referred to as 'quicklings.' Mey was considered a quickling by elven standards, but Bob never treated her as such.

In revealing her secret to Bob, she found that he already knew much of the story and could fill in the parts for her that were missing. He proved a great source of stories of her father and mother in the years before she was born. Mey loved them all the more with each story her uncle relayed. Warmth enveloped her as Bob spoke of her mother.

Deep down, Mey was hoping that her uncle knew where her father was or at least had some clue as to where he had been headed. Bob had last seen his brother when he brought Mey to visit the homeland close to fifty years before. He had not seen nor heard from him since. Hope was vanishing quickly that she would ever find her father but she never doubted that he was alive.

Mey relayed her own stories to her uncle. Speaking of Garrin and finding that she now could laugh at the memories without being sad was a welcome change. Little by little she revealed what was happening to her with the dragon blood. This last development had been the hardest for her so far. During the battle she felt that she had lost control and instinct took over.

"Uncle, I wanted to *eat* the creature! I feel like I am losing who I am."

Bob took her hands and looked directly at her eyes. "Yes, I can see changes in you. From the last time you were in the homeland to now; you are a different girl." His smile made her feel more at ease. "But I do not think you are losing yourself. You are gaining something that is part of you. It is wonderful and magical and yours alone."

"I'm not so sure I want it," Mey confessed. Tears stung her eyes as she tried to put all the emotions running through her body in check. The stubborn side came through as she kicked at a rock lodged in the dirt. "Why me? Why don't I have a choice in this?"

"Dear Quickling," Bob said. His laughing tone made her angrier by the second. "No one chooses their parents or the path their life will take. You must accept what is yours and know that there is purpose to it." His eyes took on a far away glaze.

"But I don't accept it! I *do* have a choice; I can choose to ignore this pull that I feel and to ignore the fate that the world has laid at me feet." She was being stubborn and she knew it but it just seemed so unfair. Why should it have to be *her* that everyone depended on?

"Your father would have told you the same."

"My father…" her voice trailed. Her anger faded somewhat. Convinced that he was still alive, there was a question that nagged at her. "Uncle, he is out there, isn't he?"

"I feel that he is, yes." Elves bond with their families so strongly sometimes that they actually feel the others emotions even when they are miles apart. When her uncle obtained his scar, her father told her he had felt it so deeply that he had a faint red mark on his own face in the same place for a week after. Another reason she believed so stubbornly that her father was still alive was she *felt* it.

As they sat, each in their own thoughts, the sun sinking lower on the horizon, Mey felt a wonderful camaraderie with her uncle. They had only spent two short years with one another, but had bonded as strongly as any other elves. She was glad he was on this trip with her; to help share in the struggle with who she was and to somehow find a way to bring dragons back into the world.

Almost at the same moment, Mey a bit quicker than Bob, they sprang up, weapons in hand and turned, all in one fluid movement.

Thom stood there, hands up, and a look of pure fear on his face. "S-s-sorry," he stammered.

Mey let the tension in her body relax. Her arms fell to her sides. "Thom," exasperation evident in her voice, "don't ever do that again!" She slipped the daggers back into their place at her hip. Bob was putting his weapon away more slowly.

"I am sorry. I did not want to interrupt your talk. I had cast a barrier of silence around you for your own privacy. I should not have let it down so abruptly." Embarrassment shone red on his face. "Uh…we need to, uh, speak of the Idylic."

Mey turned to Bob. The thought that he knew what it looked like had crossed her mind earlier but she had forgotten to ask.

Bob was nodding his head. "The Idylic. I suppose you need to know the story of this artifact if we are to mend it and call forth dragons."

"Uncle, have you seen it?"

"Yes. I have seen it. I have touched it and I saw it destroyed." Pain, anger, love, envy, and sadness all moved across his face as he looked at her. A hand came up to touch the rough scar that ran the length of his face.

Thom cleared his throat and said, "The Mage's Circle believes that of the pieces that were scattered across Cantor, the Heartstone is the most significant. If we can bring it together with the main body still left, it will allow the statue to heal itself enough so that one of dragon blood can call to her kin and lead them back to our world."

"What did the Idylic look like?" Mey asked her uncle. "Before it was torn apart, I mean."

Bob began to say something at the same time Thom tried to answer. They looked at one another, challenge evident in both men's eyes. Thom bowed his head slightly, acquiescing to Bob. After all, Bob had seen the actual statue and Thom's image came from the many descriptions he had studied and pieced together from books.

Bob began again. "The statue is of a dragon itself. It is the first dragon, Sundar. Gemstones adorn the entire statue, having been given in reverence over years by other dragons. The statue itself is made of marble. The Heartstone is rumored to be Sundar's own heart that transformed as it was placed to capture every dragon essence in existence. Who placed it there is a mystery. There has always been speculation as to who created the statue, but the dragons believe that Sundar himself had it made because he was vain and just liked to look at himself."

Thom cleared his throat. "The gemstones, they were used as adornment as well as being part of the statue itself, correct? Each time a dragon paid homage with a gem, he would embed that gem into the marble with magic."

"True," Bob answered. "The image of Sundar was very close to the actual dragon, although on a smaller scale. It stood about seven feet in height, with wings spread." He picked up a small stick nearby. "Here, let me try to sketch it so you have a better idea." He started scratching in the dirt.

As they watched the image form at their feet, Thom said, "The Mage's Circle believes the Heartstone to be somewhere on the Faery Isles. The level of magical activity in that area has increased over the years and is now adversely affecting everything. The people of the Barren Lands that skirt the edge of the Isles have increasingly reported strange happenings."

"But I thought the Barren Lands were empty." Mey's brow furrowed as she spoke. "No plant life, animals or people. Just flat land where nothing grows."

Bob straightened and spoke, "That is not entirely the case. The area is called the Barren Lands because it is very difficult to survive there. There are tribes of humans that dwell in this land. They have found a way to adapt and survive. However, you are right about the animals. There are not many; a few species have managed to acclimate themselves."

Thom nodded. "Yes, it is difficult to live there, but people do; and things are changing. The few animals that have dwelt peacefully with the humans have started turning on them. And the humans have been warring with other tribes as well as some small villages on the outskirts of the Barren Lands. It's like the people have been taken over by something beyond their control. There have been sightings of magical energies as well. No one can explain where they have come from or where exactly they are originating."

"So, to the Barren Lands?" Mey asked. "The four of us? When do we let Durlag in on the secret? Dragons aren't necessarily his favorite creatures. He's said as much himself. His clan was almost directly responsible for Arlien's departure."

Turning toward the dwarf who was, as usual, nursing his beautiful flask, Thom spoke. "I think he will be more accepting of our quest than you think."

Mey and Bob looked at one another. *If he isn't, Thom's magic will make sure he does.* Her uncle's smile told Mey he had heard the thought and was in agreement. Mey yawned and looked across the darkening sky. "I think I have to call it a day. We're leaving in the morning, right? It's going to be a long trek to the Barren Lands and the sooner we start the better."

"I think it would be a smart move to leave as soon as possible," Bob said. "Something tells me that we are not quite safe where we are."

Glancing at Thom, Mey told him, "I'll leave it to you to explain the dangers. I can't keep my eyes open another minute!"

****

Thom watched her walk away. He never could focus completely with her around. Sighing, he turned back to Bob, who was looking at him with a curious expression. "What?" Thom asked.

"Just a fleeting thought I was catching from Mey," Bob said. "Well, back to the business at hand. So, the Mage's Circle thinks the Heartstone is all we need to heal the Idyllic?"

Thom didn't quite trust this man yet. They had only just met and usually elves had their own agenda. How much should he reveal? He knew the location of the Heartstone; or rather, where the Mage's Circle believed the location to be.

Certainly, there was the fact that he was Mey's uncle and she trusted him explicitly. However, they had not seen one another in almost fifty years. A lot can change over that amount of time. The decision was made - he would only reveal what he had to at this point. The rest he would keep to himself. After all, there were still things he was keeping from Mey as well; all for her own good, or so he told himself.

Bob's voice brought him back from his inner struggles. "What dangers do we face, Mage? Mey told me of the Shadow Guard and the goblin attack, but surely goblins and shadows aren't the only nemesis we face."

"No, of course not. The dangers as we go along will grow. There are forces that would see this quest ended before any progress can be made."

Bob prodded him for more. "Such as?"

Struggling not to reveal information the Circle had stumbled upon, Thom chose his words carefully. "There are sects of priests who are not happy with our activities. They think we overstep our bounds and have no right to decide the fate of the world."

"Do you?" The tension between the two men could be cut with a knife. "After all, who is anyone to decide the fate of others?"

"It's not like that. We do not make the choices. We only give a small push to those that may need it." Thom was beginning to wonder if he should bow out of this conversation.

"People like my niece?"

"No." The statement was firm and left no room for argument otherwise. "People like your niece are special. People who have the ability to change the world but just don't know it yet. She is powerful beyond her imaginings and to bring that power to the surface would only lend to her existing strength and beauty." Thom stopped himself. He was going too far. He had almost let his anger carry him away.

"Well, then, I see no reason not to continue on your path to saving the world. If you feel that strongly." There was a hint of a smile on Bob's face. "Get a good rest. Tomorrow we continue your journey to the Barren Lands." With that, he walked away.

SEVEN

The terrain between Andari Point and the Barren Lands was perilous and unforgiving. Small villages and settlements dotted the route, which was mostly forestland. They decided to skirt these villages and continue on without entering, unless, of course, supplies were needed. They could live mostly off the land, what with the rabbits, squirrels, deer and other animals prowling about.

As they packed and readied themselves that first morning, Mey noticed an unwarranted amount of tension present between the men. *Now, what is all this about?* Gods, she hoped the two of them worked through their differences. The last thing she wanted to deal with for weeks or months on the road was two squabbling men. She rolled her eyes when she heard them bickering over how to load the pack horse. With conviction, she took the bundle from Bob's hands, probably a bit too roughly, and snatched the length of rope from Thom's. Glaring at them both, she looped the rope around the pack and tied it snugly to the horse's saddle.

"There," she said through clenched teeth. "We are ready."

She heard Durlag's laugh follow her as she strode toward the path to wait for the others to catch up. She would much prefer to make this journey alone if this was any example of what she was going to have to put up with. Durlag's flask was looking better and better by the moment.

With a great silence hanging over them, they left the clearing and continued on their way. Mey wanted to know more about her mother but that would mean having to actually talk to her uncle. She didn't want to be the first to break the silence especially since she had begun to feel guilty about her overreaction to their disagreement. She had been a bit of a brat and was probably too hard on them.

So she made it a point to enjoy the countryside. Trees and lush greenery showered the part of Cantor they were now passing through. Being near the sea, greenery grew in abundance. The salty smell in the air was greatly diminished but still there on the slight breeze. Concentrating hard on the smells and sights, Mey was startled when she heard a faint noise. Slowing her pace, she focused on the noise and continued slowly forward. Again, she heard it - a soft, yet distinctively frantic voice. She wasn't sure what it was saying but it was definitely yelling.

Bob slowed as well, having turned to her and noticed her reaction. "What is it, Mey?"

"Shh." Mey cocked her head to the side for a closer listen. "A voice."

At that point they had all stopped and were straining to hear. It came again. This time she was certain it was a voice and that it was calling for aid.

"I don't know how far off it is," she told them. "Someone needs help." Looking to Bob, he shrugged to tell her that he had not heard. How could it be that she could hear it and her uncle, with the finely tuned hearing of the elves, could not? Pointing a shaking finger, she said, "It's that way."

Thom started walking again. "Then we head that way." The three left behind looked at one another, and then followed.

After about half an hour, they emerged from the trees into a clearing. A house, mostly rubble now, sat in the middle. Long abandoned, the roof had fallen in on one side and half of one wall with it. A well stood off to one side. Clearly it, too, had seen better days. The stones that made up the walls of the well were mostly scattered around its base.

Too quiet. The little hairs on Mey's neck stood on end. From the bandolier across her chest, she took a dagger in each hand. Looking around to her companions, she saw Bob slowly pulling his bow from his back and nock an arrow while Thom had his eyes closed, lips moving, readying a spell to defend against whatever evil might be lurking about. They felt it too.

"This should be fun!" she heard Durlag say. As Mey glanced back at him, he was hefting his large battle axe from his back. She glanced at Bob and gave him a half-grin.

He nodded as if to say, "I'm ready."

Slowly, silently, they made their way toward the house. Then, a sudden yell stilled them in their tracks. In unison, they turned. The voice was coming from *inside the well*!

Bob cautiously took a few steps in the direction of the well. With a few gestures, he told Durlag to circle around and keep an eye on the house. Mey and Thom matched him step for step.

"Can anyone hear me?" the voice sounded again. "Please, anyone!"

"A trap?" mouthed Mey to Bob. He shrugged. Everything looked to be in its place. Bob slowly leaned in to get a look into the well. When he did, a huge smile spread across his face.

"Hey! You! Help me out! I can't hang on much longer!" The voice was definitely male.

Bob looked over to Mey and Thom. "It's a man. Human."

They both leaned over to have a look. "What are you doing in a well?" Thom asked.

"Please, help me out and I'll tell you!" the man pleaded. "I'm losing my grip!"

Thom and Bob each grabbed the rope that hung down into the well and was now supporting not only the bucket used to draw forth water, but also a man.

They heaved and grunted as they pulled. And the voice from the well cheered them on. "That's it! Almost there! Just a few more tugs!"

The rope inched upwards, until Mey could see fingers grasping at the edge of the well. As the man was getting his grip on the lip of the well, the rope that he held snapped. Thom and Bob stumbled backwards. Mey dove forward and grasped his arm before he could lose his tenuous hold. He grabbed for her with his free arm. Pulling with all her strength, she managed to get him far enough up so he could get hold of the ledge again. Then, with a little help, he was able to clamber out.

All of them, now on the ground, were breathing hard with their efforts, willing their hearts to slow, lest they leap out of their chests.

“Thank…you. Thank…you…so…much!” the man said between gasps for air.

Thom sat up. “What in the name of everything holy were you doing down in that well?” he demanded.

“I fell. Trying to get something to drink.” The man had obviously not detected the note of venom in the mage’s voice. “My name is Elerbee. I am a priest of Sirrah.”

He was dressed in white robes which, Mey noted, should have been covered in grime and filth from being down that well but were stark white. Almost blindingly white. A shock of strawberry blond hair fell over his forehead and he brushed it back with his hand, revealing soft brown, strikingly kind eyes. Mey would have guessed his age at about twenty-five human years, give or take.

“You are alone?” Bob was staring at the man as well. *Wondering about those white robes, no doubt.* Mey had already decided they were magical. With a shaking hand, she reached out to touch them. It was as if she couldn’t help herself. She saw her hand moving, was horrified that she couldn’t stop it, but she *had* to know about those robes.

Thom’s face was suddenly in front of her. “Mey?” She looked at him in confusion then slowly came to realize what was going on around her. She glanced around, all eyes were on her. Elerbee was leaning away from her outstretched hand with a look of confusion on his face. She cleared her throat.

“Sorry,” she mumbled and drew her hand back. A sheepish grin crossed her face. “They’re just so…*clean*.” Backing up a couple of steps, she wondered at what just happened. The pull of the magic was so strong! Thom touched her elbow, reassuring. Slowly, her breathing came easier.

“Yes, I am alone,” Elerbee said, answering Bob’s question. Then turning to Mey, “And, yes, they are clean. Thank you. They were a gift.” This was all the information she was going to get apparently.

“The well…?” Thom prompted him.

“Right! I was only traveling around to the settlements to see if anyone needed priestly services. I have found most of them abandoned. I was so thirsty and I figured I could still find something to drink in this old well. I leaned in to see if I could catch a sight of water or even a slight whiff." He shrugged. "I guess I leaned too far and I fell."

"Aye, I find leaning to be a bit troublesome meself," Durlag chimed in. "Avoid it at all costs."

The wrinkle in the priest's nose told the rest of them that he wasn't too keen on the dwarf's smell; the few steps he took to move away told them he wasn't keen on the filth either. The whole time this exchange took place, Mey noticed the man rubbing his hands on his robes as if to rid them of some imagined grime.

"We were just about to stop and take a respite," Thom told him. "You are welcome to join us."

"I think I will. I have missed contact with others these few weeks. Thank you."

****

Conversation was loose and camaraderie came easily to the little group. Although Elerbee had some serious quirks, he was nice enough. They didn't tell him of Mey's heritage but they did reveal that their journey would be taking them to the Barren Lands.

Elerbee explained that he had been traveling these nearby settlements offering help with crops, giving healing to the sick and infirm and praying with those who needed spiritual guidance. He was on a self-imposed mission. The other priests at the Temple of Sirrah in Jareen thought him crazy to undertake such a task.

Jareen was further north, closer to the Forest of Nott. There were many more dwarves up that way and less elves. So, Elerbee stared incessantly at Bob and Mey, curious eyes taking in all he could of their fine, angled features. Bob more so than Mey. She had the features of the elves; high cheekbones, slightly slanted eyes, though not so slanted as her uncle's, ears that pointed upward at the tips; again, Mey's slightly more rounded out than Bob's. Bob was beginning to show signs of discomfort at all the attention.

"So, you are a healing priest?" Bob asked Elerbee to break the recent staring fest. "Meylaran, how about letting him take a look at that wound on your leg? It would help to hasten the healing and we could move along a bit faster."

"It's fine, really. I haven't even noticed the pain." She moved her leg out in front of her and rolled the hem of her trousers up slightly. The bandage was getting grimy with dirt from the road. As she unwound it, Elerbee's nose wrinkled to show his distaste for the condition of the cloth. As she uncovered her calf, he leaned in to inspect the wound.

"May I?" he asked, reaching for her leg.

Thom immediately started to protest, but Mey was quicker.

"Sure," she said, and Thom swallowed his objection.

Turning her leg, Elerbee peered at the scratch that the goblin's spear had put there. She had washed it out with water and applied a salve but that's all the "battlefield" medicine she knew. It wasn't so bad.

"When did this happen?" asked Elerbee.

"Couple of days ago," she answered.

"A couple of days?" His brows came together and he looked at each person in turn. "This wound looks more like it is weeks old, rather than days."

Mey shrugged. "See, I told you it wasn't that bad. I'll just put the bandage back on."

Elerbee shuddered and put his hand up. "No. Um, that cloth is filthy. You could invite infection. Here, I'll just heal the rest of this right up." Putting both hands back to her leg, he started speaking in a low voice. Muttering a prayer to Sirrah, he moved his hands over the wound and pressed lightly on it.

Mey winced but then a warm sensation spread through her leg and instantly all pain and irritation from the scratch was gone.

She looked from her leg to Elerbee who was smiling proudly. "There," he said, "good as new."

"Impressive," she said, nodding her thanks to him. Stretching her leg out and turning it to look at where the scratch had been she could see nothing but a very clean patch of skin on the back of her calf.

"Nice," Thom's voice cracked and Mey looked at him. His eyes were wide, and staring at her leg. She had the feeling he wasn't referring to the healing skill of the priest.

Rolling her eyes, she pushed her pant leg down to cover her exposed skin. "Show's over. It's time to get back on the road." Thom's face reddened as he realized he'd been caught. Mey flashed a sly smile at him.

****

The earlier tension and all around bad mood was lifted from the band of travelers as they set out. Even Durlag had a spring to his step. Mey had to wonder if the priest didn't have something to do with that.

As they walked, Elerbee found his way to her side. "You are not fully elven," he noted.

She glanced at him. Not quite sure about this man, she decided to guard her secrets well. "No, I am not."

He chuckled. "I see. I will tell you about the robes if you will tell me a bit about yourself. I am intrigued by elves, you see. I have never met one, actually."

"Then you should be talking with my uncle. He is fully elven."

Elerbee looked at Bob. "Yes, but he doesn't seem as approachable." Looking back to Mey, he said, "I get the feeling he would rather everyone leave him alone."

"Of course he would. He is an elf." She winked at the priest as they continued their trek.

"Are all elves so secretive?" he asked.

"Are all priests so nosy?"

"Yes. We are."

Laughing out loud, she decided then and there that she liked this man. He was bothersome, but honest and he made her smile. Smiling was in short supply of late and she felt refreshed with him. Priestly presence, probably. His god working through him, certainly. He obviously believed completely.

Thom had made his way to her other side. "Elerbee, are you originally from Jareen or only there for your studies?"

There was a pause for half a heartbeat before Elerbee answered. "I am originally from the farmlands surrounding Jareen. I was born there and my family still resides just outside the city." Then ignoring Thom completely, he turned back to Mey. "So tell me, where are you from?"

She considered the question before answering. "From all over, really. I haven't had a true home since I was very young. The longest I stayed anywhere was in Seaside." A small noise drew her attention to Thom, who looked to be holding his breath. *Ah, he doesn't want me to reveal too much.*

“What about the robes? What magic is this that keeps them so clean?” Mey asked, changing the subject from herself.

“Well, they were a gift from my mentor. Once I reached Divine status, he presented them to me.” He looked guiltily at her. “If you can’t tell, I have a ‘thing’ for cleanliness. He thought it a fitting gift.”

“Yes, I think I noted that,” she said with a chuckle.

“Oh, yes,” Thom tried to interject again. “Where does that come from – that obsession with cleanliness?”

The other two looked at him, surprised he would ask such a thing. Mey couldn’t believe her ears! Her eyes wide, her mouth hanging slack, she said scolding, “Thom!”

Elerbee was obviously bothered by the attention to his relentless need to be clean. “That’s ok. Um, it’s something that’s just always been with me.” His face was red as a beet. “If you will excuse me. Thank you, Mey, for the chat.” He fell back, feigning interest in the horses and settled in walking beside them.

Mey was still looking at Thom. “What was *that*?” she demanded.

“What?” he asked. “I was only trying to stay with the conversation!”

“Nobody invited you in the first place!” Her voice was getting louder as she spoke. The anger was like a fire in the pit of her stomach, burning straight through at high speed; consuming each and every inch of her from the inside, out. From her middle, out to her limbs, the feeling radiated – and right before it reached her face, she had a sudden, terrifying thought. *Oh, no! What is happening? No, no, no, I don’t want to hurt him!*

EIGHT

Miles away, another priest sat, head in his hands. Wearily, he listened to the laments of the wizard before him.

"What you're suggesting is out of the question!"

"But, Rekho, we have to stop them! Send the demon and be done with it."

"It is not the time!"

"Then send another band of goblins, Shadow Guard or *something* to impede their progress!" the priest implored. The wizard fought them still at every turn. He had come to them wanting to help; wanting to stop the dragons from entering the world once more.

He had his own reasons, and the priests didn't care what they were. They needed him. Only the wizard could call up the denizens from the lower hells. With the rising of each new moon, the tension amongst the priests of Yenoh, the chaos god, mounted as the party that left Seaside grew not only in number but in power.

"I can't call the demons forth yet!" the wizard, Rekho, tried to explain to the priest. "I have insufficient tools here to do so." He rummaged through the shelves of a nearby bookcase. "Useless junk," the wizard muttered. "There are no farthen-crystals here! I must have the crystals!"

"They're on the way. Jost was sent to retrieve five pounds." The priest sighed and stood. "Rekho, just stop them." He turned to leave but stopped in the doorway and said over his shoulder, "I don't care how."

****

As soon as the door closed, Rekho stopped his frantic search and turned to the work table. There, hidden under strips of cloth was a small farthen-crystal. Pushing the cloth aside he bent close and spoke the words that would activate the magical properties of the stone. A picture shimmered before him.

He could have chosen to join the conjured image and become part of it, but he had to keep his distance. Silently, he watched.

The half-elven girl and the mage from the Circle were speaking heatedly. The two seemed to disagree more than any others. *NO!* Rekho screamed silently. The changes that were happening with the girl! Eyes wide, he focused on her.

A red glow flickered into existence, starting in her mid-section. The glow slowly rode outward, spreading to cover her entire body. It was very faint, but Rekho knew it for what it was. “No,” he whispered aloud, pain enveloped in that one word.

Her beautiful green eyes started to change. The silver radiance shone more brilliantly than any other time her unstable dragon blood had surfaced.

He *did* have to stop them. This was happening way too fast and if it continued, he would be unable to do anything at all, no matter how many demons and monsters he threw at them.

Making his decision, he stepped into the spell and found himself surrounded by trees. He checked to make sure he was still incorporeal before moving forward. Slowly sliding up to the girl, he made sure not to touch her. She would sense him, surely, but no one would see him in this state - he had not allowed himself to fully enter the spell.

He began to whisper to her, soothing words of comfort. He must get her calm. She would destroy all of those around her and he could not allow that sort of melee. There had to be another way to stop her and her companions. There simply *had* to be. He could not permit the dragon blood to overtake her. All his efforts would be in vain.

Gradually, her breathing slowed and her eyes focused on the dark-haired human before her. She was frightened, of that he was certain. Whether fear for herself and what was happening or the knowledge of what she could have just done to those around her, he did not know. He continued speaking softly to her.

The girl turned her head toward him slightly. Confusion replaced her rage as the red glow surrounding her diminished; her arms fell limp at her sides. Ensuring she would imagine this was all in her mind, he conjured images to disorient her. Energy spent, she sank to the ground.

With lightning reflexes, the young mage moved, catching her up in his arms and cushioning her fall. Together, they collapsed in the middle of the road.

Rekho retreated, breaking the spell, his disembodied spirit joining once again with his physical body.

The magical energy in the crystal winked out. Exhausted, Rekho lifted a hand, massaging his temples. Withholding his temporal form from the transference spell was always taxing. But it couldn't be helped; he had to remain unseen. He reached for the crystal, now depleted, and it crumbled like dust beneath his fingertips.

The crystal would have lasted longer had he not manipulated it improperly. Bending the magical energy to fit his needs had destroyed its delicate essence. It was his last until Jost returned. Deep in the Forest of Nott, in the Caverns of Endless Time, the crystal thrived and multiplied. Like an organism feeding and growing off of the land itself. The crystal was in abundance there. The trick was getting in and out of the Caverns in one piece.

****

What Rekho could not know was that Jost had located the crystals and was preparing to transport them back. But many denizens of an underworld so dark and rank with evil were set to guard these caverns. Taking the crystals was like ripping pieces of their very life-forces from them.

A figure rose up behind the priest, silent and deadly. It watched as he loaded his pack full of the life-giving crystals. When the man turned, he came face-to-face with one of the guardians of the crystals. Part human and part animal, the creature lifted its red eyes, flattened the ears that sat atop its head and let out a cry so terrible that it froze Jost in place and he dropped the pack he carried.

With a trembling hand, Jost reached for the stout mace that hung at his belt. He was not a novice to battle, which was why he was chosen for this particular task; however this otherworldly creature would be unnerving to even the most seasoned of men. Its long body was humanoid, covered with patches of skin and sparse hair. The other patches were the muscles that *should* have been on the *inside*. It glistened from ooze that constantly ran from every inch of its abominable body. The face was human; however it sported animalistic ears and a slightly elongated snout. Set within the snout was a wide mouth revealing two rows of razor-sharp teeth. Its cries were decidedly feral. It stood before Jost snarling and ready to protect what belonged to it.

"Yenoh lend me strength," muttered Jost as he pulled the mace forward. The weapon glowed with an aura of godly magic. Jost felt the power of his god flow through him and into the weapon as he brought it above his head. The thing charged.

Just as the creature slammed into him, Jost brought down his mace on its head. Howling in pain, for the gods' power lent strength to the priest's arm, the creature lunged straight for his throat. Snapping teeth found the soft flesh of his neck. Again, the mace found a mark on the beast's head. The two, locked together, rolled away from the wall and the crystals spilled from the bag.

In only moments, the snarling beast stepped away from the man. Jost's unseeing eyes stared. Circling, the creature licked its lips free of blood and gave special caution not to go near the weapon that lay in the lifeless hand. Making its way around to where the crystals lay scattered, it picked one up. It held the crystal lovingly and gently, and then placed it among the others on the cavern wall. The wall seemed to absorb the crystal. It took only moments to replace all the crystals and when he was done, the beast turned back to the man on the floor.

It howled. Three times the long, mournful cry sounded and echoed throughout the caverns. Others beasts emerged from the blackness and gathered around the dead priest on the ground. They made short work on the body and when they finally stepped away from the spot, the only thing left was the glowing mace that none of them could touch.

****

She knew that voice! Where did that come from? As Mey opened her eyes, trying to push herself up, she realized that strong arms held her.

"Don't move." The command was firm.

Looking around, things swam back into focus and she concentrated on just being able to see. "Wh-what…?" she managed to croak out, but her throat was hot and dry. It felt like she had swallowed a mouth full of dirt. She took in a deep breath and let it out very slowly.

Three faces loomed above her and she recognized all of them. The looks of fear on Thom's, Bob's and Durlag's faces confirmed that *something* had happened.

"I'm fine," she finally said. "Just let me up."

"No, not yet." Thom insisted. "Mey, that was…are you burned?"

"Burned?" She was a bit confused at that question.

"You…you…were covered in fire," he said, adding quietly, "I've never seen anything like it."

"Lass, there were flames all around ye! Like they came from inside ye and then just ate ye all up!" Durlag looked very frightened. Mey remembered the story he had told them. She felt a little guilty.

"I'm sorry." The statement was aimed at Durlag because she truly felt sorry that she had brought such fears back to him. His face changed and what she saw there now was more akin to worry.

"Ye're alright, then?" he asked.

"Yes," she answered. She struggled in Thom's grasp. "Just let me go, now. I need to stand and get my bearings."

Bob stepped back and offered a hand. He had not said a word during all this but his eyes told her this was not the first time he had seen such a sight.

Thom was hesitant and his arms tightened slightly about her. "You're sure? You can stand?"

"I am fine!" she snapped. Twisting her head around to look at him, she was shocked at his look of sheer terror. He was intently focused on her. "I am fine," she whispered to him, more gently than before. She even managed a smile. What? Why was she trying to reassure him? He was the one who started all of this in first place! But the need to calm him far outweighed any anger she was feeling.

His arms loosened and she started up. Her limbs were shaky and she was unsteady but Thom was quick to support her and once she made it halfway, Bob took her hand and steadied her.

She saw Elerbee had stayed back, near the horses, his eyes wide. She managed a smile in his direction. He didn't move.

"Well, what are we waiting for?" she said to them. "Let's go. We've got a lot of ground to cover."

Coming to her side, Thom said, "Mey, don't you think you should take it easy for a bit? Rest some before we continue on?" The look of concern had not left his face.

"No, why? I'm fine. We're on a time table, are we not?"

"Well, yes, but…"

"Then, let's go." She picked her pack up, dusted it off and set to readying herself. Bob was close behind her. The others slowly followed suit, picked up their gear and continued at a somewhat slower pace.

As they walked, Mey slowly began feeling more like herself. She breathed in the fresh scents of the world around her. They were on a dirt road that connected the farms with one another. The lands were flat and the grasses grew to knee height. The road hadn't been traveled recently, given the debris and over-growth that littered it. Most of the farm houses they passed had been abandoned. If they followed it, this road would take them straight into the next populated town.

Until the noises returned, she hadn't noticed the eerie quiet. Small insects buzzed around them and birds cried above in the skies. Reflecting on what had just transpired, those noises were conspicuously missing until just now. Mey peered up into the sky, squinting against the brightness of the sun.

Glancing at her uncle, she took in his mood and tried to figure out what it meant. He didn't seem worried about what had happened – he didn't worry about much. He had been the only one who was not shocked and disgusted.

The dragon blood, she was sure, had almost consumed her that time. She couldn't dwell on what she had almost done to those around her. It was too frightening for her to think on. But she had calmed and controlled it. Told it to retreat and it had obeyed. All she really recalled was the soothing feeling and images of the time she spent in the elven land with her father and uncle. If she could control it, then she could possibly stop it, right? She wasn't ready for this yet and couldn't say if she ever would be.

Looking at the eastern sky, she noticed the dark clouds that were massing in the distance. They were far away, but the look of them was threatening.

"What does it mean?" she said aloud.

Her uncle answered her question. "I do not know. But I feel that it does not bode well for any of us."

NINE

Once the group reached a spot near the last settlement, they called a halt. The growing darkness in the east troubled both Mey and Bob. They brought it to everyone's attention over the scant dinner they had pieced together; each one contributing something of what they had left.

"I do not know what it means," Bob was saying, "but the feeling I get when I gaze upon it is very unpleasant."

"Yes," Mey agreed. She could feel the unease of the entire group. "I think we should set a double watch tonight. Then be off from here as early as possible."

Thom set down his plate. "We still have to cross the Dahrst Hills and that will take at least another week to reach. Once we cross the Hills into Sorga we can stock up and prepare to enter the Barren Lands." He paused and looked at no one in particular. "Crossing the Dahrst Hills will be rough going."

"Aye," Durlag chimed in. "The Hills be haunted. Haunted by the thousands of soldiers, who, under the command of Borgan Dahrst, lost their lives protecting their homeland." He took a long draw from his flask. "Heh," he tittered nervously before he added, "But who's believin' in ghost stories! Not meself!"

All the others eyed him. Swallowing hard, Elerbee nodded. No one wanted to voice their opposition to the ghosts that were said to live in the Dahrst Hills.

"We'll figure a way through," Thom said as he stood. "I'll take morning watch." He left the rest to work out details of the remaining watch hours. Mey watched him go. He pulled something from a pouch at his hip and disappeared into a copse of trees. Tempted to follow, she stood.

"Where do you think you'll be goin' now, lass?" Durlag asked. "Yerself must take a watch! Which one's for you?"

"Put me anywhere," she said absently and waved him off. "I just need to go check something…" Words trailing, she absently walked in the same direction Thom had taken.

"Hrumph," Durlag said to her back. "Let her have the middle watch! That'll show her to pay attention when it's needed!"

His words did not register, however. She was more intent on finding what the wizard was up to. He always radiated magical energy but whatever he took from his pouch was stronger than his normal aura.

****

He was chanting when she found him. A spell! Mey watched silently from the shadows. A faint memory of her father assailed her. She'd heard these words before, had she not? Silent as the wind that passed through the branches of the trees, she crept forward. However, he must have been in a state of heightened awareness. His back stiffened and he slowly began to turn.

Mey thought about quickly hiding but her curiosity got the better of her. She stood, in the open, ready for him to berate her for the interruption.

It caught her off guard when he turned to her with a smile, one that lit up his eyes and made her feel like he was truly glad to see her. *His eyes are so blue.* And after that one thought, everything else seemed inconsequential.

"You're following me?" He seemed more amused than angry.

"Wcll…sort of, ycs." She stammered. "Actually, I was following whatever that is in your hand, there. It's magic." She spared another look at those amazing eyes, careful not to linger, lest they pull her in where she could not escape.

He glanced down. "Oh, yes. A farthen-crystal. I had intended to communicate with the Circle."

"Farthen-crystal," she repeated. "I remember my father having these."

"Your father?" That seemed to take him off-guard.

"Yes," she said. "He dabbled in the magical arts, you know."

"Dabbled!" Surprise was the only word she had for what she saw on his fine features.

Confusion threatened to overtake this moment. But she wouldn't let that happen. She changed the subject. "What is it that you will tell your wizards? That I am more and more unstable with each passing day? That we are no closer to retrieving the Heartstone of the Idylic than we were when we started?" She felt smug and powerful to hang this information over his head.

"What? No, I was only…keeping them aware…of my whereabouts." He was definitely hiding something. This whole time she had felt that he was not telling her the entire truth and now she intended to find out what it was.

Pointing an accusing finger at his chest, she said, "You have kept your secrets too long. It ends now."

He didn't budge. "I will not be bullied into revealing anything." His icy stare pinned her in place. She swallowed hard. She was expecting him to at least show some fear of her. Now she didn't know *what* to do. That had been her plan; the whole thing. He stepped in closer. She could smell his unique scent of bitter herbs and sweet flowers. It made her head swim and she lost focus. *What now?*

"I will keep any secrets I see fit to keep. My task here is to make sure you are safe." Did his voice just break? He cleared his throat.

She stepped closer. "So, is that what I am? A task?" She softened her voice and held on to her emotions for dear life. "I thought we were becoming friends."

"Mey…" he began, a cross between an invitation and a warning. Something melted behind his frosty blue eyes.

The way he said her name, the way he smelled, it was too much. She couldn't hold it together anymore. Mey closed the distance between them. Without hesitation, she pressed her lips to his.

Thom's body went rigid, his hands coming up in a firm grasp on her shoulders. He inhaled deeply. Surely he didn't mean to deny her? Though his lips were awkward and unyielding against hers, Mey knew he *had* to feel something. She hadn't mistaken the stolen glances; his possessive glare while Elerbee had examined her leg.

Desperation urged her closer. Just when she thought he wouldn't relent, his hands loosened, tension easing from his grasp. His thumbs, warm and smooth, traced a small circle over her collarbone. Heat infused her limbs; pooled low in her belly. His lips molded against hers as his hands found their way down her spine, resting at the small of her back. Pulling her closer with the slightest movement, Thom matched her enthusiasm, making her gasp as her body pressed closer to his.

Gods, he tastes as wonderful as he smells! Mey felt as though they had tumbled and floated in emptiness, just she and Thom. Tiny prickling electrical shocks hit her every nerve. All she knew was this moment; this sensation that she never wanted to end. Her arms moved of their own volition, twining around his neck, pulling his body closer. A low, primitive groan stirred in Thom's throat. His hands pressed harder against her back, his lips firm and demanding. Mey curled her fingers in the collar of his tunic, desperate to anchor herself.

Then something changed. He started to pull away. Mey wanted to scream. *Oh, no! Don't end this.*

Thom moved his hands back to her shoulders, pushing her back to arms length. His breathing was fast, labored. "I…can't…" He shook his head, swallowed.

"Why?" Her own breath was coming in short gasps. "We both want this, don't we?" She moved closer. "Since the first touch. Tell me, Thom. *Tell* me you didn't!"

He lifted trembling fingers to his brow. "I…I don't know, Mey…of course I did!" The statement shocked her. She had indeed expected him to protest. His eyes were shut against his feelings. "But, Mey, this is only the dragon blood taking over. It has heightened all your senses. Even this one. It strips away all reason. One of us has to keep a level head!" He sounded more as if he were pleading with her.

As he opened his eyes, she could see his agony in making this decision. It angered her even more. He *was* rejecting her! Men didn't normally reject her and this took her by surprise. Especially since she *knew* he wanted this as much, if not more, than she did. She stepped back.

"Fine." She bit the word off. Another step back. She could feel anger creeping in way too fast. She tried to push it away. Even through her anger, she didn't want to hurt him. Quickly, she turned. If she didn't get away from him now, she wasn't sure if she would be able to control the emotions.

She heard voices as she hurried through the camp and past everyone there. Her intent was to get far enough away that she could let go of these feelings without hurting anyone. She wanted to scream! How could he? She had revealed herself to him on a most personal level and he had thrown that back at her like it didn't matter. She was so sure of his intent. He was as easy to read as an open book. Carrying everything in his eyes; eyes so frosty blue that they chilled her even as she thought of them.

She walked faster, almost at a jog. *Stop it! Focus.* Stopping under a great oak tree, she leaned against it and slid down. Her hands fell next to her and she felt the roots of the tree. She grabbed on for dear life for it felt as though she was sinking. The harder and more desperately she held on, the more stable she felt. Tears that had threatened for so long finally spilled over and she let them run, unchecked, down her cheeks. She missed Garrin desperately; and her father. She had never missed her father so much as she did at this moment. She wanted someone she could trust that would let her tears soak their shoulder and they would remain silent while she emptied all the poisonous feelings.

"Meylaran." Her full name. Looking at her uncle, another flood of emotions came. He looked so much like her father.

"Uncle," she acknowledged him, but she couldn't let go of the tree just yet. It was her anchor and her hold was tenuous at best.

Kneeling next to her, he moved his hand over one of hers, gently freeing her fingers from their grip on the roots of the tree. He held it in both his hands. His smile was full of concern and love for her.

"*Ah la'du utahn,*" he whispered. *My beloved child.* Not having heard nor spoken elven since she left the homeland, she still knew what he was saying and the inflection of care in his voice was unmistakable. Her father used to say the same thing to her. Giving in, she threw her arms around him. He let her sob until she felt that she had nothing more left.

"Here, now," he said finally, and lifted her chin with his delicate fingers. "What is this about?"

"I don't want this! At any given moment, I could kill those I care most for and not even be able to stop it!"

He looked at her thoughtfully. "You know, I saw your mother get angry more than once. She never hurt anyone she did not intend to hurt. What you have to do is learn to *control* it."

"And how exactly do I do that? With no other dragons, who will teach me?"

"Well, that wizard seems to know a bit about it." He hesitated, but only slightly. "Why not ask him?"

Snorting with derision, she started to feel her hurt returning. "Right! He doesn't want anything to do with me!"

"Ah," Bob replied. "So, now we get to the heart of it."

"What do you mean?"

With a slight hint of a smile on his lips, he continued. "He has hurt your feelings." Again, he caressed her chin. "I can see you care for this human. In your life, you will have many people whom you care for. They will not always return your feelings."

"But he does! He said as much. I just don't understand why he rejects me!" She had said it all before she even meant to. If she had thought about it, she would not have told her uncle all of this.

"Rejection is part of life, Meylaran. Perhaps his own fear keeps him from showing you his true feelings." He dropped his hand from her face and stood. "Now, let us return to camp."

Just like that, he had said what he was going to say. Oddly, it was comforting and she felt better for the distraction but it really didn't answer any questions or solve any problems for her. She would have to be conscious of letting her feelings get the better of her, since everything was in such a heightened state of awareness. Especially her anger. She had found some good friends she could trust in and she didn't want to lose any one of them. Soon she would have to explain all of this but for now, she just needed to keep it under control.

"I'll be right there. I just need a moment." He nodded and started to move away. "Uncle, wait!" He turned back to her. "Thank you. *Holuran ad'nay.*"

Inclining his head to her slightly, he said, "I honor you, as well." He turned and walked back toward their camp.

Mey breathed deeply and took in the scents around her; the trees, the earth, the animals. She closed her eyes and focused on her breathing. It was a calming technique Garrin had taught her and it almost always worked. She let her mind float free of all worries and worldly happenings. She brought to mind those she loved most. Her father, smiling at her with loving approval; Garrin next, his easy grin and happy eyes sparkling. She felt a slight ache in her heart for missing these two. Then she drew up her uncle's image. He was so much like her father! Lastly, she held an image of Thom. How could she hate him? He was certainly beautiful but more than that, she was drawn to him. He had been kind, he saved her life. Perhaps he was right; they should keep their task foremost in mind. That was the right thing, she decided; of course it was. How could she have behaved as she did? Slowly, she brought the world around her back into focus and opened her eyes. She stood and made her way back to their camp.

****

Upon entering camp, she could feel the eyes on her but when she would look up, they all quickly looked away. All but Thom; his eyes never left her.

The fire was small, the nights had not yet become too chill, but Mey set her bedroll out closer to it. The light comforted her. As she lay, staring into the flames and drifting to sleep, her mind called to her protectors, as it did every night. The faces of her father, Garrin and, no matter how much she wanted to ignore him, Thom.

The next thing she knew, she was awakening to the sound of her name. She rolled around, trying to avoid the annoying noise. Quickly, she became alert, knowing she had to get up for her watch. Opening one eye, she looked right at a smiling Durlag. "Time fer yer watch, girl," he said.

The smell of the spirits he constantly drank washed over her and she almost gagged. *That* was surely their best defense against any creature who thought to venture too close! Maybe they could just have Durlag breathe on their enemy and they would run, screaming back where they came from.

Immediately seeking a way to avoid another wave of the nauseating smell, she sat up and rubbed her eyes.

"Yes, I'm up," she mumbled through her sleep fog.

"Much as they say elves don't need sleep, you lot sure can snore to wake the dead," he said over his shoulder as he made his way to his own bedding.

"I do not snore!" Playful indignation colored her words as she stood and put on her bandolier and sword belt. Checking her secreted weapons in her boots, sleeves, at her waist, and even strapped to her leg, she asked, "Who's on watch with me?"

The dwarf yawned and rolled to his side facing her. "Yer own uncle, to be sure. That's yer first watch. I'm thinking that our young priest has tried to bribe 'im into getting the next with ye." He winked at her. "I'm thinkin' that one's smitten."

She cocked an eyebrow at him. "I think not. Just curious about elves." She hadn't thought Elerbee's attention to be more than that. Was it? She shook the notion off and continued about her business.

Her uncle was at the perimeter of the camp on the southern edge. She almost walked right past him but at the last moment, her keen sight caught his heat signature.

"I will start here at the southern point. You start at the northern. We will make a circuit of the camp, slowly, to cover all ground." Her uncle was nothing if not thorough.

After two hours, they had circled the camp three times. Bob looked weary. If she had not forced him to go rest, she was sure he would have tried to stay on a third watch. Reluctantly, he dragged himself to his bed. Shaking her head, Mey could only ponder on his dedication to their safety. When she thought back, he always took more than one watch. Rarely did she see him sleep. And when he did, his sleep was troubled. Perhaps no rest at all was better than what awaited him behind his closed eyes.

Her second watch was indeed with the priest. Once awake, Elerbee was enthusiastic to share time with her. The small clearing was lightening as the sun began its rise, so they had little need to run the perimeter – Mey could see most of it. Human eyes wouldn't be able to detect the changes she could see, but Elerbee trusted in her when she told him that everything was clear.

He had not traveled much with others and was a bit unused to having to watch out for people, he confided to her.

"How, then, do you keep yourself safe while on the road?"

"Oh, now, *that* is the fun part," he winked at her. "These robes that you are so fond of; they keep me safe. They are my shield."

"What do you mean?" Mey wanted to know. "Like armor?"

"Exactly! They also keep me from freezing in cold weather or overheating when it's hot." With a flourish of his hands, he showed off the amazingly clean robes. He chuckled. "And they stay clean."

Trying her best not to just reach out and touch them again, she opened her senses to the magic they exuded. The familiar pull of the energy was there but this time she tried putting herself outside of it rather than directly in it. It was working! The pull lessened and she was still able to sense the energy and follow its path. Her urge to know more about the magic and to experience it was still there as well, but the overwhelming need to possess it was not. Her uncle was right; all she needed to learn to do was to *control* all of this.

Elerbee held out an arm. "You may touch them, if you like."

Mey looked from him to the robes and back again to be sure, before she reached out her hand. She was trembling with the effort it was taking to keep her urges under control. The moment her fingertips brushed the fine white fabric, it was like an electric bolt was unleashed throughout her entire body. Magical energy flowed through her in such a rush, she jerked her hand away. The moment she did, it was all gone. She smiled in spite of herself. Looking at Elerbee, she found him smiling as well.

"It's you, isn't it? *You* are the descendant of the dragons." Excitement danced in his eyes. "I knew it!"

Hesitation would not serve her here. Immediately, she answered him. "What are you talking about?" She placed a careful look of innocent confusion on her face.

"I had my doubts at first, but then, that fire…" he broke off. He had a smug smile on his face and Mey was getting more nervous by the minute.

"You must be mistaken. I'm sure I don't know what you're talking about." Turning away to continue moving on the perimeter of the camp, she abruptly stopped. Something was amiss. Sniffing the air, there was only the smell of the people in this camp. She could see nothing and her ears picked up not a sound.

"What?" Elerbee pressed as he moved closer to her. "What is it?"

"I don't know," she admitted. "Maybe nothing."

He muttered quiet prayers to his god and the barely perceptible glow of magic engulfed them both. At the same moment, a dagger hit the invisible force in front of her and fell harmlessly to the ground.

Quickly, Mey drew a dagger in each hand. She turned to Elerbee, who was holding his own weapon, an ornately wrought, silver warhammer. *Now where did that come from*? Instinctively, she crouched and moved to the nearest tree.

Elerbee's voice was right next to her. "You are covered by the spell. Priestly armor; but it will only last a few minutes."

"Did you see where it came from?"

"No." He didn't seem as frightened as she would have thought. Fleetingly, she noted his comfort in handling the hammer and the general situation of danger.

"We need to wake the others." She let out a long, low, whistle. Bob was at their side in almost no time. "Elerbee, go. Get the rest up!"

He nodded and moved off. Mey continued to scan the camp and its surrounding area with all her senses. But she could come up with nothing. Whoever it was knew what they were doing.

"I don't know where they are!" She ground her teeth together with frustration. "That dagger," she pointed to it, "came at my chest. Elerbee's armor spell stopped it."

"I'll take the higher vantage point." Slinging his bow over his shoulder, Bob scrambled up the tree they hid behind. Once he was out of sight, Mey let out the breath she had not realized she had been holding.

She could hear the others stirring now. Durlag first, then Thom. As they made their way over to her, she could see Elerbee's divine power shielding them all. Durlag brought up the rear and was swatting at his arms and face in distaste of having the magic touch him so closely.

Just as they passed into the tree's shelter, another dagger hit the armor spell covering Elerbee and clattered, useless, to the ground.

He bent and picked it up. The group huddled together. Quickly, the decisions were made; Durlag moved off to position himself opposite the group on the left. Thom moved to take up the right, and insisted that Elerbee stay close to Mey with his healing magics at the ready. Elerbee blessed each as they made their way to their points.

They waited. Mey closed her eyes and opened a mental link to her uncle, above them. *Do you see anything*?

At least six. She heard the sound of an arrow fly and a grunt. *Five. They move in shadow. My guess would be a band of highway thieves.*

She whispered this information to Elerbee, who hefted his hammer and nodded once. *Where*?

They will come from all sides. They are splitting up now.

TEN

Things moved quickly. A few more daggers flew in, but once they met with Elerbee's magical armor, they fell harmlessly to the ground. Still Mey could not hear, smell nor see anything. One of the filthy rogues was almost on her before she spotted him. Where in the hells had he come from? She focused on the black paint that covered him head to toe, even his clothes.

Ah, invisible midnight. A trick she learned almost from her start as an apprentice with Garrin. Mixing the right herbs would give one a black, inky substance that would shield you from prying eyes if used properly. It also rendered any smell almost nonexistent. That would explain much.

A slow smile curled her lip as she circled him. He never took his eyes from her either. She kept her senses open, trying to determine if any of them were sneaking up from behind to pin her in and get the advantage. The only weapon in his hands at this point was a garrote. He had planned on taking her out silently, had he? Well, they had lost their advantage of surprise. Now, they had to stand and fight and they were ill prepared for that.

Her opponent took a swipe at her. Mey side-stepped and came in with her own lunge, dagger leading. She managed to nick his arm as he turned to parry her move. He spiraled to the left, drawing a sword as he moved. Not her preferred mode of attack, but, swords it was. Mey drew her own but kept the dagger in her left hand. Sword-play worked much better for her if she had a dagger to balance it out.

"Come on, girl," the man said through gritted teeth.

"Oh, must we have all this talking?" Mey sighed and came in with a backhanded swing, which he managed to knock aside with the flat of his blade.

They matched each other move for move. He was good. Her blade locked with his. They were so close she could feel his hot breath on her cheek.

"Maybe I could show you how to handle a sword," he said with lewd intent.

Blinking once, his face froze in a grimace and the life started fading from his eyes. Warm blood ran over Mey's hand as the dagger sank to the hilt. "Maybe I could teach you a thing or two about underestimating a woman with a dagger," she whispered as he slid to the ground.

Dropping the sword, she turned in time to see Durlag engaged with two of the highwaymen. Almost at the same instant, small darts of light from Thom's spell found their mark on one of them. Scanning the small campsite, she spotted another man on the ground, arrows protruding from his back and neck. That was two down. Where was Elerbee?

A loud cry resonated from behind, and had her grabbing two more daggers as she crouched low. The sight of Elerbee holding his hammer above his head, ready to bring a smashing blow down on his opponent answered her question. The weapon glowed with a radiance bright and pure as the hammer passed through the air. Elerbee's booming call to his god had the other man's eyes wide with fear. At the last moment, the man managed to twist himself back and the blow landed on his shoulder. Apparently, Elerbee had not anticipated missing and he was not ready with the follow-through swing. The thief managed to get his weapon in hand and up for a strike. The sword was headed for her new friend's chest and surely would fell him.

"Not today," she whispered and raced toward the two. Throwing one of the daggers, it deflected the blow enough so it met with his arm and not his heart. A look of pain crossed Elerbee's face and by that time, Mey was behind the rogue, grabbing his filthy hair and pulling back as hard as she could. He grunted in protest. A dagger appeared at his throat.

"Mercy," she heard the man whimper.

Her hand stopped for only an instant, but a clear urge to

continue the task was forefront in her mind. She pierced the soft flesh and drug the blade across his throat. Warmth flowed over her hand and she heard her own voice, "Mercy is for fools!"

She closed her eyes, almost able to taste this moment. A sudden vision exploded behind her lids, speeding through her mind: The magnificent creature stretched its powerful limbs. Sunlight shone and sparkled on its royal blue scales. Leathery wings rose from its back and it rolled its head around to stare directly at her. It was the most beautiful thing she had ever seen. The compulsion to kneel before this majestic being was almost so strong she couldn't escape it. Golden eyes held her and laughter encompassed the entire countryside.

"Welcome, sister. Thank you for waking me."

She dropped the dagger like it was molten hot and the vision was gone. Looking up at Elerbee, eyes wide, mouth agape, she wondered if he had seen it too.

He stood, holding his arm, his gaze still on the dead man at his feet. Mey looked down. The man's head was nearly completely severed from his body. Revulsion swept over her.

Had *she* done that? There was no time to dwell on it now. The sounds of battle assailed her ears. She decided to leave the dagger where it lay. To touch it again was not a thought she relished.

Finding Durlag still engaged with one of the rogues, and Thom sagging against a tree trunk, urgency moved her feet. Elerbee was right next to her; healing his own wounds as they moved. They stopped next to Thom, who was several feet away from the dwarf.

"Are you hurt?" Elerbee asked Thom.

Thom only shook his head. He looked too tired to even speak.

Bob approached. "What do they want?"

Looking at one another, all three had to shrugged, admitting ignorance. Suddenly, Mey had to know. What *did* they want? "Elerbee, can you stop him without killing him?"

"Yes, I can. But Durlag…"

"I'll take care of Durlag. You just stop our friend, there. And make sure he can still talk." She flicked her wrist and a dagger fell from beneath her shirt sleeve and she moved toward the dwarf, circling around so that he would see her approach.

Plainly, Durlag was having fun. One hand held his battle axe, a large and definitely well-used weapon, and the other held his ornate flask. He swilled the concoction after almost every swing. Mey had to chuckle at this sight. The poor rogue must think his opponent crazy, and he wouldn't be far off. She knew, however, after spending these few weeks with Durlag, the other man was doomed.

A twinkle of merriment lit the dwarf's eye. Durlag dipped his chin; a barely perceptible nod to acknowledge he had seen her. Now she had the task of trying to pull him away from a fight. This wouldn't be easy. Durlag prepared to swing the axe low, bringing it around easily with one hand. The man jumped at the last moment, avoiding the blow. Mey moved a little closer, trying to communicate her intentions to the dwarf.

The rogue was covered with invisible midnight. Also carrying many pouches and a fine sword. These men were not amateurs. They knew what they were doing. One of those pouches surely contained the pay this one received to complete whatever job it was he was sent to do. Only a couple of more steps brought her closer to Durlag.

"We want this one alive," she said in low tones. "Retreat and let Elerbee lay his trap."

"Hmpf," the dwarf snorted. Hoisting his axe once more as if to land an overhead strike on the poor man before him, he took one step back as his opponent's sword came in. Barely missing the short-statured dwarf's nose, the sword sang through the air. It was a fine weapon, with a glow of iridescent green light, hinting of magic. Whoever hired these men paid well and this made her ever more curious to know why that was.

"Durlag, trust me," Mey whispered. "Fall back."

Another snarl from the dwarf. Letting this go was hard for him. Dwarves never backed down from a fight. But, out of the corner of her eye, she saw him slowly moving away. The man in front of her laughed.

"You filthy coward!" he yelled at the dwarf. "Leaving so soon?"

Mey knew if she did not let Elerbee throw the spell, they would lose their chance. Durlag wouldn't stand for the foolish taunt no matter how much his friends wanted the man alive. Knowing what was coming next, she prepared to throw herself into a backward roll. She would stop Durlag's charge so any spell would not affect them as well. As she threw herself back, she yelled out, "NOW!" Her momentum took her straight into the dwarf's legs and knocked him to the ground. His battle axe flying from his grasp to land somewhere behind them.

Screams sounded around them as they tumbled and came to a stop about ten feet back.

"Me drink!" Durlag had managed to hang on to the flask, sacrificing everything else to use both hands in securing its safe landing. "Dratted girl! What d'ye mean, nearly parting a dwarf from his spirits! Have ye gone daft?" His grumbling was lost in the wailing and maddening screams coming from the rogue.

Mey looked over her shoulder, her mouth gaping at the sight. The man was on his knees, wailing, screaming and spouting gibberish. Her brow came together in a confused pucker and she immediately turned her attention to Elerbee, who looked very proud of himself.

The others started raising their hands to their ears. The screams were continuous and becoming frightening. Mey watched as Durlag stomped past her and straight over to the man. Without a word, he drew his fist back and slammed it into the other's face. The screams stopped instantaneously and the man fell with a hard thud to the ground.

Mey was on her feet, uncoiling a length of rope from her pack. "Help me tie him up." She looked to Elerbee. "How long will it last?"

"Only an hour or so."

"What did you do to him?"

"I-I only did what you asked of me." Taking the defensive, he said, "I stopped him, didn't I?"

"Right." She bit the word off before she said something she would be sorry for later. "Will he have his mind to give us the information we need from him?" Anger was beginning to surface. They couldn't lose this chance to know what these men were after.

"I didn't drive him mad; only gave him a fit of screams. His mind will be intact."

His feelings were hurt, clearly. Damn. Well, he would just have to get over it. The world was not a kind place and sometimes you just had to do the job whether you liked it or not, then move on without regrets. Regrets would only slow you down. Truth be told, he reminded her of herself after her father left. She turned to help the others secure their prisoner.

Bob was helping Thom to the campsite. It was obvious that this fight had taken a lot out of him. His power drew mostly from his own energy with help from the various gems and stones he carried. Durlag had suffered only a minor wound and that was from the fall he took when Mey barreled into him. In trying not to spill the contents of his flask, he had let go his axe and sliced his own arm in the process. Elerbee was more than willing to help heal the dwarf, but Durlag only grumbled something about nuisances and rummaged in his own possessions for what he claimed was a potion of healing.

Only in this after-math could Mey focus on what had happened when she used the bone-handled dagger. As she gathered up the weapons she had thrown, she came upon that one last.

She crouched next to the body that she had nearly decapitated. Forcing herself to look upon the man, she studied him, starting with his feet. She stopped briefly before letting her gaze continue to his neck and head. The injury was one of the most ghastly she had ever seen; and she had seen many, both received and inflicted. This, however, had more effect on her conscience. She had felt driven to take this man's life, even as he begged for mercy. Her hand was guided by something more powerful than she had ever felt. Her eyes fell to the bone-handled, bejeweled dagger next to the corpse.

Remembering that she had only bought this weapon because she felt drawn to it, Mey reached trembling fingers out to retrieve it. Her hand stopped, wavering above the weapon. She swallowed hard to rid herself of the lump of fear that had gathered in her throat. *It's just a damn dagger!* But, she knew that wasn't the truth. There was more to it. At first glance, one would assume this weapon was only for show. It was not practical to actually use with all the jewels set in its handle. When she thought about it, she didn't remember this one feeling any different from the other daggers she used every day. It had fit perfectly in her hand.

This is ridiculous! Berating herself for her fear, she shoved her hand forward and grabbed the dagger. *Makagesh…*the word whispered through her mind. It was not one she recognized from any language she was familiar with. A breath hitched in her throat but she gritted her teeth and slammed the dagger back in the sheath hanging at her waist. As she stood and turned, her eyes caught Thom staring at her, a question in his eyes. He had seen and surely noted her struggle with the dagger. Avoiding having to answer any questions, she made her way to the next body, to search for any useful items.

****

They all held their breath as they watched the man come awake, anticipating the screams. There were none. Enough time had passed for the spell effects to fade. His head lolled to one side and he groaned; eyes opening slowly. Mey wanted hers to be the first face he saw upon sliding back into the conscious world. She was eager to know what these men had wanted.

Bob convinced her to let Thom question the man first. After all, he had spells that would pry answers even from the most stalwart.

They all watched as he looked up. Immediately he tried to move his hands and feet, finding them bound. The set of his jaw changed, his eyes darting rapidly from face to face. He understood he was a prisoner. Thom knew this man would not give up information so easily. A spell to loosen the man's tongue would help. He spoke the words quickly and carefully, while holding a small pearl.

"Who are you?" Thom asked him.

"Barton Johns." Surprise colored his face as he answered. He had obviously not intended to tell them his real name. Such was the power of the spell; if you opened your mouth, the truth was going to come out, whether you liked it or not.

Mey pushed forward. "Why are you here?"

Thom held out a restraining hand discouraging her from getting any closer. Her moods seemed a bit unstable and he couldn't chance her hurting or even killing this man before they gleaned the information they needed. She glared at him, obviously still hurt from his earlier rejection. He would definitely have to fix things between them, but right now, he had to find out what this thief wanted.

"Barton Johns," Thom began. "What do you want from us?"

The man shook his head, refusing to speak. He struggled with his bonds in a useless attempt to free himself.

Leaning in a bit closer, Thom whispered, "I can strengthen this spell and dig the words from you mind, if you prefer." Barton's eyes widened, throat flexing as he swallowed hard. "So, I ask you again, what do you want from us?"

Barton lowered his eyes as he answered. "We were sent for the mask."

Shock settled among them. They all turned to Thom in question about what this man was talking about. Thom was surprised, to say the least. When his gaze turned to Mey, she too, had a look of surprise. Could he mean the mask she and Garrin had stolen? Could the Mage's Circle's theory be correct? Did this mask have something to do with calling dragons back into their world? He had so many questions, and not nearly enough answers. Unfortunately, he would have to wait for those. His attention turned back to the man before him.

"Who sent you?"

Again the man struggled, his discomfort growing by each passing moment.

Mey again made it past the others and before Thom could stop her, she was in front of their prisoner. "You will die either way," she said to him. "You might as well make it a quick death rather than a slow agony. For, I promise you, you will beg for mercy as your friend did." She gestured to the man whose head lay askew from his body. "It did him no good."

Thom could only guess the mention of this mask brought only pain for her. Her mentor and friend had died trying to secure the item. And no matter how much she tried to portray she was too tough to be hurting, he knew it wasn't true.

Eventually, Thom could attain his answers, but it would leave the man broken and his mind in a state which could never be healed. He had to kill him. It didn't appeal to him, but he knew what had to be done.

Turning to the others, he said, "I need a few moments with him. I will concentrate better alone."

He saw their looks of concern, unsure suspicions and, from at least one, desperation. One by one they turned and left him. Mey was the last, reluctant to leave.

"He doesn't deserve any comfort you may give," she said,

tipping her chin at Barton Johns. “Death surrounds this mask. Why should *he* escape unscathed?”

“Mey,” Thom started toward her; she backed away, mouth set in a hard line. He looked her in the eye; her beautiful green eyes, liquid silver flowing through them. “Trust me.”

“Garrin’s life was taken for that mask. He obviously has something to do with that! How can I let that go?”

She had a valid point, but how could he let her see what he was about to do? “You have to let me do this. I’ll get the information we need. I’ll find out what exactly this mask has to do with us and our quest.”

“Thom, all I want is a chance to find out why Garrin had to die.” An edge of pleading had come into her voice.

“I will get what we need. I promise you.” His heart ached for her, of course it did. How could he ignore any pain she felt? What he really wanted to do was to take her face in his hands and promise her that everything was going to be alright and that she would never have to feel hurt ever again. But that was a futile thought – it would never be true.

“He should die in agony,” she said.

“I’ll take that into consideration.”

Silence hung between them for what had to be an eternity. Finally, she gave in, but nothing in her face changed as she turned and left him.

He went about this task unerringly, leaving no memory or thought unturned. The information he sought was there along with much, much more. Useful snatches of remembered conversations, accidental encounters with the right people at the right time. It seemed Barton Johns had been a lucky man; until now. His luck had abandoned him and his last agonizing breath gave Thom a bit of satisfaction. “For her,” he murmured as he watched the man’s life ebb out of his eyes leaving an empty shell.

****

When he approached the rest of the group later, he couldn’t help but feel the heavy burden of what he had done. He had the man’s blood on his hands, not literally, but he had mercilessly killed him all the same. Looking at the expectant faces, he only nodded to indicate his task was successful.

Mey pushed past him, heading for the spot where they had left Barton Johns and Thom.

"Mey, don't..." he began, but then had to sprint to catch up to her. He didn't want her to see what he had had to do.

When he finally got to her, she had come upon the body and was standing still as stone in front of what used to be Barton Johns. He couldn't see her face and he reached out to grasp her shoulder.

When she turned to him, she did not have the look of disgust he had imagined she would, but rather, she was smiling.

Opening his mouth to speak, he found he had no words. He should have been repulsed by her elation at the twisted face of the thief. Mouth open in a silent scream, the skin of his face torn where he had dug his own nails in trying to remove the intruding force from his head, Barton Johns had definitely died agonizingly and in sheer horror.

As she left the clearing, she reached up and touched her hand to his face. "Thank you."

Her touch was always like an electrical shock to him. His breath caught in his throat. He watched her move around the others, who had all followed them, until he could no longer see her.

The group of faces looking at him now showed mixtures of awe and respect. Shouldn't killing this man in such a manner be something he loathed? It wasn't right that he used his power that way. The thief had been defenseless against it. But everyone seemed to approve of the ghastly scene before them.

"Ye got what we need, then?" Durlag asked.

Thom didn't trust himself to speak yet, so he only nodded slowly. The dwarf clapped him on the back as he followed the same path Mey had taken, getting as far away from this place as he could.

That night, as they camped, he made contact with the Mage's Circle. Familiar faces and voices assailed him as the spell carried him across time and space. He found himself seated in the middle of their sacred Circle. Careful to open only the parts of his mind that he wanted them see, he began to speak.

"You were right. The mask has something to do with our journey and bringing the dragons back. I don't know yet exactly what it does." He described the attack on their camp leaving out the details of how he gleaned the information, he told them the rogues were sent by a sect of priests of Yenoh that would stop at nothing to make sure dragons did not return. They believed that, if returned, dragons would destroy the world; that only darkness would follow them into this realm and the priests would lose their hold over the people. These priests were zealous in their beliefs that dragons were unnatural creatures and had no place among the other races of the world. Mostly, they feared the power that dragons would bring with them.

"We travel now with a priest of Sirrah. Apparently, Sirrah blesses this quest and his worshipers are on our side. Elerbee is not one of those intent on destroying our mission. I will work on getting more from him, but I believe his particular sect is intent on lending their aid to us."

"Be careful, Thom," the old man warned him. "At this juncture, no one is to be trusted."

"Mey's uncle has also joined us. He is a warrior of great skill and has been most helpful with her history." He opened his mind and let them see the group, as he knew them.

"The dwarf could pose a problem," a female voice rang in his ears. "I see he carries the Flask of Aruk. That clan is not so fond of dragons."

"He is not like other dwarves we have met. I believe his life has been a hard one and has shown him more compassion than most dwarves see in a lifetime." Thom smiled. "I think he likes us."

The old man laughed. "You will have to explain yourselves to him soon enough."

"And what of the girl?" another voice interrupted. "How is she coming along?"

He had to be careful here. "She changes more and more every day. She fights against it. Acccptance comes slowly." He tried to keep his voice calm and even, all business. He couldn't allow his feelings to show in front of his superiors. His heart thudded in his chest and he was sure it would betray his true feelings.

Thom continued, "She carries a dagger made of dragon bone. I'm not sure, but when she used it today, I think something happened. It looked as if she were afraid to touch it again. I will question her further about it and report back."

"Where are you bound next?" another man asked.

"We must cross the Dahrst Hills into Sorga. From there we can make our way into the Barren Lands."

The stone walls around him wavered. Thom knew he was tiring and the spell wouldn't last much longer. The others sensed it as well.

"Thom, study the mask. See if you can discern some of its properties." The old man was stern. "There can be no mistakes when the time comes. You can find me away from the Circle if need be; I can always relay your information to them."

What? He couldn't be sure, it was all slipping away so fast, but was that an invitation to meet alone with the Head of the Circle? Confusion clouded his thoughts as he slid back among the dirt, trees, and sky of the camp. *He knows!* Surely, he wasn't thinking straight, the spell had sapped most of his energy. He was so careful to keep the image of kissing Mey out of his thoughts. How could he know? Well, he couldn't very well contact the Head so soon after expending his energy, he could barely lift himself from the ground to find his bedroll. And as much as he was sure his thoughts were separate from him, they surged at him as he closed his eyes to sleep; her warm lips and smooth skin against him. He wanted to lose himself in her and the world be damned! He knew he didn't have the strength to deny her again.

ELEVEN

During the continued journey south toward the Dahrst Hills, Thom explained what he had taken from the thief's mind. Well, most of it, anyway. The mask he carried was magic and very valuable. He was careful not to reveal all of its properties as Durlag and Elerbee were still in the dark concerning Mey's dragon heritage.

Just a few days outside the Hills, Thom finally approached Mey. The group stopped for a respite and Mey used the time to tend to her weapons. Each of her daggers had been laid out neatly on her cape for proper cleaning. As he approached, Thom noticed one dagger conspicuously missing from the line-up.

"What about that one?" he said pointing to the bone-handled dagger sitting off to the side.

She shrugged, not bothering to look up. "It takes care of itself, it seems."

"It certainly is beautiful. Hard to use, I imagine, considering all the gemstones set in the handle."

Mey stopped and glared up at him. "Do you have a purpose for interrupting me?"

"Yes. May I sit with you?"

After a moment of hesitation, she relented, moving a few daggers back to their places along the bandolier. "Sure. Mind you don't cut yourself."

"So… I remember when you picked that one up." He really wasn't very good at this small-talk. "What was its appeal? The jewels?"

"Your *purpose*?"

"My…purpose…" he stuttered, distracted by her shirt which was unlaced a bit too far, revealing more flesh than made him comfortable. He could barely pull his eyes away; but managed to look her in the eye. "Right." Clearing his throat, he gestured to the bone-handled knife. "I wanted to ask you about this dagger."

"What about it?" she shot back.

"I noticed you used it." He watched her carefully, ascertaining more from his scrutiny than any words she would willingly tell him.

"It was the first one I grabbed." Her eyes narrowed. "What exactly is it you want to know?"

He supposed he might as well say it. Thom rubbed his hands together, unable to help glancing once more at the skin exposed from her unlaced shirt. "Well, I noticed you were reluctant to touch it while you were gathering your weapons. I just wanted to know the reason."

He could tell she was about to say something, but she looked back to her work and began cleaning the next weapon. "I don't know what you mean."

"Well, would it surprise you if I told you that the dagger has magical properties?"

"No," she replied. "Anything that tacky would have to be magical. I'm sure you see the aura as well as I."

"But I didn't see it until you used it that day," he tried to explain. "The magic in this blade was dormant until then. What happened when you used it?"

"Nothing."

"Nothing?" His exasperation with her was building. Why was she so stubborn? By the gods, he would make her talk to him. "I saw the way you were afraid to touch it. Something happened!"

Again, she seemed on the verge of saying something, instead opting to shake her head and shrug.

"*Fine*. We won't talk about the dagger." Maybe leaving the subject alone for a while would help. He decided to broach another subject they had to face. "You know, we have to tell Durlag the truth. Elerbee as well if he is to continue with us."

"Elerbee knows."

"What?" He was shocked by this response.

"He knows," she repeated. "Right before that scum attacked our camp looking for the mask, he asked."

Thom pushed for more, "What did he say?" This was a bit of news he had not known.

"He simply asked if I was the descendant of the dragons. Things moved too quickly afterward for us to continue our conversation. He hasn't raised the subject again."

So *that* is what his looks meant, Thom thought. He had noted how Elerbee watched her. He watched her every move and when he spoke directly to her, he was very reverent.

Thom felt a little guilty for mistaking the attention as something more. He had even had bouts of jealousy. What was happening to him? It wasn't like him to be so rash in his judgments. His thoughts whirling, he didn't realize his gaze had again gone to the low neckline of Mey's shirt.

"You know, if I take the shirt off, you get a better view," she snapped.

Immediately, heat infused his face. He tried to stammer an apology but it only came out sounding pathetic and weak.

Ignoring his attempt at an apology, she said, "So, Elerbee knows about my heritage. We must tell Durlag." She placed the last dagger in the bandolier. "No better time, I guess."

He was sure she was trying to avoid being alone with him for too long. He deserved her coldness. But he couldn't let it continue.

"Mey, we have more matters to speak of."

She cocked an eyebrow in question. She was so exquisite; her beautiful dark auburn hair trailing in strands into her face, half covering one silver-green eye. He could stare at her without speaking for eternity, he was certain.

"We need to speak of the mask." He hesitated for a moment. He wanted to add, *and I need to explain myself.*

The impassiveness she had set so carefully on her face wavered. "What about the mask?"

"As I told everyone, it is magical. But what *you* must know is that it has to be used in calling the dragons. I'm not entirely sure why yet, I need more study, but you would have to wear it."

He watched as she struggled with composure.

"Does it frighten you?"

"Of course it does," she answered. "It is unknown. Everyone

fears the unknown."

"We can talk about this, if you like." He was offering to open up to her; to share his own thoughts as well, but would she accept?

She was quiet, so he tried again. "Mey, I can tell you things about your heritage that will help take away some of the fear. I'm trying to help you."

She sighed. "I know. I have to come to terms with this and I *am* trying. My uncle has told me to speak with you on this as well."

He saw the opening and had to take the chance. It would give him more time with her. Time in which he was sure he could fix all he had done wrong. "What would you like to know first?"

"I think that the first thing I need to learn is how to control all these emotions." Looking him straight in the eye, she said, "I can't lose control again."

He relaxed a little now that she was talking. "Emotions can overwhelm anyone. In your case, they are all at a heightened level. Dragons were infinite beings and could feel everything acutely: anger, fear, pride, love." The last word lingered in his mouth, tasting like bitter fruit. There were so many other words he wanted to say but he held them back. This was not about him; it was about helping her to control her emotions.

"Love…" she echoed the word. Her brows had pulled together in confusion. Then, shaking her head, she said, "I can feel these things most times, coming upon me. Now that I know they have the potential to overwhelm me, if I concentrate hard enough, I should be able to control it, right?"

"Yes, you should. But some will be harder to control than others. You should spend time each morning in meditation. It would help you to relax and think through all these things." He let a smile touch his lips. "I read that dragons spent weeks and sometimes months in a meditative state. Perhaps this is what they were doing, as well."

A small laugh escaped her. The sound had a profound effect on him. It was the most wonderful sound he had ever heard. He swallowed the lump in his throat that was forming. *Stop this!* If only she could see how he was indeed putting his own lesson into play at this very moment, it would help her understand. His own nervous laugh helped release some of his tension. How much of what was happening to him was the pull of her dragon essence and how much was true feeling? That thought disturbed him.

"You know," he said, "dragons had a power that was innate. A power to dominate. This is the one thing that people were most frightened of. There were dragons who purposely used this power to have power over whole races. It was out of control and they were responsible for a lot of the wars that led up to their banishment."

She shook her head vigorously. "I would never control someone's free will. That would be wrong. I don't want to do that."

"You need to consciously be aware of this power. People are drawn to you. Your mystery and magical essence attracts people whether they like it or not." The look that crossed her face told him she understood that he was confessing his feelings of confusion at his attraction to her.

"Oh. I would never…" Her words trailed off.

"Not on purpose. I know that." She looked so sad, it drove deep into his heart. He had to assure her somehow. "You can manage this, as well. Just be aware of it."

There. He had explained himself without actually having to mention their kiss. A kiss he found himself thinking about almost every moment of the day and dreaming of every moment of the night. The truth was he wasn't sure if his feelings were genuine. They felt real, and most importantly, they felt right. But there was a doubt, so he had to be certain.

"Maybe we should talk to the others now. They need to know things as well." She paused. "We're in for a rough time from here on out, I suspect. The darkness in the north is growing."

Thom turned and looked at the sky behind him. Black clouds roiled in the distance. It looked like the most hideous storm massing that he had ever seen. "What *is* that?" he whispered aloud, not really expecting an answer.

"Come on, let's find the others." Mey was on her feet in a split second. Thom rose, and with his eyes still on the dark clouds, murmured ascent.

****

Mey looked at the stunned face of the dwarf. The others were, of course, not shocked. But Durlag stood, staring, mouth agape, his eyes locked on her and a look of confusion spreading fast across his hard features.

He shook his head slowly, as the words she said were sinking in. "But I've fought beside ye," he protested. "Ye're walkin' on yer two legs. Those ears belong to an elf or I'm an ogre's uncle!"

"I am a mortal being, yes," Mey told him. "But the blood of dragons runs in my veins. They are my kin. My mother was dragonkind until she chose to stay in mortal form with my father." There was no way to tell which way this would go at this point.

His head never stopped its back and forth momentum. His fingers fumbled at his wide belt. When he didn't find what he sought, his attention went to his hands. Patting all around the belt, his search grew more frantic.

Mey produced his ornate flask from her boot and held it out to the dwarf. With a slight grin, she said, "And I am still the thief you met in Seaside." His scowl deepened and he snatched the flask from her hand. "Sorry. Old habits." She shrugged.

"Dratted girl!" He unstopped the ornate flask and took a long draw. Stopped, breathed, wiped his mouth and took another long draw. With a deep sigh, he sat on the large trunk of a fallen tree.

"That's why the fire ate ye." He pointed an accusing finger at her and his voice rose. "That's why, ever time I look at ye, those eyes are different."

Thom stepped in. "That's right, Durlag." He glanced back at her. "Mey's dragon blood is surfacing and there are things about her that are changing. But she is still the same person she has always been." He was trying to reassure the dwarf, but Mey also heard the tone of persuasion in his voice. Looking to his hands, she spotted the glint of the gemstone he held. A mistake, she thought. Dwarves resisted magic and Thom's attempt to ensourcel Durlag was bound to backfire.

Sure enough, the next thing she heard was Durlag's roar of discovery. "Ye're workin' magic on me?" he yelled at the mage. "Ye don't think I can decide for meself whether or not I intend to follow the girl?" He snatched the gem from Thom's hand, and holding it close so Thom could watch, crushed it in his palm.

"What are you doing!" Thom said frantically, scrabbling for the bits of what was now just another pretty rock. "It was my last rubinite!"

"Humpf," Durlag snorted. "Use magic on me, will you? Ye're lucky ye didn't find *yerself* broken and ground into the dirt! I won't be treated in such a way. I am over 100 years your elder, lad!"

Before Thom could retort, Mey stepped between the two, leading Durlag off to one side. "I understand your apprehension. Your clan was mighty and was shamed and brought down by a dragon. But, that wasn't me, Durlag. The dragon you faced was an evil representation of what dragons are meant to be."

Durlag eyed her suspiciously. He probably thought her words were a trick as well. After all, dragons had a natural persuasion, Thom had told her. But she was honest and sincere. She liked the dwarf and did not want, in any way, for harm to come to him.

"It ain't natural," Durlag grumbled, kicking a piece of the red stone in Thom's direction. "I knowed something was different in ye, but I never imagined…*this*!"

Suddenly she wanted, no, *needed* his acceptance. "Durlag, listen to me; I would never betray you. I would never seek to control you or take away your free will. I am not that type of person."

"But ye'll swipe me drink when I'm not lookin'!" A glint came to his eye and he smiled a little. "Don't ye know better, lass? A dwarf's drink is his life!" His chuckles died down and he looked at her, squinting to impart his seriousness to her. "I pledged me axe to ye, girl. I will see this journey to its end. Me word means something." He took a drink from his flask. "But ye try swipin' anythin' from me again and ye'll find yer fingers in the same shape as that durned mage's stone! I won't have it!"

Mey's smile spread across her face and touched her eyes. "I would expect no less, sir." He nodded at her and continued off.

Bob put his arm around her shoulders. "I do believe he likes you." His laugh was musical and her smile widened. "That is no easy feat."

"I think he likes all of us." She watched him grumble to himself as he found a spot that he could sit and drink. He accepted her but his distrust of dragons ran deep. That was something altogether different that he would have to make his peace with. She was not like those dragons who held his clan captive. She did what she had to do to get along in this world, but she could never imagine holding an entire city captive to do it.

Mey sighed and turned back to the others. Her glance briefly fell on Thom and then slid over to Elerbee. All other eyes moved to him as well. The stares obviously caught him off guard.

Looking one to the other, he said, "What?"

"You knew me for what I was." Moving to stand in front of him, Mey took on an accusatory tone.

"I – I…" he stammered. He rubbed his hands on his immaculate robe.

"*How* did you know?" she persisted.

"I didn't know it was you…at first. I only knew there was *someone*. I was sent..." He shut his mouth, pursing his lips together tightly.

Mey narrowed her eyes and advanced on him. "Sent?"

Elerbee backed up a step and put his hands out in front of him. The shimmer of magic immediately came up around him. "I am a priest! I am here to see your quest finished to the end! There are those of us who don't believe as our brethren."

Mey felt hot rage boiling in her middle, starting to fill her limbs.

Thom's voice was in her ear. "Breathe. Tell it to stay at bay."

Concentrating on the air flowing into and out of her lungs, she closed her eyes and thought, *I am in control here. I am not angry.* She opened her eyes and felt her breath slowing and the heat receding.

Elerbee let out a gasp. "You're eyes…" he began. His own were wide with surprise.

Panic almost won the moment over, but she managed to keep her breathing even. "What? What about my eyes?" She turned to Thom. "What's happening?"

"Calm, Mey. Stay calm! It's nothing that hasn't been happening all along." Mey saw him glance sharply at Elerbee. They were keeping something from her! She hadn't thought of it before and she wasn't a very vain person so she had not sought out her reflection. Now she desperately searched around her for any source that would reveal her own face.

The small stream where she had cleaned her weapons was close. She turned and headed that direction. Dropping down by the clear waters, she looked in. Staring back at her were eyes she didn't recognize; the pupils elongated and silver, like a liquid lake flowing through the green, ever moving, shimmering. A small sound escaped her. Strangely, it was not frightening. Almost beautiful. Were these *her* eyes? Reaching out to touch the reflection, the image broke as her fingers brushed the water.

"Mey?" Thom's timid question caused her to turn.

"Have they stayed this way? You said it's been happening all along."

"No." He dropped down next to her. "They change when your dragon side starts to emerge. Each time, a bit of silver seems to stay." He gestured at the water now. "There. Now look."

She turned once again to the stream. "Oh," she breathed. These eyes were familiar; the pupils round, sitting amongst the forest green of which she was accustomed. There were small silver streaks, however, running through the usual color. Her thoughts stayed there only a moment before she turned back to Elerbee.

"You don't get off the hook that easy." She narrowed her eyes. "Talk, priest."

Nervously picking invisible lint from his pristine robes, Elerbee said, "I didn't happen to be in that well by accident." He kept his eyes down. "I was transported there…by a spell."

"By whom?" Mey pressed.

"Apparently an idiot apprentice mage who swore he had been to that area before." His voice turned quieter, "Or maybe it was purposefully done…he never liked me anyway…"

"Elerbee." The warning in Thom's voice was evident.

"Oh, right. Thom knows that most of the priests on Cantor are against dragons returning to our world. They are afraid. But, there are some of us who believe wholeheartedly that they should reenter our world." He grew more excited as he spoke and he knelt in front of Mey.

"We found writings from an old prophecy that said there would be one who could call them back. Someone to restore the balance in our world."

"D'yob's Prophecy," Thom whispered.

"Yes!" Elerbee said, looking up at him. "The writings of a mage…in a book of spiritual history! Can you imagine? We are so divided these days that no one remembers that priests and mages once lived and worked together." He looked back to Mey. "Our world was balanced."

Mey was not sure she was taking in everything he was saying. "So, your sect of priests found this prophecy? I still don't understand what you're doing here and *why*."

"My sect is one of the few that believes this prophecy. We have been working secretly with the few mages residing in Jareen." To Thom, he said, "They knew that your masters would seek out the Descendant. After they contacted their informant, they told us that the masters had sent someone to Seaside. From there, they tracked your magical energy so we knew where you were headed."

Thom's mouth hung open as he listened. Mey knew what he was thinking; if he could be followed that easily by priests, who else would be able to get to them?

"Once we saw you were on the move," Elerbee continued, "we acted. We knew one mage alone could not get the Descendant to her destination. We knew because," he hesitated, "most of the priestly orders are trying to stop you."

"Trying to stop us?" Mey asked. "How exactly are they doing that?"

"Well, we're not sure, but we think the priests of Yenoh are working with someone. A rogue mage that is willing to call creatures of the foulest kind to stop you."

"A rouge mage…" Thom's voice trailed off. Mey looked at him, trying to decipher the look on his face.

Turning back to Elerbee, she asked, "Why you? I mean, there had to be other priests. Why were *you* sent?"

"I am Chosen. I have been touched by Sirrah." Turning, he pulled the neck of his robe down, so that they could see the symbol of Sirrah, a circle surrounded by line bursts of differing lengths. The skin was raised as if the symbol were underneath, pushing out.

"Does it hurt?"

He turned and smiled at her, shaking his head. "No. I woke one morning with it there. You know that feeling that you've had the most wondrous dream but you can't remember it?"

She nodded.

"That's what it was like. I was ten-years-old. I have trained as a Chosen ever since. We are educated beyond other priests, taught to fight, and are put to tests no others could endure." His eyes held a sadness that Mey couldn't identify, but it was gone quickly, replaced by the special light his brought.

Thom had fallen silent, but now spoke. "Do your elders and scholars have any idea who this rouge mage would be? The Heads of the Circle have guessed at this same scenario."

"No," Elerbee conceded. "They only know it must be a mage. Priests cannot work the arcane spells necessary to call up dark creatures. Our magic relies solely on the divine; we cannot control evil."

Mey listened until she felt numb with information. She just couldn't take in any more. She excused herself to find her uncle. She had questions of her own to ask him.

For one, he had been a quickling while dragons still roamed on Cantor. She wanted to know more about the blue dragon she had seen when she used the dagger. It had whispered a word to her…*Makagesh*. Perhaps he could tell her something. She was hesitant to mention this to anyone else until she knew what it meant. The dagger called to her silently and constantly. She recognized that it had a conscious of its own but she had been able to push it away for the most part.

Mey felt a sense of urgency. She needed to know things before they approached the Heartstone. This dagger, the mask, her growing abilities; they all fit somewhere. Someone had to be able to help her put this puzzle together. Her uncle was the oldest. She was certain he would have some answers.

TWELVE

The amount of information Mey took in before they reached the Dahrst Hills threatened to overload her mind. The dagger, with its sentient dragon, spoke to her daily. Bob was familiar with the word, *Makagesh*, and told her it was the name of a blue dragon that had been defeated when he tried to dominate a group of mages living in the western region of Cantor, just off the coast of Dronos. The dragon had made its home on the Faery Isles. Isolation and the whisperings of the fey creatures that inhabited the islands had driven the dragon mad over time. The voices convinced him he could take on the group of more than fifteen mages that were assigned to this coastal region and possess the magic they held in abundance. Needless to say, he failed; the mages drove his conscious being into the dagger she now carried. Bob was amazed she had this relic. It had traveled a great distance to end up on a peddler's table in Seaside.

Mey was familiar with the concept of sentient weapons, but had never actually seen one. So far, she was able to keep the influence of the dagger at bay. It spoke to her, but she ignored the voice urging her to hold it, to use it, sate its thirst for blood and vengeance. The one time she actually used the weapon, the image it inundated her with stayed with her. Makagesh was magnificent and the image of him was burned into her mind.

She worked relentlessly to control her emotions. Taking her cues from Thom, and on occasion, Elerbee, she learned to make meditation part of each morning and night. Bob and Durlag worked with her on skills in sword-play and the exercise was wonderful at burning off any unspent energy.

She practiced at her daggers alone, however. Well, alone to everyone else's eye. Her memory of Garrin was with her in these moments, recalling his training. His jests at her early attempts to best him, his patient urging to push herself farther than she thought her will and stamina could go. He was still her teacher, even in death.

The hills of Dahrst loomed into view on the fifth day. Dark mounds against a fading sky, they looked like huge boulders set in the middle of the land. They were grey and lifeless just like the dead things rumored to inhabit them.

"There they are," Durlag quietly commented as the group entered the forested expanse that led right up to the edge of the Hills. His face was pale, eyes wide and the tone in his voice hinted at his fear.

All of them looked up to gaze on the mountains as they disappeared behind the trees surrounding them on all sides.

Mey swallowed her own fear which bubbled up from the pit of her stomach. The sight of the Hills was unsettling, but more disconcerting, the voice that echoed through her mind. The voice of the dagger that hung at her hip. It was hungry and eager to feed itself on the evil lurking within the approaching region.

The forest became denser further in. They weren't making much progress and Mey was now certain they would be camping in the forest this night. True to what her instincts told her, they cleared a spot to settle in. Elerbee and Durlag went off in search of wood to build a small fire while the rest finished preparing the site.

As Mey unpacked the horses and set food before them for their own respite, a sound that had been faint before, rose to an almost earsplitting pitch. A moan, slowly swelling into a wail, floated through the clearing. Bob threw his hands to his ears, obvious pain reflected in his expression. Mey felt some discomfort but not to the level that her uncle clearly did. She looked at Thom who was just sitting, scratching odd symbols in the dirt.

"What is it?" she asked to no one in particular.

"What is what?" Thom looked up. When he caught sight of the other two his brow pulled together in confusion.

The wail grew to a level that finally made Mey put her hands to her ears. Bob was on his knees, crippled by the noise, eyes wild with pain.

Then it was gone. Mey released the breath she didn't realize she had been holding. Her uncle had tears in his eyes when he looked up. "The trees…" was all he could mutter.

"Oh," whispered Mey. She understood now. Her father had once explained the connection elves had to nature. No wonder Thom didn't hear it; he couldn't.

"They're in pain," she continued. "I could tell that much from the sound of it."

"Yes," Bob nodded. As an afterthought, he said, "Durlag and Elerbee!" He got to his feet, ready to head off when the other two entered the small clearing, carrying armloads of freshly chopped wood.

"You cut the trees?" Bob demanded of them as they approached.

"'Course we did," Durlag said. "Couldn't find any fallen limbs. Had to get our own. This priest here climbs a tree like nobody I e'er seen!" He chuckled as he dropped his armful, oblivious to the incredulous look on Bob's face.

Elerbee, however, did catch it. "Why?"

Bob turned to Mey. "We will have to fix this. It will not do to camp here while they are so unnerved and distraught."

She nodded. "Sure. Um, what about the others? Shouldn't they be a part of it since it was their fault?"

"What are ye two elves babbling about?" Durlag asked.

"You've upset the trees." She tried to explain. His look of confusion deepened to surprise.

"Upset the *trees*? What kind of mumbly-jumbly elf talk is that? We only took what we needed." His voice started to rise. "If the durned trees had been considerate enough to drop a limb every now and again we wouldn't have had to cut them!"

"Upset trees, upset dwarves…now we've done it," mumbled Thom as he moved past all of them to begin building the fire.

As Thom reached for the pile of sticks Durlag had unceremoniously dumped in a heap, Bob sprinted over to him. Catching Thom's hand, he said, "No. Let us first ask their permission. Give us a half hour, at least."

Clearly too tired to care either way, he shrugged and moved away to set his bedroll out.

****

Mey and Bob moved away from the group to find a proper place to make their connection with the forest. They found a spot where the trees formed a half-circle. Rising above most of the others, these trees soared into the sky, and then bent inward, leaves flourishing out and intertwining with one another. The sight was beautiful and Mey found herself admiring the tall trees.

"What are we supposed to do?"

"Just follow me," her uncle told her.

He knelt before the nearest tree, placing his hands on its trunk. "Open your mind to them, Meylaran. They will talk to you. They long for it."

A bit unsure, she moved to the next tree and knelt, as her uncle had. She reached out, fingers sliding along the rough skin of the tree. She pushed her palms to the trunk, letting her body relax and her mind open to the world around her, just like she did when she meditated. A faint humming sounded in her ears. Gasping she pulled her hands away quickly. Was that its' voice? She let her hand drift back to the tree. The humming sounded again, resonated through her fingers, into her bones and rose until she could make out actual words.

There were so many voices! The humming was all the voices talking at once. *Elves! There are elves in our forest!* She heard the proclamation more than once. Mey concentrated and could single out one, clearer than the rest. *You are more than elf. What are you?*

She knew the voice was addressing her but words stuck in her throat as she attempted to answer. The amazement she felt was almost overwhelming.

There is no need to speak your words. You can impart your thoughts to me.

That made sense. Breathing deep, Mey tried again, this time conveying her feelings in thought to the tree, just as she did when she Mind-spoke her uncle. *I'm talking to the trees!* the thought came before she could stop it. The words sounded clear, just as if she were speaking them aloud.

Laughter from all around her rang through her mind. How beautiful. *You feel different than the other elf. What are you?*

My ancestors were dragons, she answered.

Dragons! We've not spoken to a dragon in such a long time. Even longer than the last elf we spoke with.

Mey wasn't sure how much they knew about the world around them. Would they know what events had transpired? *Dragons have been gone from this world for a long time. The races rose against them in fear. They were driven away, into exile.*

A wave of sadness flowed over her. Other emotions came fleetingly: anger, frustration, confusion. *Please*, she said, *we are here to apologize to you. Our friends cut your limbs. We heard your pain.*

There was a moment of silence. Then the tree's voice sounded again. *Yes, my sisters have told me. It was painful, but we heal very quickly. Your apology is accepted. We grant you permission to use what you need from us, Dragon.*

Thank you, you are very generous. She wasn't sure about trees, but she felt that flattery was always a useful tool when begging forgiveness.

Then the voices rose again to a jumble. So many thoughts came at her at once; they mingled together and she struggled to decipher words from the mass of voices. Her confusion must have been imparted to the tree, because when it spoke, it acknowledged the emotion.

We are sorry to cause you confusion. My sisters excite easily and we have not spoken to another being for so long. They tell me you are being followed, Dragon.

Followed?

Shadows. They seek you, specifically. Their thoughts are easily read, as they are base creatures.

Mey's heart quickened. The Shadow Guard. How did they find her? Thom was making sure to cover their magical imprint. Perhaps his efforts weren't enough.

Do not be afraid, we can delay them. Oh, what fun this will be! We have not been able to help elves and Dragons for long years. We will instruct the forest to aid as well.

Thank you. I must tell my friends. You are a generous being.

Dragons and elves have long been a friend of the trees. We are at your service. This parting thought drifted in Mey's mind as she removed her hands to break her bonding connection with the tree.

Darkness flowed through her mind and crept over her body, through every pore. There was no pain, but when she opened her eyes…nothing. Where was her uncle? He had been right next to her. She couldn't see or hear anything. Numbing panic started to set in and she jumped to her feet, reaching for her weapons.

****

Rekho saw his chance. What good fortune that the girl had opened a bonding pathway. He quickly opened his own and joined it with hers. He connected to her easily. Her mind lay open for his suggestions.

In fleeting glimpses he caught pictures from her memory. He found her unconscious thought and delved deep. "Meylaran, *ah la'du utahn*."

Those words brought all of her attention to him. He felt her concentrate only on his voice. "Father?" The word broke as she said it. It touched his heart to hear her speak to him again. As soon as he thought it, a pain gripped him and he steeled himself against the emotion.

He had to act quickly. The bond was tenuous over such a distance. "Mey, you have to stop this quest. The world will not benefit from having dragons back here to exact their revenge."

Confusion floated in the open pathway. If she felt it, so would he in this state. "But there will be no revenge. The world is sinking, Father. Dragons will right the balance once again. Their presence is natural to this world and without them we are doomed."

"NO," his voice boomed. "It is trickery! You are being led to slaughter. You will be killed in the process." He calmed his voice. "Please, *tae'wa*, I would have you live your life and be happy."

Silence reverberated through the pathway. Then, in almost a whisper, she asked, "Are you dead, Father?"

He chose his words carefully. "All deaths are inevitable." Better to let her think him gone. He didn't want her to know what lay ahead of her would be his doing. He had to stop her. That much he was completely sure of and he warred with himself knowing what he had to do. All the same, he let his love for her soar through the path and directly to her essence.

There were so many confused emotions coming from her. It must be happening, he realized. She was changing and no matter what he did at this point, it would not stop that process. That cinched it. He knew what he had to do and the pain of that realization nearly crippled him. She was not his little girl, she was a maturing dragon and the dragons had to be stopped. Whatever the cost.

He started to sever the bond, but felt her anxiety when she realized he was leaving. "Father! Wait! I feel like I am losing you forever."

"Meylaran, my sweet *tae'wa*, I will always love you. Please, forgive me." He couldn't bring himself to say more, so he cut the last tie holding them together.

When he opened his eyes, tears were trailing down his face and running over his cheeks. Anger immediately overtook him. This life had taken everything from him; his beloved wife, his kind and trusting nature, and now his only child.

No matter what became of him, he could not let the threat from the retreating dragons come true. Even if it cost him his life, he would try to stop her.

A sound brought his attention back to his surroundings. Composing his face, he turned toward the doorway. A priest stood just inside the entrance. "Well, what?" Rekho demanded after a moment of silence.

The other man cleared his throat. "We have not received the crystals Jost was sent to retrieve."

Rekho stood, his imposing height had him towering over the smaller human. His dark eyes narrowed dangerously. "I have to have those crystals."

"Yes…sir…" the man stammered. "B-but we've lost contact with Jost. The last report came just before he entered the Caverns to retrieve the crystals."

"Has anyone searched for his magical signature? His weapon?"

The priest's eyes widened. "N-no. I wasn't aware…" his voice trailed as he shrunk from the mage's vast anger and towering presence.

"Of course you weren't," Rekho muttered. He stormed past the other man and down the dank hallway to the makeshift laboratory.

He found a bit of glass and placing it in a bowl with a pinch of powdered steel, he took a deep breath and started reciting the words that would tell him where Jost's powerful weapon was located. The essence of the godly weapon could be traced through magical means. To track the man would require the blasted crystals that seemed to be in short supply around this priestly commune; a prison, it felt to Rekho.

He could feel the weapon's presence, but it was veiled. Like a thin fog surrounding the weapon. *It must be inside the Caverns*, Rekho thought, *otherwise I would see it clearly*. Something was blocking the strength of the magic.

To do more would require the damned crystals. Each spell required a certain stone, but a farthen crystal could be used for just about anything. It could be substituted for many spells. It was an invaluable magical anchor. He had to have those crystals!

He turned to the priest that still hovered near the doorway, ready to run at a moment's notice. "Inform the Elder, I will leave at dawn for the Caverns."

The other's eyes widened. "Th-the Elder?" He swallowed hard. One more look at Rekho and he choked back any protests he may have had. Backing slowly out the door, he said, "As you wish, sir."

Rekho turned his attention back to the room. He scanned the small chamber, littered with paper, books and nubs of candles. His eye stopped on a small leather-bound tome. Taking it in his hands, he let his fingers brush over the slightly raised lettering on the front, *The Princess of Orphana.*

It was her favorite. Mey would have him read it over and over when she was avoiding sleep. Of course, he would oblige. He could never deny her anything, his sweet *tae'wa*. She would snuggle close to him and before he finished the second time through, he would hear her soft snores. A smile played at the corner of his lips. Slipping the book inside his tunic, next to his heart, he continued gathering what he would need for the trip to the Caverns of Endless Time.

An hour later he sat waiting with an entourage of priests that were to accompany him. His scowl deepened when the prisoner was brought to meet them. "Why does he need to come?"

One of the priests looked at Rekho. "This one is to die. The Elder has decreed we take him to his fate at the Caverns." The priest's eyes hardened. "It was ordered."

It would definitely slow them, but how could he argue with an order from the Elder himself? Rekho shrugged. "I hope he can keep up." With that, he turned and set a quick pace for the march, the prisoner and his keeper stumbling behind.

****

Mey felt groggy as she sat up. A dream? She had dreamt of her father. It had felt so real. So real, in fact, she had the overwhelming urge to cry. Vaguely, she started to recall something about trees.

Slowly, movement and voices came into focus around her. She must have slept right through her watch. Why wouldn't Durlag have wakened her?

"Meylaran?" Bob's voice broke through the veil of sleep that clouded her head.

"I just had the strangest dream," she said, putting her hands to her head. "About my father."

"Did he say anything?" Bob knelt before her, concern etched his face.

She was confused at his reaction. Confused at everyone's reactions, for that matter. "He was saying goodbye. That's all I can remember."

Their glances told her that something more was going on here. "Why?"

Elerbee finally broke his silent brooding. "We have to hurry." Looking at Bob, he said, "Didn't you say the trees told you that Shadow Guard were here? In the forest." He wiped his hands continuously on his white robes.

Looking to her uncle, she concentrated hard on her memories. They were talking to the trees, she *did* remember that. But when was it? Everything was all jumbled out of place. She shook her head slightly, trying to clear it of the fog that didn't want to dissipate.

"Come," Bob offered his hand. "We have to go."

As she got to her feet, she repeated, "It was so real."

Bob smiled at her. "I know. We can talk about it all later, but right now, Meylaran, there are Shadow Guard coming. We have to leave."

The sleep-fog was slowly falling away and she could think more clearly. Yes, she remembered the trees had told them about the Shadow Guard. Looking over to the tree she had communicated with, she was a bit surprised to find them bent, lower than before. Like a protective canopy over their little group.

They're shielding us. Her amazement was complete when a path opened up before them as the limbs closed in behind. She was jostled into the middle of the line, with Elerbee and Bob leading, Thom and Durlag bringing up the rear. All around them, she could see a faint outline of glowing light. *Elerbee's armor*, she thought.

Something felt very out place, however. The forest was thinning as they sped through to find an exit. Mey's mind kept going back to the dream of her father. He had told her to stop her quest. That she was in danger if she did not. Was that true or was it just her own fears coming out in her dreams?

As they came upon a clearing, the trees moved aside and they emerged onto rocky ground. All of a sudden, the feeling that something wasn't right made sense. It *wasn't* right. It should have been daylight; the bright, round ball of the sun should be shining brightly. Instead, as Mey looked around, darkness flooded this clearing. Looking up, she squinted at the dim light from the moon.

Glancing at one another, all of them clearly confused, Thom said, almost in a whisper, "The first sign."

THIRTEEN

"What do you mean?" Mey demanded. "What sign?"

Moonlight flooded the earth in a soft veil. Morning should have broken well over an hour ago. She turned toward the forest behind her, wondering what was happening, as the limbs closed in on the retreating path.

Mey looked first to her uncle, who wore the same confused expression likely reflected on her own face, then to Thom who had muttered something about a sign.

"The prophecy," Thom said, turning to her.

"Again with this prophecy." All this vague information was really becoming annoying. "Enlighten the rest of us."

"There will be three signs foretelling the dragons' return. Unending darkness will fall upon the world. The next will be continuous light." He paused. Mey's tapping foot propelling him into rapid speech. "Finally, when all is ready, the stars will align to create a path; a doorway back to this world where they will explode into being as they enter."

She had to admit the last part had her curious to know more. "Will they all come through at once?"

"No one really knows," he said. "I have read books on the account, but they are just guessing. The only thing we know for sure is it will be a wondrous sight to behold."

Smiling despite her irritation, Mey said, "You make it sound amazing." Her heart raced at the thought of finally encountering her ancestors.

"Mey, it will be beyond our greatest imaginings." As she looked into those frosty blue eyes that always seemed to pierce right through her, he took her hands and his smile widened. It was dazzling and full of…what? What was he feeling? *Damn this dragon blood.* With all the tumultuous emotions, she could never quite read other people correctly. Looking away, she broke the spell of his gaze before it could capture her. His smile disappeared almost instantly.

Slowly, she loosed her hands from his firm clasp. Catching her fingers before she could break contact, he forced her to look at him again. "It will be incredible," he whispered.

She caught a fleeting emotion pass through his features. He released her hands but kept his eyes on her.

She hesitated, cleared her throat. "So, we continue on?" When no one protested, she continued, "The Dahrst Hills can't be more than a few hours away. We have to cross them to get to Sorga and then to the Faery Isles."

They each fell into step behind her, weapons at the ready.

****

Misty rain began to fall as the group marched toward the Hills, making the rocky path slick. Every step had to be carefully placed; Mey had already fallen twice, cutting and scraping her palms on the small stones littering the pathway. One gash in particular was deep and throbbed with every step. Ignoring the stinging pain, she gripped her daggers tighter.

Elerbee made his way to her. "Mey, let me heal you." Blood ran down her fingers, mingled with rainwater and fell in drops on the path.

"I'm fine, thanks." She had suffered worse wounds and lived.

"This blood will leave a trail for any beast of prey that might be following us," he insisted.

She stopped abruptly. Elerbee took another two steps before he realized she wasn't beside him. Thom bumped into her from behind.

Looking closer at Elerbee, she noticed he was bone-dry and seemed very comfortable in the damp, chill rain. "Wha-?"

His answer was quick, as if he knew the source of her

confusion. "The robes," he explained. "They keep me safe from the elements." He shrugged and reached for her hands.

Mey let him grasp her cold fingers. Amazed at his warm, dry touch, she knew he truly was totally protected from the elements around them. He turned her palms up to examine the cuts that were filled with debris from the road. Elerbee grimaced at them.

"These are filthy." He muttered. "It's a wonder infection hasn't already set." He rubbed them lightly with his thumbs, she winced at the stinging pain. Concentrating on one at a time, he closed his eyes and asked his god for the gift of healing that would make her whole once more. Elerbee's soft touch and the reverence on his face was entrancing. His brow wrinkled with concentration.

Mey felt a fluttering grow within her belly; she tore her gaze away from his face and looked down. The bleeding stopped instantly and the ragged skin knitted itself together under his gentle grasp. She let out a soft gasp of surprise. The pain was fading rapidly and her mood felt lighter. As if a great burden was lifting from her soul. His god, she realized. The peaceful feeling was all-encompassing.

Elerbee quickly healed her other hand. She admired his devotion to a being he couldn't see or touch and was compelled to understand it further. As she put her healed palm to his cheek, he smiled at her. His skin was warm, dry, smooth and perfect. He literally glowed with divine energy. His brown eyes sparkled and were full of understanding.

Thom cleared his throat. "We should move on." As he passed, his icy glare lingered on Elerbee.

Elerbee reddened as he took a step away from Mey, breaking her touch. He worried his robe, nervously picking at the invisible lint that seemed to habitually plague him.

As they made their way toward the Dahrst Hills, the rain strengthened and lightening skirted the clouds hanging in the sky.

How long would they be inundated with night? Already Mey was confused as to the natural time of day. Her body was sore from the strenuous march. She wanted desperately to lie down and let the rain sing her to sleep.

There was no shelter between here and the Hills, only the rocky slopes of the terrain with little to no plant life to speak of. Bleak, gray and now miserably cold. Mey was soaked and the cold seeped right through to her bones. She shivered.

"Cold?" Thom asked.

She nodded, lips trembling; she couldn't speak without great effort.

"Here," he offered his cloak. It was dry. She looked at him in surprise. "A spell. The cloth can be protected from soaking up the water."

"Y-you had th-this ability the whole t-t-time?" Her teeth were chattering furiously and getting words out was difficult. But the nerve! How could he not have shared this earlier?

"I put the spell on the cloak before we ever left Seaside. I didn't know for sure we would run into rain."

Mey was beginning to warm up, but no matter how grateful she was for the thoughtful gesture, she was still mad. If he could do this once, surely he could have done it for the rest of them. When she looked at her friends, they were all soaking wet and looked miserable.

"And you don't feel compelled to share now?"

He sighed deeply. "Mey, I only had one stone to cast this spell. I am not prepared. If we can find more limestone, then, yes, I will share." His voice was rising. She could see that he was becoming irritated but she didn't care. Damn him, she was getting mad.

"Perhaps you could consider 'protecting' the others in your company next time." Blood was roaring in her ears and she had no idea why this made her so angry but it did. She wasn't about to let it go without a fight.

His pace started to quicken and Mey doubled hers to stay with him. He wasn't running away this time, she would make sure of it.

"Oh, yes, and perhaps I'll read the future every time I make decisions to journey with temperamental women so that they will never become unhappy," his teeth were gritted together as he spoke. Water plastered his hair to his head and ran in rivulets down his face.

She realized all of a sudden what she was doing. He was sacrificing his own comfort for her and here she was chastising him for it. *What's wrong with me?* A profound thought came to her just then. *He is not running away from me; I am pushing him.*

"Can't you just appreciate the gesture and say thank you?" His voice had softened somewhat, to a defeated tone.

"Th-thank you," she stammered.

He walked beside her for a moment longer. His face was etched with fatigue. He nodded, eyes lingering on hers for only a brief moment before he dropped back to move in behind her.

Was it sadness that she always saw when she looked in his eyes? There was always something more beneath the surface. He was hiding it carefully. This miserable atmosphere let it slip out and she saw it plainly. She had to get her emotions in check. She couldn't keep treating her friends as though they were targets for her poisonous emotional arrows. He had every right to be sad.

****

The rain eased and a thick fog rose from the earth. It swirled at their feet and clung to their ankles as they walked. They had to slow their march, not being able to see anything past a few feet.

"We are here," Bob announced.

"How can ye tell? I can't see me own hand in front of me face!" Durlag was trailing at the back of the small group.

"Can you not feel it? The air is different." Bob turned around trying to see past the fog.

A low moan sounded in the distance behind them. Or was it in front? The sounds confused Mey's senses and the darkness already set her body's clock in the wrong direction. She felt lost in chaos. Another moan sounded, closer this time.

"Shouldn't we keep moving?" Mey asked suddenly. Something was urging her not to stop.

"Wait," Elerbee said, coming to a central point between them. He kneeled and bent his head reverently. Praying to Sirrah, he asked the god to give him the power to shield against the undead creatures.

Mey listened carefully. Light spread from the symbol at the base of his neck and moved outward toward the rest of them, like a blanket covering from head to toe. He rose, smiling that warm and comforting smile. "Now," he said, "we can go. The protection only lasts a little while."

"We should cover one another," Bob said. "Meylaran, you are in the middle."

She rolled her eyes, but moved between the others as he

suggested. She was a bit tired of being protected. It made her feel like a child who could not take care of herself.

They moved cautiously. Noises sounded from all directions: moans, screams, muffled voices, swords ringing as if locked in battle. Every so often, Mey would catch a face out of her peripheral, but when she turned to look, there was nothing.

After all of them had asked "Did you see that?" or "Did you hear that?" at least a hundred times, they quit asking. It was apparent that they were not all hearing or seeing the same thing. They pushed on, trying to ignore the unnerving, ghostly clamor.

Rock rose higher on either side of them, creating a path etched out of the very hills. At best they had traveled for at least an hour when Elerbee called a halt. "The shield is fading. I will try to bring up another but be prepared, the spirits will be able to reach you until I do. Do *not* look directly at them."

Swallowing hard, Mey tried to speak past the fear forming like a fist in her chest. "The-the faces I keep glimpsing...they'll get closer?"

"Yes." Elerbee's eyes darted all around. "This shield will be weaker and won't last as long but, I have a few other spells that will aid us." Turning to address the group as a whole, he said, "Weapons are pretty much useless at this point. Unless they have some sort of magical property." His stare came to rest on Mey, slid to her hip where the bone-handled dagger hung.

Did he know it was magical? How? She wanted to ask, but at that moment, he whirled, shouting. A glow emanated from his extended hands and shot forward, finding solid purchase on a form that appeared right behind him. Mey watched wide-eyed as the form hissed, broke into tiny droplets like dew and slowly fell to the ground.

Without hesitating, she took the bone-handled dagger from her hip, feeling helpless and completely at someone else's mercy. A very unsettling feeling for her. Durlag cursed a stream of colorful words that, even in the tension of this moment, had her smiling. The only thing magical he possessed was the flask. Thom had his spells, Elerbee his divine intervention and Bob had a sword from the elven homeland. Elves inherently possess a degree of magic that seeps into all they do; weapon-making included.

They circled Durlag and her, the two most vulnerable. Mey

closed her eyes, drawing on the power of the dagger and calling up the sentient being within it. The image formed behind her closed lids, revealing shimmering, royal blue scales and golden, luminescent eyes. Makagesh breathed a contented sigh and asked, "Why do you call me, sister? You have spent so long pushing me away."

She communicated her thoughts to the dragon. *I have need of you now. We will work together or I will put you back into your slumber.*

"Oh, very well," Makagesh grumbled. "What is our purpose?"

We are in the Dahrst Hills, surrounded by ghosts of the soldiers who fought here in past battles.

One gleaming eye lifted in interest. "The Dahrst Hills?" he asked. "This should be fun. No blood to be had, but lots of fun."

She was careful to take charge of the interlude. *You will work with me and follow my lead. Can you destroy spirits?* she asked him.

"Of course," the dragon replied, a bit miffed at being given orders. "Some of them."

What do you mean, 'some of them'?

"Well, I can't just rid you of all of them! I will do my part, but you must do yours. Being close enough to touch one is essential." The dragon snorted. He could feel her fear, she realized.

Hardening her resolve and opening her eyes, Mey discovered ghastly forms pressing closer, transparent and flowing. Most were dressed in tattered shreds of uniforms from a long-lost army. There were still others who were clothed in plain workaday clothing and some in piecemealed armor. Some had glowing eyes and were more solid in form. Mostly men, but there were some women and a few children. There had to be hundreds of them.

Elerbee had extended another protective shield around them. It held for now but they had to get moving. And quickly.

"Forward," Elerbee called. They started ahead as one, moving as far and as fast as they could.

The glow from the ethereal creatures helped them stay on the path that led through the rock and, hopefully, out the other side.

As they walked, Mey watched the forms around them. Some ambled aimlessly while others followed them with purpose and still others shrank from Elerbee as he moved forward into their path. The ones with the glowing eyes looked as if they were waiting for the shield to drop so they could rush in for the warm flesh that the living possessed. It was unnerving, so she concentrated on Elerbee and Thom in front of her.

She had to put her trust in them. They were the only ones with enough power to get them all through this. She knew that Makagesh was on her side as well, but it gave her little comfort. Giving trust was something she had only done very few times in her life and it had hurt her every time.

Mey could see the shield weakening. The magical glow was thinner. She breathed in, steadying herself. A fire had begun to burn in her belly, growing and eating at the fear her mind insisted on. Thankfully, the fire was winning out. It was familiar to her now; this warmth that spread over her and consumed her being. She would not allow it to overtake her, she must let a part of herself mingle with it. The work she put into controlling her dragon blood was paying off.

The first indication that the shield was broken was the incredible shriek that sounded behind her. Unbearable to hear and chilling to the very bone. *Bob!* She turned to see her uncle leap, avoiding the sweep of an incorporeal great sword. The figure in front of him was wild-eyed, ghostly hair flowing out in all directions. The wail flowing from its open mouth was meant to distract and it was working. Concentration on anything else was impossible. Mey shook her head to clear it of the spidery sounds that crawled and tangled all thought.

Just at the point she wanted to let her own screams out, silence fell all around her. Surely the creature had rendered her deaf with its incessant and ghastly wailing. She turned to find Thom with a smirk on his face; he winked at her and pointed to his ears. The silence was his doing. She didn't think she'd ever been so grateful. Swallowing the fear that threatened to overtake her, she smiled her thanks, sighed and turned back to the breach. There was no more time to dwell on it. It was time to fight; time to die, if need be.

As she came up next to him, Bob's sword sang through the air and found solid purchase on the being in front of him. Mey countered with a sweep from the dagger in her right hand. Her concentration was almost lost again when she felt it sink into soft flesh. The only difference from a living being was how cold it felt.

Instead of the warm flow of blood, a numbing chill flowed out as the ghost shimmered and just disappeared from view. Would it come back? They'd find out that answer soon enough.

The group inched slowly on as the forms closed in. The gap in the shield was widening. Steadying her breathing, nodding to her uncle, she made a gesture to indicate the breach was growing wider. His soft, brown eyes hardened, the only indication that he was at all affected by their situation. His sturdy stance never wavered.

Mey admired him so much. He was so strong and she fed off of that strength. He had been a rock for her, a solid presence in her suddenly tumultuous world. She positioned herself so that her back was to his. If they were going down, it would be together and fighting.

Mey and Bob concentrated on the widening breach in the shield, and another ghostly form slipped through. Its mouth was open in what she assumed to be a deadly wail. It headed right for Bob, who burst into action. Every movement was fluid and his swordplay reminded her of a dance. This form had a weapon as well. The silence when the weapons struck was somewhat disconcerting, but reminded her again of Thom's saving spell. She smiled, as she looked to find him weaving a temporary armor around himself. His hands moved with speed and precision. Delicate, yet strong and sure. Movement behind her drew her attention back. She readied herself for any threats.

Bob had already dispatched another form. Two more were slipping through the gap. It was fading faster and desperation tugged at Mey. She knew in just moments they would be overcome with these creatures. Her head needed to be right here, not thinking of magicians and their beautiful, delicate hands.

"Makagesh," she whispered. He could hear her, if no one else could. "It's time." Laughter touched her ears, although she knew it to be inside her own head. He was ready.

Not a moment too soon. The shield burst and completely faded. Three forms moved right in front of Mey. Warmth spread over her body and tugged at her limbs. Makagesh was infusing her with his will and she let him nudge in, if only in small amounts. Mey's legs moved with a speed she had never known she possessed and the dagger in her hand flew into action. She had a dance of her own;

the dance of dragons. It took her into a whirling spin, ending in a semi-crouch, one leg extended, blade slicing through the form nearest her. The form exploded into droplets and fell to the ground.

Mey rose from her stance, and flowed evenly into the next, dagger leading. Jumping to avoid the sweep of a ghostly sword, her body carried its momentum over into a roll and she flipped over the form, landing solidly behind it, driving her blade upward into what had once been its spine. Again, droplets of dew formed and tumbled to the ground. With no hesitation, her next move followed. Heat spurring her on, and a feeling of absolute comfort encompassing her whole being. Straightening her legs and bending backward to avoid another sword, her arms swung wide for balance. Snapping up as the sword passed, she came in low at the form. This one had been a good swordsman, apparently. It avoided her lunge with practiced ease.

Following the forward motion through, she turned just in time to counter the next attack. When her dagger connected with its sword, a bone-numbing chill ran through her body, mingling with the heat. She shuddered and nearly stumbled, Makagesh roared in her head, keeping her from completely losing herself to the shock of the ghastly touch. Gritting her teeth and growling from low within her stomach, Mey moved with a slow sway, looking for any opening.

When the ghost came in again, she was ready for him. His sword sailed through the air, coming in from the right, she parried the blow and his sword flew wide. Again and again the sword came and each time she eluded the deadly blade. The ghost wasn't going to tire, but she was. *Enough of this game*. Moving as if she were going to come straight at him, she stopped short of following through and sidestepped quickly, driving the blade into its side and dragging it through as she moved. The fiend's mouth opened to scream in defiance even as he shimmered and flew apart, the droplets hitting her and sending small shivers throughout her body.

Taking stock of those around her, Mey noticed her hearing slowly returning; at first, everything sounding muffled and then cleared. Finally realizing the rushing sound was her own blood flowing in her ears. Bob was gracefully dispatching ghost after ghost, Elerbee was clearly tiring but he rebuked scores of the creatures at a word. Thom threw bursts of light, shattering many at a time. But the most disturbing sight she found was Durlag.

The dwarf was laughing wildly while swigging down huge gulps from his flask. He looked to be doing a strange, stomping dance. *He's finally gone mad. The ghosts have addled what was left of his brain.* Taking two steps in his direction, thinking to try to sooth him, Mey noticed his stomping feet had a purpose. Bones. He was stomping on a pile of bones.

Her mouth fell open and her brows came together in complete confusion. He noticed her stare and yelled, "Ha, Lassie! Watch!" He pointed to the ghosts nearest him. With a yell, his foot came down, hard atop the pile of bones. When it did, two figures shimmered and dissipated. Over and over he stomped on the pile of bones. Randomly, a ghost would disappear. "HA HA HA! Found their rotten bones, I did! Bye, bye, ghosties!" And with that, he took another swig from the flask and continued his stomping.

Mey shook her head. He had found a way to combat the ghouls even without a weapon, save his own two feet. That dwarf was an enigma.

"Mey!" The yell brought her around just in time to see one of the red-eyed monsters close enough to embrace her. And it seemed he was about to do just that; arms outstretched and a frozen grin on its face, showing the razor sharp teeth inside.

Out of nowhere, Thom was there. He shouted a few words and lightning burst from his fingers, shooting into the creature. It shrieked. A horrifying sound that had Thom paralyzed and falling to his knees. Mey moved to bring her dagger around. Quicker than she thought even possible, the wight reached out a hand and plunged it through Thom's chest.

Thom jerked as the wight's grin widened. A pain seared through Mey's body as well. Gripping her heart and twisting it. Anger was the first to hit her and she let it flow with the heat, burning so hot that she was sure her skin would melt from her bones.

"Yes," a voice in her head whispered. "Yes. Let it out."

She felt the scream forming in the pit of her stomach, bubbling on the molten waves of her blood, searching for a release through her throat. A deafening sound burst from her and she could do nothing to stop it.

The wight quickly let go of Thom to reach for his ghostly ears.

When it did, Thom slumped to the ground, skin pale as death, lips blue. *Too late*, the thought hit her. *He's dead.*

Her lamenting scream went on, advancing on the creature as it shrank from her. Pinning it with her voice against the rock wall, she never let up. All the pain, anger, passion, and fear flowed out in that one shriek. The wight broke apart into tiny dew droplets, showering her. Then from all around, droplets of dew hit her as she turned to watch the remaining forms burst and fall to the ground.

FOURTEEN

They looked at her in shock, but there was no time to figure out what the stares meant. *Thom! Oh, no, Thom!* She fell to her knees beside him, almost afraid to touch him, she reached her fingers to his face, pale as death. His lips blue from the chill the creature sent through him, freezing his blood and his breath.

His skin was icy to the touch. *No, not again*, she thought frantically. *I'm losing everything that means something in my life…again.*

"You will *not* die," she whispered through gritted teeth.

A pair of gentle hands touched lightly on her shoulders. Shaking them off, she bent closer to Thom. The hands persisted, this time with a firm, hard grip that took hold and pulled her back.

"Let go!" She tried to twist out of their grasp, but the hands held her firm.

"Meylaran, *eldu rahl*," her uncle's firm voice admonished, "Move away; let Elerbee help him." Bob moved her back so that the priest could take her place beside Thom.

"Please, Elerbee," she pleaded. "Don't let him die." She looked into his eyes, searching for the comfort she always found there. He appeared spellbound for a moment, and then he slowly nodded and turned his attention to Thom.

His hands moved over Thom's neck, pausing there for a moment, then on to his chest where the wight had penetrated flesh.

"He's breathing," Elerbee sighed. "I will do what I can, but we need to get him to Sorga. The temple there will be better equipped to help."

Mey let out a shaky breath. Under her uncle's gently urging hand, she moved to help them construct a litter to carry Thom. Everything was so surreal, every movement sluggish and without purpose. She kept telling herself over and over, *he's not gone, he's not gone*. She chided herself for all the unkind things she had said and done in the last weeks. Those are the things you remember when someone you love is facing death.

Love? Do I love him? Since she had never felt love for anyone other than her family or Garrin, which was more love one would have for a brother, she couldn't be certain. Her heart was breaking, she knew that. The ache sitting in her chest threatening to squeeze her heart into pieces was as real as any feeling she'd ever had.

"Come, now, lass," Durlag said, interrupting her thoughts. He took the cloak from her hands. "The priest will help him, surely. You needn't fret."

"Right. Elerbee knows what to do."

"'Course he does!" An awkward silence hung between them, then Durlag said, "Here." The ornate flask appeared in front of her eyes. "Just don't drink that last drop, girl, or else I'll lose me supply!"

Mey looked at him, dumbfounded. He was offering her the only consolation he knew. The dwarf's gruff demeanor had slipped ever so slightly. He was refusing to meet her gaze but his gesture meant the world to her all the same. Tears tugged again at her eyes. "Thank you, Durlag," she managed to say and took the flask.

"Hmpf, if it'll get ye back to work, I'd offer ye my arms!" He stomped away to finish the litter.

By tying their cloaks together, they managed to create a crude stretcher. Bob and Elerbee each lifted a corner of the litter. Thom, who was still pale had started to toss about slightly. Every time he moved, he let out a groan of utter agony.

"Is he hurting?" she asked Elerbee. "Can you stop it?"

"He's feeling the effects of the wight's touch. I've done what I can. It would be worse had I not."

Mey worried her bottom lip and nodded. Insisting on walking next to Thom as they traveled, she could keep an eye on his level of discomfort and alert Elerbee whenever it increased.

At least the rain had stopped. She took out the flask Durlag had handed her earlier, contemplated actually drinking the contents, but decided she was better off clear headed. Looking back over her shoulder to find the dwarf trailing far behind, she stuffed the flask back in her belt.

"We'll have to make camp at some point," Bob said. "It takes a day and a half to get from these hills into Sorga. We'll just have to guess at the passing time." He shrugged.

"I'd rather not stop, if we can help it." She felt desperate to get Thom to someone who could restore him wholly to himself.

Bob was ready with a retort, but Elerbee intervened. "Mey, back there with the wight, do you remember what happened?"

That caught her off-guard. "You all saw what happened. That thing nearly killed Thom and could possibly still do so."

"I mean with *you*. You managed to destroy what was left of the ghosts and wights. Do you remember?"

"I remember a sensation of soaring out of myself; like I was on the outside looking down on it all. I was angry…and scared." She swallowed back the tears that were forming in the corners of her eyes. "The heat was there. The heat that comes when my dragon side is emerging."

Bob glanced at Elerbee. "I do not think now is the time…" he began, but Elerbee cut him off.

"I think now is the perfect time." He lowered his voice, but she could still hear them. "She has changed. Physically. If she's not aware already, she should be. It will need to be hidden when we enter the city."

"What are you talking about?" Mey quickened her steps to walk beside them, hesitating briefly to make sure Thom was comfortable.

Elerbee continued, "Mey, we saw something happen when you attacked those creatures."

"Something? What? Elerbee, spit it out!"

"It seemed as though you shifted between two beings. One of them you, of course, but the other…the other was a dragon."

On rare occasions was she ever left speechless, without a thing to say, but now was one of them.

"*Tae'wa*, it's only the natural progression of what your mother handed down to you." Bob shot a sideways glare at Elerbee.

Finding her voice, she finally said, "Please, explain to me what you saw, Elerbee." She wanted to know but there was also fear.

Not understanding what was happening to her left her vulnerable. She had to know; *needed* to know.

Elerbee's face reddened and his obsession with invisible lint emerged. He used his free hand to pick at his immaculate robe, but managed to stammer on.

"Um, well, I didn't see the attack on Thom…" His voice was barely above a whisper.

"Elerbee," Mey pleaded, "I need to know, you said so yourself. This is happening and the more informed I am of what is going on, the better I will be able to control it."

His pained expression softened somewhat but there was still a degree of reluctance in his eyes. "Right. OK, I only saw what happened after."

"Just tell me what you saw."

"I was turning a group of spirits when I heard the scream. At first it threatened to deafen me, it was so loud. That's when I turned my attention to what was happening. I spotted Thom on the ground and then saw you with the wight."

They slowed their steps enough for Durlag to catch up. He still hung back, pretending not to listen, but Mey knew he was eavesdropping.

"You were, well, *shifting*." Elerbee's focus strayed as he recalled the events to her. "The sound I heard started as a scream but then changed to more of a roar. Your face, your body, started to shift. Like you were two different beings. You took on the shape of a dragon. A purplish-black dragon with the most astonishing silver eyes." His voice took on a touch of awe as he looked at her. "I have only seen anything so wondrous one other time, and that was when Sirrah came to me to bestow his blessing."

Mey felt numb. Each breath seemed to stick in her throat and she had to force each one out. "I turned into a dragon?"

They had stopped walking altogether now. She looked at each of them in turn as they nodded.

"And now ye've changed some more," Durlag put in. "Yer hair, it's streaked with that purply-black color and yer eyes…" He shuddered and didn't continue.

Her knees felt weak, like they wouldn't be able to hold her much longer. Finding a large boulder, she sank down to it with a sigh.

"I could hear Makagesh urging me to let go," she whispered. "The power felt so massive, like I would split in two if I didn't let it out. I knew I had to destroy the spirits. That was the only thought in my mind. Then I felt the warmth and the sensation of leaving myself and looking down on what was happening." She lifted her trembling hands to her face.

Bob knelt before her. "Meylaran, your mother gave you a gift. You should not be afraid to use it. It makes you more precious than anyone else in this world. And you controlled it magnificently."

Looking up questioningly at her uncle, Mey said, "What do you mean?"

"The power you unleashed could have been strong enough to destroy everything around you for miles. A dragon's voice can create or end life as it desires. You focused yours only on the immediate threat – the spirits. It would have been very easy to kill all of us as well. You showed great control." His smile was full of pride.

The thought of ending life at a whim did nothing to quell her fear. It was starting to sink in just how powerful dragons had been and would be again. Almost godlike if you thought about it. No wonder people had become afraid of them. They held everyone's life in the balance. Was she doing the right thing, bringing that back into the world? There were races that didn't want them here; the priests of Yenoh, for sure, thought it was a bad idea.

This was about more than just her. "Uncle, what happens to the people if I release the dragons and they decide to take revenge instead of pity?"

The silence that followed sickened her. The fate of the world lay with her decisions and hers alone.

Preparations for camp went on around her. She volunteered for whatever watch they would put her on, she wouldn't sleep this night anyway. She moved to Thom's side. He groaned and tossed his head. Reaching a hand to his forehead, she smoothed the dark curls away.

He quieted at her touch. She slid her other hand into his cold, pale one. "We'll get you help," she said to him quietly. "I won't let you go."

****

The wight was coming for Mey. He couldn't let that happen. *She has to stay safe.* He uttered a few words that had him at her side in an instant. Exhausted though he was, he still had a few spells left to him. Thom knew his strength was fading, but he used one of the more powerful spells anyway. He couldn't let anything happen to her, she was his responsibility.

As the tiny bolts of electricity shot from his fingertips into the wight, it let out a horrific wail. The spell had hurt it, he could see the tiny holes through the creature's chest. But it's wailing response was deafening. Thom felt as though he were nailed in place. He couldn't move.

Sinking to his knees, his thoughts lingered only on Mey. She had to make it to Sorga, and beyond to the Heartstone so she could mend the statue. They were so close. But the thought of leaving her bothered him the most.

An icy chill seared his heart and he looked down. The wight's arm was protruding from his chest. He tried to take a breath but it caught in his throat. Numbness crawled out from the fingers gripping his heart and flowed outward to the rest of his body. Darkness tugged at the edges of his sight and he knew he was dying.

I won't leave her. This thought played over and over in his mind as the darkness finally overcame him and he fell to the ground. Swirls of color snaked behind his closed eyelids.

One pinpoint of light hovered in the center. It was so far away, it would be impossible to reach it, but he knew he had to. He concentrated on that light and tried to move forward.

As if granting his wish, light was all around him. He had thought about going toward that light and then, there it was. He had read about the two planes of existence but actually experiencing them both was beyond comprehension. His body lie on the physical plane, and now, his mind had wandered into the spiritual plane. It made perfect sense, really.

The wight was not of the physical plane. When it struck him, it set him on a journey into the spiritual plane. He would become an incorporeal being just like those creatures they battled. As this thought sank in, panic welled. He didn't want to be a creature of spirit! *You have to fight this*, he told himself. The panic rose steadily from his stomach to his throat, making it hard to breathe.

Frantically searching around him for any sign of what he should do, he stumbled and fell to his knees.

"Don't be frightened." The voice startled Thom and he froze.

A feeling of calm washed over him like warm water. He could feel it seep into his pores and wash through his body. He took a deep breath and let it out in an audible sigh.

"There," the voice continued, "that's better. Now you do not feel so chaotic."

Afraid at what he might find when he looked up, Thom kept his eyes on the ground beneath him. He was curious, however, and it seemed that his curiosity was winning this one. The voice was male and full of authority. Was this a god? If he looked upon a god did that mean he would certainly die? He warred with himself and these questions, but the scholar in him *had* to know.

He let his eyes swing upward. There was nothing in front of him but light. Slowly, he looked to his left and then to his right. He tensed again; it must be behind him.

Steeling his resolve, he turned. Nothing. The only thing around him was the bright light. "Who are you?" he called out.

"A being forced to live between the planes of existence."

"Why won't you let me see you?"

"I'm not sure you're quite ready for that." A shuffling sound came from his left and Thom turned quickly. He only caught a glimpse of something that shimmered and then vanished from view.

"I am not interested in your games," he called out, getting to his feet. "Reveal yourself! I assure you, I am a scholar, I can handle whatever it is you have to tell me."

When no answer was forthcoming, Thom tried another approach. "Are you a god here to tell me that I am dying?"

Laughter boomed all around him so loud he had to raise his hands to his ears. "You are a scholar, are you? Well, scholar, do you know where you are?"

"I am fairly certain I am passing into the spiritual plane. I was wounded by a wight. But I will do whatever I can in my power *not* to let that happen."

"Yes, I feel that about you. You're a very determined creature."

Cool wind gusted around him and he had to wrap his arms around himself to guard against the chill. He could hear what sounded like buffeting wings, as if a giant bird was alighting. As the ground shook, the air before him shimmered and sparkled. An image formed, vanished and reformed several times. A large image. Then as if the air itself were melting away, the image stayed.

Its head cocked to the side, an enormous dragon stood before him. Thom's mouth hung open and his mind felt blank. The creature had to be at least thirty feet tall. The scales that covered it shone with golden brilliance. It had a tail that curled behind it, ending in a barbed point. The talons on its forelegs were as large as a man. It snaked its head down to look Thom straight in the eye. Oh, it's eyes! They were rosy pink and they glittered just as a handful of crystals in the sunlight. It blinked.

The creature seemed to be scrutinizing him. Sizing him up with those amazing, clear eyes. Thom was nailed in place, he dare not move a muscle. After a moment, the dragon seemed satisfied and sat back on his haunches. It might as well have been a god for all the awe Thom felt at this moment. His legs felt weak beneath him and his heart thundered within his chest as though it would burst through.

"You – you are a dragon," he managed as he sank down to his knees again.

The dragon chuckled. "Yes, I am. My name is Yndaryandrus. You can call me Yndar."

Thom took a seated position right where he had been standing. "What are you doing here, in this place between planes?"

"It's my home," Yndar said simply. "Tell me, has it become customary for humans not to reveal their names once another creature has done so?"

"Oh, no, I am sorry. I am Thomas Uray, Mage of the Circle. You can call me Thom," he added almost as an afterthought.

"A Mage? Of the Circle?" Yndar seemed taken aback by this revelation.

"Yes," Thom said. "I was born in Val and raised to hone my gifts. My life's work has been to locate the one that the prophecy promised would bring dragons back to our world."

Thom wasn't sure if dragons could be surprised, but Yndar certainly seemed to be shocked by his revelation about his life's work. The dragon's eyes had grown wide and he ruffed his leathery wings once before settling them back in place.

Yndar stared at Thom for long moments. Thom was uncomfortable under the scrutiny. Just as he was beginning to fidget, the dragon spoke. "How does the world fare without us, Mage Thom?"

"Not well, I'm afraid. The balance that dragons kept while on Cantor is failing. The Ruling Council now leans heavily to the side of the priests. All but one of the divine factions are intent to impose new laws over the lands."

"New laws?" Yndar roared. "The priests have always been hungry for power and could not stand that we held it and not they!"

"The Provicary Council has become inundated with priests, especially those of Yenoh. While Sirrahn priests remain in favor of the dragons' return. Irohna has always been neutral but somehow the priests of Yehoh have been able to gain their support in trying to stop that from happening. Each race has a priestly representative on the Council. The laws and treaties that were drawn up in the time of dragons are being overruled and amended to fit the priests' whims."

A low growl sounded from Yndar as Thom told him the history of the ruling Council of Cantor since the departure of dragons.

"They must be stopped!" Yndar's eyes flashed with anger.

"It is the Yenohan and Irhonan sects of priests who push for the take-over. The Sirrahns work diligently against the others, but there are not enough of them these days to make a difference." Thom shook his head. There were far too few priests who served the gods of good.

Abruptly, Yndar stood, nearly knocking Thom backward. He paced back and forth, growling through clenched jaws. "We need a way back! When the Keeper tore the Idylic, she eradicated any chance of us returning."

Thom stood. "But she didn't! You must remember one of your kin stayed behind. She chose to stay in mortal form."

Stopping his pacing, Yndar turned to Thom. "Tanahil," he whispered. "Yes, she stayed with her elven lover."

"They had a child."

Yndar smiled. "Good for her. Is she still with this elf? How does she fare?"

"She died in childbirth." Thom saw the light in Yndar's eyes darken, so he hastily added, “But her child lives. She is the one the prophecy promised could bring you back; all of you.”

“Prophecy?” That had gotten his attention.

“Yes, at the time when the dragons left Cantor, the Head of the Mage’s Circle was Naoj D’yob. He foresaw that Tanahil would have a child. He left a prophecy that told us that one day, there would be a descendant who could bring back the dragons.”

Hope sparked behind the rose-colored eyes. Thom could see that Yndar was thinking of being back home. Back where there was more than just this endless, stark light. Hundreds of years spent here would drive a lesser mind insane.

“I have found her, you know.”

“Who?” Yndar asked.

“The Descendant. The one who can free you and bring you back to the world.”

The dragon maneuvered itself to look right in Thom’s eyes. “But you are stuck here just as I, mage.” Yndar narrowed his eyes. “How do you propose we get to this Descendant?”

He hadn’t thought about that. It took him off guard. As much as he wanted to fight what was happening to him, so much depended on what they were doing to save him on the physical plane. He would deny death as long as his mind would allow, of course, but if they couldn’t save his body, well, then his fight was lost.

“We’ll think of something,” Thom said quietly. His heart ached again when he thought of Mey alone on her journey. He knew he had to get back if for nothing else but to see her face again. To wrap his arms around her, pull her close and hold her. Things he wanted to do the whole time but had restrained himself from doing for fear of…fear of what? His Master? The Mage’s Circle certainly would frown on him taking a personal interest in her, but what, ultimately, could they do to him?

They could banish him from Val and from the home he had always known. They could deny him the right to practice magic legally. He could become a rouge mage, of course, like so many who had trouble following rules did. Would he do all this for her? Yes, he would.

“Mey will find a way to bring me back so that I can help her bring you and all your kind back to the world.”

“And while we wait, mage, tell me of what has happened in the world and of this Descendant." The large body shook the ground as the dragon lay itself down in front of Thom, settling in comfortably to await stories of a place that had largely forgotten him.

Thom sat cross-legged in front of Yndar. He began by filling the dragon in on more of the political upheavals the priests had facilitated over the years. When he spoke of Mey and the journey they were on, Yndar's interest increased and he asked many questions.

"So she is half-elven? That makes for an interesting mix," Yndar commented. "Dragons, of course, make the most beautiful mortals, whichever race they chose to manifest as."

"They certainly do." Thom's thoughts were on Mey. Her face, her smile, the exotic look her slight elven features gave her.

"Hmmm, you are in love with her."

"What? No, I…what gives you that impression?"

"It is written all over your face when you speak of her." Yndar shrugged. "You could do worse than a dragon, I suppose."

"But, I am only on this journey to see her safely to the Idylic, to mend it and save our world from falling to the priests who would ultimately destroy it."

"Now, that sounded rehearsed." Yndar rolled over to his side and stretched his massive body to a more comfortable position. "Why lie to me, mage? After all, you may never leave this place. Lies do you no good here."

He *did* love her, he knew that within himself but he had not admitted it outwardly. To do that would mean he was willing to give up the life he had always known. To give up his position with the Circle and be willing to become rogue. Everything he was would change. He hadn't been ready. But if he never left this place, it wouldn't matter, would it?

Closing his eyes, he thought of her. His mind went always to the kiss they shared. That kiss had solidified any feelings he may have been doubtful about. It had broken past any misgivings and apprehensions about who he was or what his purpose in this life was. His purpose was loving her, being with her, giving her everything he could offer of himself.

Opening his eyes, he studied the golden creature before him. Thom let out a long, cleansing sigh.

"You are right, Yndar," he said, smiling. "I love her."

FIFTEEN

Sorga had been in upheaval for quite some time according to the priests still residing in the temple of Sirrah. The group would be allowed to stay as long as they didn't overstep the boundaries set by the Yenohan priests. Their power was rooted deeply in Sorga and the people followed them blindly with the promise of living forever with riches beyond imagining.

Ushering them inside, the priests took Thom and carried him to a large room at the back of the temple. There were beds along one wall but none of them occupied. Mey watched as they laid him out and began removing his belongings. His pouches were placed reverently on a stone table, along with a small dagger that hung from his belt. Funny, she had never noticed a weapon on his person.

"Elerbee," Mey said quietly, "what are they doing?"

"Removing his magical elements." Elerbee laid a comforting hand on her arm. "They place them on the stone to ground them to the earth. Interference from their arcane power makes it harder for the priests to do their work."

A boy, dressed in plain wool robes with the symbol of Sirrah stitched on the left breast, timidly approached. "Pardon," he began. "We have prepared a place for you. Please, follow me."

Mey hesitated, looking back at Thom. He looked so fragile lying there, pale and still. His thrashing had ceased sometime on the road to Sorga but Mey couldn't pinpoint when that had been. She had stayed by his side the whole time but her thoughts were scattered.

"He's in good hands," Elerbee assured her.

Swallowing hard and nodding, Mey followed the others. Elerbee walked beside her and she could feel his calming aura reaching out to cover her.

The boy showed them to a large room. It was plain, just like everything else in this temple; there were three cots along the back wall and basins of fresh, clear water next to each.

"I'm sorry it's not more," the boy said. "But you can wash the dust of the road away and rest. There's plenty of food in the kitchens. We will bring you something to eat."

The boy turned to Mey, wide eyes the only thing giving away his shock at her appearance, and continued, "Madame, if you will follow me, we have quarters prepared for you as well." He hurried ahead of her.

A small smile curled the corner of Mey's lips. Of course, she thought, men and women were not housed together under the temple roof. The boy led her down the hallway to a smaller room.

"Thank you," she said when he opened the door and gestured her inside.

He bowed at the waist and was gone without another word. Mey let out a sigh and sank onto the cot. She was exhausted, but her mind refused to slow. Her thoughts were constantly running over what the others had told her.

Looking at the basin of water, curiosity got the better of her. What *did* she look like? Slowly, she stood and stepped to the little table holding the basin. Careful not to shake the table, thereby disturbing the water, Mey took a steadying breath and leaned in.

She froze. These were not her eyes. One was completely silver; the other still held a mixture of the green she had always known. But both of the pupils had elongated, reminding her of the old tabby cat she used to feed scraps to. Her hand trembled as she reached to touch her own face. *This can't be*. Only then did she notice her hair.

Running a hand over her long, dark tresses, she untied the leather strip at the nape of her neck and, tenuously, held the silken strands away from her face. Its color had always been soft auburn. Now strands of deepest violet ran thickly throughout. It was a color she was unfamiliar with; purple, yes, but more than that. She didn't have the words to describe it. Hot tears seared the corners of her eyes. *I'm losing myself.*

A knock on the door startled her and it opened almost immediately afterward. Bob stepped through, holding a small bowl of something hot, judging from the steam rising from it.

"Meylaran?" He walked straight to her and started to hand her the bowl, but stopped at the sight of her tears. "Why are you crying?"

She turned fully to face him and stared into his soft green eyes. Silence hung between them a moment longer. He didn't turn away as she expected. "You don't find this frightening?"

"And what, exactly, would I find frightening?"

"The eyes! The hair!" her voice rose uncontrollably. "This isn't me, Uncle." Tears rolled freely down her cheeks now. "I am losing myself and I can't do a thing to stop it!"

A smile broke his usually stoic features, almost obliterating the white scar that ran the length of this face. He was beautiful when he smiled. People might think the scar took away from the hauntingly exquisite elven features. But for Mey, it only added to his charm and made him more interesting to look upon.

Not for the first time, she thought how much he looked like her father when he smiled.

"Perhaps you are *finding* who you were truly meant to be, not losing who you were." Mey loved him more because he could always make her reevaluate her position in the fewest words possible.

He offered her the bowl. "You should eat. We need to strengthen ourselves while we can."

"I'm not hungry." She ignored his outstretched hand and turned to the basin. The cool water felt heavenly against her skin as she splashed it to her face. Grabbing the towel and dabbing at the moisture, she continued, "I want to see Thom as soon as possible. I was planning to go to the main temple and wait."

Outwardly struggling to compose his disapproval, Bob set the food on the small table and moved to position himself in front of her door. "I think you should eat and rest."

"I'm not in need of a nurse maid," she snapped at him. "I am going to the temple." Moving forward to pass him, his solid form did not sway. "Uncle, let me pass."

"No, *tae'wa*. This time you will listen to me. Eat. You are no good to anyone if your body fails. I will not concede on this." His mouth set in a straight line, his eyes hardened and a small muscle in his cheek ticked. He meant what he said.

"Fine. I'll eat, but then I will go see what progress the priests have made in helping Thom."

He nodded but stayed where he was. Trust was obviously something she hadn't completely earned with him yet. He knew her too well.

"You are so much like your mother," Bob told her as she ate. "She was very strong-headed as well."

"But did she carry the weight of the entire world on *her* shoulders?" Mey mumbled through bites of the warm stew.

"Yes, she did."

"She did?"

"You forget she was the last of her kind. People did not know what to do once the dragons were gone. They had always turned to dragons when an unfair lord decided to overstep his bounds with their land, money or food. Or to settle disputes that surely would end in bloodshed otherwise." Bob seated himself on the edge of the small bed. "Not knowing where else to turn, they sought her out. And with it being in her nature, she felt compelled to help them."

"How? If so many people demanded her attention, how did she manage to help them all?"

"She could not help them all, *tae'wa*. Hence, the weight she burdened herself with." He reached out and stroked her hair, not at all apprehensive of the changes in her appearance. She loved him so much more for that. Even Durlag and Elerbee had stared, making her feel a side-show freak somewhat. But not her uncle.

In an almost inaudible whisper, Mey voiced the thought that weighed on her so heavily, "But I *can* help them all. I can bring back the dragons."

Smiling at her, Bob stood and moved toward the door. "We will meet you in the temple."

Nodding absently, she set the bowl aside and moved to the small window in the far wall. The streets of Sorga held so many people. Many begged for money or a bit of bread to feed their families. Children ran, without shoes and little clothing, up and down the filthy road, oblivious that the rest of the world did not share their plight. Hollow stares looked out from almost every doorway. *Helpless*, Mey thought, *they think their situation helpless*.

She watched as a man dressed in comfortable robes made his way up the moonlit street. Stopping before a woman holding a small baby, he spoke, gesturing to her neck. She cried and shook her head vehemently, clutching at whatever the priest had obviously gestured to. Mey couldn't hear what was being said, but it was obvious that the man was demanding something and the woman did not want to comply. The child in her arms wailed.

As she tried to comfort the infant, the man reached up and yanked something from her neck. She tried to grab for it but he struck her with the back of his hand so hard, she fell back against the wall.

Heat rose in Mey's middle. Concentrating hard on the robed man as he turned, she took a good look at his face, imprinting the details in her mind. The large strawberry mark he tried to hide with his beard would be the only detail she would need. That, and the fact that his robes held the mark of Yenoh. She watched him until his small figure turned the corner of the street and disappeared.

Looking back at the sobbing woman holding her child to her breast, Mey let the heat crawl through her limbs. Even welcoming the voice that urged her on. Makagesh was ever-present, even now when the blade was not physically with her. He held no dominance over her, she had conquered that demon. Yet he still talked incessantly. Mostly she could ignore him, sometimes she let him ramble and now she welcomed his voice, encouraging her to let her anger take her to a place where he was sure to find bloodshed.

Turning from the window, Mey strode to the door. Determination and anger flowed through her, but first things first. She would check on Thom.

****

Entering the big open room in the main temple, where Thom had been housed, Mey's footsteps echoed as she approached his bed. The stone table where his magical elements had been laid was there, at the head. A lone priest sat vigil, monitoring his condition.

The priest briefed her. While he still walked the plane between spiritual and reality, they had managed to stabilize him further; his breathing and heartbeat had grown stronger.

Mey noted his color looked much better. His lips were no longer blue and his skin had regained some of the healthy pink tinge it should have. A wave of relief washed over her and she breathed a bit easier.

"Can I have some time alone with him?" she asked the priest. He glanced at her, eyes widening before he was able to compose himself. Nodding, he stood and bowed as he exited. Mey took the seat next to the bed.

Thom looked more peaceful than he had on the journey into Sorga. He no longer thrashed, but rested comfortably. It even appeared he had a slight smile on his lips. Mey took his hand in hers; it was still colder than it should be given the warmth of the temple.

"Thom," she whispered close to his ear, "we have made it to Sorga. Come back to us. I need you here; I don't know what to do next."

Mey wasn't sure if she was seeing things but he reacted to her voice, slightly turning his head in her direction. And she could have sworn she felt him squeeze her hand. It was almost imperceptible, but it was there. Could he know what was going on around him while his mind wandered another plane? Moving in very close to him, she tried again.

"Thom," she said. "Thom, if you can hear me, squeeze my hand."

Nothing. Watching him closely, she could discern no movement of any kind. Her hopes sank; she had imagined it. Breathing in deeply, she could smell the familiar mixture of herbs and flowers. Lowering her forehead to his arm, she squeezed her eyes shut against the tears that threatened to break through yet again.

Letting her mind drift to thoughts of others she had lost, there was no stopping the warm flow of tears that found their way down her cheeks. Her father, vanished while on a trip to the elven lands. Garrin, ripped from her life by thugs who thought they could bully him into revealing the mask they had acquired. Was she never to be allowed any happiness? Any time someone that made her happy was in her life, something happened to take it away.

Thom made her happy. She loved him, she was sure. A conclusion she had come to when the fear of losing him sent waves of panic and anguish through her heart.

"What am I supposed to do?" Her voice echoed off the walls and rang back at her, empty and hollow.

A whisper made her start and sit up straight. Expecting to see the priest, she quickly wiped at her eyes to obliterate any trace of tears. But, when she looked around there was no one there. Certain that she had heard someone, she called out. "Who's there?"

When no answer came, Mey tensed, and reached for a dagger at her hip. "Damn!" They had given their weapons up on entering the temple. Well, they had given most of them up. She reached down to her boot and slid the small knife from its hiding place. Crouching low, she moved around Thom's bed, listening for any more sounds. She was positive there was a voice. A male voice. But she couldn't make out what it had said. Moving around, she made her way to the head of the bed where the stone table was placed.

The pull of the magic was so strong. Almost as if she couldn't control them, her eyes moved down to the table to look at the various gems, trinkets and the dagger. Everything here glowed with a magical aura, some stronger than others.

The feeling that someone watched her was stronger here. Glancing around, Mey noted everything in the room in just seconds. There was the bed where Thom lay, with several other cots folded and stacked against the wall to her right. The room had two entrances. The one she used and another to her left. That one must open up to admit the higher clergy. Tapestries hung on two walls, left and right; none of them long enough to hide a person. And windows lined the top, allowing light to enter. There was no light from these at present, it was still nighttime outside and the moon had hidden behind clouds for at least two days now.

Mask... The word whispered through her mind and made her jump. Jerking around to look behind her, she found no one. It was plain as anything and somewhat familiar. "Mask?" she repeated.

Looking down to the table before her, she scanned its contents. There, half hidden under Thom's pack, was the mask she and Garrin had acquired. *Mask*... the voice floated through her mind again. This time she was convinced she knew it.

"Garrin?" she asked with a shaky voice. Surely she was going crazy. It couldn't be.

Glancing at Thom, Mey saw he had not moved. She shook her head but looked back to the table where the magical elements were laid out. The mask glowed just as everything else here. Reaching a shaky hand, Mey slid it from beneath the pack and held it at arm's length. It was slender, only large enough to cover the eyes. Made from cloth and covered in thin gold sheets, there was leather on either side to tie it around one's head. It was cold to the touch.

What was it that Thom had said? The thieves that had come for this mask said it had something to do with calling the dragons. She hadn't paid much attention at the time. She was too angry. What else did he pull from the man's mind? Did he ever say? Damn! She couldn't remember.

She replaced the small knife in her boot and held the mask in both hands. "What do you want me to do, Garrin?"

Mask... the voice came again. How was she hearing him? So many strange things had happened to her, she had stopped questioning some time ago. After all, she saw Garrin most every night in her dreams. But she was awake and supposedly of sound mind.

Nodding once in determination, she brought the mask to her face, stopping inches from letting it touch her. "I trust you, Garrin," she whispered and closed her eyes. Mey placed the mask to her skin and tied it behind her head.

Slowly opening her eyes, at first all she saw was a bright, blinding light. Then things began to focus and take shape. It was the same room she had been in but considerably different now. Her breathing came fast and in short gasps. The feel of the magic was starting to flow through her and it was the most exquisite sensation. Everything around her shimmered. She scanned the room and saw that now only two tapestries hung on the walls, one on each side of the second door. The only furniture the room housed was the table and the bed on which Thom lay. The other cots and the chair the priest had used were not there.

Strange. Where did everything go?

Moving around to Thom's side, she placed each step carefully as the floor looked farther away than she remembered it. Her movements felt cumbersome and heavy. He still lay unconscious, but with a more marked smile on his lips. Satisfied that he was alright, she moved to the tapestries that hung by the door.

Each depicted dragons, some flying, some on land. On the first, a city burned as a dragon flew above. Looking closely at the creature, Mey could see it had tears in its eyes and the tears fell to the city below in large drops. The next scene showed bodies laid in a field while a dragon crouched over them, wings spread covering and enfolding. There were words written throughout the pictures:

From mountaintops to valleys low,
The softest chimes or trumpets blow.
Make whole the sick.
Bring home the lost.
Lay hidden the secrets to cleanse the sin,
The spoken word of dragon-kin.

Below the words were the same scenes, but now with a town made whole and the people all well and standing in the field.

As she stood and stared at the woven pictures and words, a memory of something her uncle had said came back to her. *A dragon's voice can give or end life as it desires.*

Give life! A dragon can give life. It was the answer all along! Mey's heart soared and felt near to bursting with happiness. *She* could save him; she could bring Thom back.

Quickly making her way back to his side, Mey reached for Thom's hand but stopped suddenly when she looked down. The hands reaching for Thom were not her hands. These hands were covered with deep purple scales, almost black, and the fingers curled into talons. Jerking back, the hands she watched mimicked her movement. She moved her arms to hold them in front of her and the strange arms moved as well.

Looking down at her legs, they were also covered in scales and had elongated. No wonder her movements felt awkward. It wasn't the magic, it was her. Reaching up, she yanked the mask from her face. Everything was as it had been when she first entered the room. There were dozens of tapestries on the walls, the furniture was in place and most importantly, she was herself again. Her arms and legs were covered with skin, not scales and had the fleshy tone they had always carried.

Wondering at this, Mey slowly put the mask on again and held up a hand in front of her. It was covered in the purple scales. Without moving her hand, she used the other to remove the mask and the arm and hand transformed back to normal. *Amazing*. This mask was showing her the dragon side that resided within her blood. Mey found it strangely beautiful, curious and a bit frightening all at the same time.

Then she remembered Thom. Looking back to him and replacing the mask on her face, she reached to grasp his hand. What was she supposed to say? The tapestry did not tell her if there were any magical words, only that she must use her voice to help him.

She decided that she would recount their time together, starting with their meeting in Seaside. Mey began speaking, making sure to concentrate on the goal of waking Thom. After a few words a fine, spidery mist flowed from her mouth and curled around him. The mist twisted through his hair and circled his head, moving over his body. Hope filled Mey's heart and she spoke faster, talking of their search for companions to help on their journey, the first meeting with the Shadow Guard, and Durlag's story of the Flame Soul that devoured his friend.

The mist worked its way down and around Thom, completely enveloping him. The further it moved the more eager Mey became.

It was working!

She lifted her hands to his face and cupped it while she spoke, focused on him and blocking out everything else around her.

****

Something was tugging at him. It was a slight pull but enough to be annoying. Opening his eyes, Thom saw Yndar, peacefully dozing, chest moving rhythmically with each breath.

Another tug. *What is going on?* Rolling over to see what could possibly be pulling, he almost fell straight into a big black pit. His heart pounded wildly as he scrambled to back away from the gaping hole. *Gods! Where did that come from?*

The tugging sensation happened again. The pull came from the hole, as if drawing him in. Steadying himself and looking closely into the darkness, he could make out shapes. It looked to be a large room, mostly empty. But if he focused, he could see a figure lying on a bed with another beside it. There was a strange mist floating across the figure lying on the bed.

Snatches of whispers came to him, although he could not make out the words. Concentrating harder on the two figures in the room, he could make out the other figure had scales along its arms; its mane flowed like hair rather than the hard scales Yndar had running along his back. *Another dragon?* But this one wasn't quite a dragon. It had a more humanoid shape.

A gasp escaped him when the figure moved to reveal the face of the person lying on the bed. It was him! Is this what was playing out back on the material plane? He crept a little closer to the edge of the pit, hoping for a better view. The whispers grew louder and he could make out a few words. *Elerbee, Sorga, wight...*

Fascination at what was transpiring had him ignoring the tugging feeling so when he came back to himself he realized he was perilously close to the edge of the great pit. He moved back again, coming up against something solid.

"You should heed the call," Yndar said.

"Do you see it, too? What is going on?"

"I do not see it, but I recognize the voice of a fellow dragon. I can hear that she calls to you. If you allow it, she can bring you home."

"She…?" The word trailed off. Thom leaned a bit closer. Surprise at whose profile he was studying burst forth. "Mey!"

"There is power in her voice," Yndar observed. "You should go now before the chance is lost."

Thom hesitated briefly. "But what about you? Can you follow?" He looked up at the magnificent creature.

"No, the call is for you alone, mage."

Mixed feelings flowed over him, not the least of which was fear. He had no idea what would happen if he stepped into that pit. The possibility that he would never awaken was foremost in his mind. But even stronger was the possibility he could be with her again. A gentle wave of calm settled around him and he smiled up at the dragon.

"Thank you, Yndar."

Focusing all his energy on Mey and the placid whispers she spoke, he closed his eyes and took one step into the oblivion before him.

SIXTEEN

The apprentice cowered as glass vials and bottles of all kinds smashed around him, showering small pieces of glass over the room. Rekho's temper was something one would be wise to shrink from. Every last one of the thieves he had sent to recover the mask had failed. Every one.

"Where do you find these incompetents?" he shouted at the young man. "I ask for professionals who can accomplish a simple task and *this* is what you give me?"

Another shower of glass and an explosion of power from the mage's hands. If he wasn't forced to work with these priests, he'd be out there doing the damned job himself. It would have been over a long time ago.

"Master, I must tell you that the group is now headed for Sorga. The mage who travels with them is injured and they seek the protection and help of the Sirrahn temple."

A small sound started low in Rekho's chest and bubbled up as a growl that he released to ease the aggravation at his crumbling plans. His gaze landed on something in the back of his makeshift laboratory. For at least the tenth time since they arrived at the Caverns he considered smashing this bothersome bug. His eyes locked with the eyes of the bound and gagged man.

A small shudder raced down Rekho's spine. He wanted rid of this one simply to obliterate that annoying feeling. There was a challenge in the other's eyes that left no doubt to Rekho that after his usefulness, he would have to be disposed of. A sneer curled across the mage's face and he turned quickly back to the apprentice cowering at the door.

"They have not used the mask yet but it is only a matter of time." He paced across the room. "They *will* eventually figure out that it is a key piece to this puzzle."

Obviously it was useless to go about stopping them this way. By all indications, the mask would lead them to the Heartstone and in the end they would find the Idylic, dooming his daughter and releasing the dragons to rain their vengeance on the unsuspecting world. And him.

His divinations with the priests had given them knowledge that the magical power contained in the Heartstone of the Idylic was concentrated on the Faery Isles.

Reason told him that they would head for the Isles next. It was close to their current position and their mage had mentioned having to cross the Barren Lands. This would be Rheko's next destination as well.

He couldn't touch the Heartstone, it was only safe for dragon-kin to handle it, but he could certainly put roadblocks in place that would stop the group before Mey could lay hands on it. If he was lucky, that mage of theirs would die in the hands of the incompetent priests of Sirrah and he would not have to worry about them getting much further.

Unlikely. This Uray fellow was strong. Infused with the power of the Circle, no doubt.

To the apprentice, he said, "Ask the Elder if he will see me." The young man moved quickly, knowing that if the mage asked, it was best to comply hastily.

Less than an hour later, Rekho sat in an ornately decorated room off the main path of the Caverns. Apparently priests had no problem using their divine gifts to surround themselves with trinkets and luxuries. Disgust twisted through his stomach and sat heavy. He didn't like this arrangement but what other choice did he have?

His disdain for the priests went back, far into his youth as a quickling in Orphana. There were very few elven priests, mostly because the elves revered nature as their god and protector, not some pale imitation of a being so powerful it could control the very destiny of the world.

He had known one elven priest, however. After his mother had been taken in by the wretched fool, and given over every precious heirloom the family held sacred in exchange for a promised divine place among the gods for her and her children, the priest had disappeared. No one ever heard from him again and his mother's spirit had been broken so severely she never quite recovered. Her nighttime wanderings and one-sided conversations with herself in search of a god who likely did not exist had left Rekho mistrustful of any and all priests he had come into contact with from then on.

"Master," a voice broke into his reverie.

"Do not refer to me as such," he sneered before composing himself and turning to face the Elder. "I am no longer of the Magister's Order."

"Of course," the soft-spoken man before him said. "Rekho."

"That will do." Rekho sat in the nearest chair, covered with velvet no less. "I need to travel. I will require the assistance of some of your most seasoned priests. If you have any Chosen, they would be most beneficial."

The Elder raised an eyebrow and moved to seat himself across from Rekho. His robes were the softest spun silk this side of Cantor, the mage was sure and wrapped with the sash delineating his station, sewn from golden thread. The man himself was middle-aged, as humans went. Just into his fortieth year if he had to guess.

"And where would you be traveling?"

"Our target will head next to the Faery Isles. I must arrive before them to prepare a…surprise welcome, shall we say." Rekho was quite uncomfortable under this man's scrutiny but he would never allow the man to know as much.

Moving to retrieve a small glass along with a colored decanter, the Elder looked up. "Wine?" he asked. Damn him and his flippant attitude. This was not a social visit. Rekho ground his teeth together and shook his head. Enduring this man was a challenge in itself. The 'Elder' had inherited the position from Keelan Bor, recently deceased. *And likely at this one's hands*, Rekho thought cautiously. This Elder took no chances that he would suffer the same fate as his predecessor. Spells of detection were always placed strategically about him. You never knew if he was privy to your thoughts or if he was prying into your soul.

Rekho swallowed his ire and contempt. "Elder, I have a plan that should stop them from acquiring the Heartstone that is located on the Isles."

"And how do you know the Heartstone is on the Isles?"

"Reports of mutated fey creatures that inhabit these isles are pouring in as of late. The sprites, gnomes and nymphs are warring among one another, with detrimental effects upon the gnomes I hear. The sea creatures that have lived peacefully in those waters for centuries are altered. Fishermen have shunned the area for some time now."

"The same things that are happening in Chal, I presume? And the outskirts of Val? The sightings of Gnor are dramatically increasing." He drank the wine in one gulp and poured another. Rekho supposed he had to repress the haunting deeds of his conscious somehow.

"Yes." Rekho's gaze wavered slightly before he said, "And I plan to call the Zar'leith."

"So, you have deemed it necessary to bring in a denizen of the dark, have you?"

Swallowing his apprehension, he replied with amazing surety in his tone. "The demon will be instructed only to protect the Heartstone."

"A demon that follows orders?"

"It has no choice. I hold its essence."

"And how did you ever come by something so valuable, Rekho?" The sly smile on the Elder's face widened. He would love to know the secrets Rekho carried from the Order of Mages, but he was not so idiotic as to reveal that information.

Rekho remained silent. The Elder laughed and poured another drink. "Very well, Rekho. You may have ten priests to accompany you, three of them Chosen. Suitable?"

"If they can handle traveling the roads of magic, yes. We must arrive quickly and I can take no chances at crossing the Anarhet Sea with the reports of the abominations that plague the fishermen."

"Very well. They will be ready within two hours. I must assemble them and then give my own instructions." His intent was quite clear. He would have to instruct them not to let the mage out of their sight. Trust was not something that he found within the ranks of priests.

Rekho moved to leave the Elder to his drink, but was stopped with the man's next question.

"What of that prisoner you keep?"

Heat flowed to his face and anger colored his pale cheeks. "He will be left untouched for now." It was not a request.

"I wonder, Rekho, what you're intending for that one? What value does he hold other than to allow for mistakes to be made?"

"That is *my* concern. I assure you that once his usefulness has faded, he will be disposed of." Anger fueling his steps, Rekho pushed through the curtain hanging in the doorway. He stopped abruptly just outside and took a deep, cleansing breath, blowing it out slowly.

He had to endure these priests. It was the only way he had any chance at stopping Mey and her friends from going too far with this quest. Funny, the empty hole where his heart had once been only ached slightly when he thought of her.

The insatiable need to stop her had grown so large it had eaten away at most of the tender feelings he had had trouble overcoming when he first offered his services to the priests. With every hour he spent plotting against them, the hole grew. Evil plans rushed to fill the void. He almost couldn't pull up the memory of her face the last time he tried.

He had severed the last thread between them when he let her believe he had died. She probably didn't believe it, but no matter. He brushed the thoughts out of his head and proceeded back to his laboratory. There was much work to do.

****

Under the canopy of stars that had twinkled in the sky now for nigh on a week, Rekho looked over the priests sent by the Elder.

They would suffice. The three Chosen were all servants of Irhona. The only female deity of the three gods worshiped by the races of Cantor, they bore her mark over their hearts. A circle struck through with an "X". She would claim not only their allegiance, but their souls as well. One of these men had decided to show his devotion by carving the deep X over his eyes. Rekho shuddered as he looked at the mutilated face of the priest. The extremes some of the devout would go to for their god was disturbing.

Going over the plan to call the demon forth, Rekho had to be sure he left nothing out. It was tricky business to deal with the dark demons but he wasn't overly worried. He had done this before, although on a smaller scale. The particular demon he wanted to summon this time, however, was unfamiliar with his presence. He would have to be careful to let it know he was someone it could trust.

As Rekho checked his store of farthen-crystals, he thought of how best to deal with the prisoner. The Elder wanted him dead. He couldn't let that happen before he gleaned all he could from the man. He knew more than he was telling willingly. Chanting the words that would produce a cloaking spell, Rekho blanketed the man with silence and shadow. No one would see nor hear him. He placed additional magical locks and alarms and traps all around and at the entrance to his laboratory.

Most priests here wouldn't dare to enter the mage's laboratory. But the Elder, that was an entirely different matter. The man was brazen beyond all good sense. Surely he was aware that Rekho protected his work with powerful spells. And if he wasn't, well, that was a mess Rekho would have to clean up once he returned.

One of the priests who would be accompanying him approached. "Sir, we're prepared to leave at your leisure."

Nodding, Rekho turned from the doorway of the deep grotto he chose to house his laboratory and walked the short distance to the mouth of the Caverns. He and the priests occupied the spaces closest to the entrance to the Caverns of Endless Time. Further in and deeper down, time meant nothing. It sped up, slowed down, suspended itself and churned backward constantly. You couldn't trust that you wouldn't be ripped to pieces if you entered unprepared. Closer to the surface, his magic combined with the divine powers of the priests, could hold any negative effects at bay.

The priests and Chosen waited for him in a clearing not far from the Caverns. He had instructed them to build a small altar with the handful of kyanite stones he had given them. Once he arrived, he grunted his approval at their handiwork. He stood near the stones as the priests circled around him. They knew what was required of them as they all joined hands to arms around Rekho. So, the Elder had honored his request at seasoned priests; good to know.

Murmuring words that would infuse the stones with the magic they would need to facilitate a journey to the Faery Isles, Rekho closed his eyes and concentrated. The words came faster, but never above a whisper as he chanted. The sensation of wind blowing over him lasted only moments before dying down. The sharp smell of salt air hit his nostrils. He slowly opened his eyes and looked around. All ten priests and Chosen had made the journey unscathed.

A wave of weakness passed through Rekho before he felt comfortable enough to move his legs. Breaking past the circle of priests he walked to the shoreline. There were three islands in the region known as the Faery Isles. Each was inhabited by a unique collection of fey creatures. Their destination had been Inispry, home to the sprites. It was likely they wouldn't see any of the small, elusive creatures while they were here. They tended to shy away from contact with outsiders.

"Sir, where do we find the Heartstone?" The tallest of the priests, who also seemed to be the one designated as leader of the bunch asked.

"We head toward the center of the island." Rekho was certain it was here, the pull of magic was strong. They would find it first by the mutated land around it. The power released by the stone was of the purest kind. Dragon magic was clean and undiluted. When the Idylic was broken, the magic from its Heartstone was allowed to seep into its surroundings, changing things slowly over time.

He led the men up the sandy beach into the dense trees. Laughter on the wind blew past them as they entered. "Only sprites," Rekho threw over his shoulder as he continued walking. "They are harmless, really. If you leave them alone and do not meddle with their homes." He smiled devilishly, then added, "Mind where you step."

All ten priests' heads snapped to their feet as they all froze in place. Looking to one another, they slowly began moving after Rekho who strode boldly through the wooded terrain, chuckling.

The islands were abundantly green and lush with flora. Every now and again a buzzing would sound. The curiosity of the sprites would get the better of them eventually. They would follow the mage and priests but they would not show themselves unless provoked. Rekho did not know any of the names of the men who accompanied him, he didn't really care. "You," he called to the tall man, "can you clear a path?"

The priest hesitated, not eager at altering the homes of the sprites. "Oh, for the love of stars, just do it. We are in no danger from sprites." Rekho's ire began to flare. Simple minds irritated him to no end.

The priest threw one unsure glance around to his brothers, but he brought his hands together in prayer. The thick vine and brush began to snake back, forming a path large enough to walk in a line. Without another word, Rekho turned and stomped on, fuming at the stupidity he was forced to endure.

As the group trudged further into the wooded island, Rekho began to notice the trees were increasingly twisted around one another. Inky black spots covered the leaves and trunks. There was a distinctive smell wafting on the breeze here as well. Rot. He kept a steady pace. Dead birds began to dot the floor of the woods, in various stages of decomposition. The further they traveled, the larger the animals they found dead and dying along the path. The trees had begun shedding their leaves and the decay littered the ground.

The smell had gotten worse as well. All indications that sprites were about had ceased. Likely they did not travel into the area of magic. The pulse and pull of it drew Rekho forward. It was close. The priests behind him had begun to tie cloths about their faces in an attempt to block the smell.

Rekho stepped into a large clearing where everything was bare. All the trees were skeletal remains of the beauty they once held. A sound, akin to a heartbeat pulsed in Rekhos' ears. A glow broke through a mass of dead plants and animals. He headed in that direction as the pulsing grew louder and threatened to make him turn around and walk away as quick as his legs would carry him. It was the dragon magic protecting itself. Falling to his knees, he peered through the tangled mass of skeletons and tree branches.

There, he saw the origin of the glowing and pulsing magic. No bigger than the palm of his hand, a grey stone, pocketed with pores from centuries of wear, sat among the debris. His breath caught in his throat.

"It's here," he breathed. Images assailed him as he gazed upon it. A beautiful, silver-eyed woman whose hair shimmered with a purple hue in the sunlight. His wife. A single tear burned a path down his cheek. "Tanahill."

A hand fell heavy on his shoulder. "Sir?"

Rekho snapped back to himself with an angry growl. He swiped at the tear and composed his face before he turned to face the others. "I need to set up a workspace." He slung the pack from his shoulder and opened it. He pulled out a small, iron brazier and a large, flat stone. Laying the stone on the ground as close as he dared to the glowing Heartstone, he placed the brazier on top of this. He instructed the priests to bring him some of the dried leaves that had littered the pathway and twigs. These he put inside the brazier to start a small fire.

He had brought only those potions that would be used in the summoning of the Zar'leith. Carefully he removed a small metal box. Opening this, he removed the delicate vial swirling with a colored liquid from the velvet lining. The essence he would need to demand that the demon follow his commands.

"Place your men twenty paces around me in all directions. Do not come nearer," he told the tall one. "No matter what you may hear." The warning in his voice was clear. The priest nodded and began issuing orders.

The three Chosen stood before Rekho and he eyed them critically. How strong was their faith? He would know soon enough. The one he had dubbed 'Scar' carried a long chain barbed with spikes and ending in a heavy, solid ball of metal. He chose this one to stand with him as he summoned. The man's eyes were void of anything, especially fear, so he should be able to handle what he was about to see. The other two Rekho told to only move in if the demon tried to lash out.

Rekho prepared his brazier, adding several drops from the three vials and the fire sputtered and shot sparks. Holding tightly to the vial of Zar'leith essence, Rekho muttered the words of conjuring that would open the depths of darkness and allow the demon to pass into their plane. A curtain of inky black opened and extended to the size of man, then elongated growing taller and taller.

As he chanted, Rekho inserted the name of the Zar'leith between breaths. A low rumbling sounded from the black hole that now stretched to ten feet. The ground around them shook and fissures shot outward from the chill blackness. Rekho chanted relentlessly. The men around him started to fidget nervously, except for Scar who stood still as a statue beside the mage. The only indication that he was alive was the free hand at his side curled into a fist that had his knuckles whitened with the effort.

With a rush of fetid air, a long, thin reptilian creature stepped out of the darkness. The body glistened in the moonlight. Three sets of arms stretched outward, it unfurled a set of wings that included every color known in existence and perhaps a few others as well. They were mesmerizing and gorgeous. Odd that they would be attached to such a hideously evil creature. The face of the beast resembled that of a bat but only one large eye sat in the middle of its face. Its elongated snout ended in a stubbed nose and opened revealing very few teeth, however the ones it had were thin, sharp and dripped with poisonous saliva. Pointed ears sat on either side of its head. It was brilliant red, the color of the fire burning bright from the brazier.

"Who summons me?" The voice that roared forth from it was actually several voices, male and female alike. It set every nerve in Rekho's body on edge. When it spoke, the smell of sulfur engulfed them.

"I…" Rekho nearly choked on his words. "I have summoned you," he said more forcefully. "Rekho Moonshadow of the elven land of Orphana, fallen Master of the Circle of Mages." Adding in that he was a 'fallen' mage would indicate to this creature that his intentions were less than pure, an important factor to the demon.

"Fallen Master," the demon said. It laughed, causing the two Chosen behind him to grasp their ears. Scar merely gripped his fist tighter. Rekho smiled.

"You dare summon me, mage?" it shrieked at him. Demons were notoriously uncooperative. It wouldn't obey unless either persuaded or forced. Rekho had little patience for persuasion.

"I do," he said. Holding the vial in front of him that contained Zar'eith essence, Rekho uncorked it, his smile never wavered. "I am in need of your services."

The demon hissed as it sniffed the air, recognizing the scent that came from the vial. Another rumble and the ground shook beneath their feet. The demon was obviously unhappy at its situation. From the corner of his eye, Rekho saw two of the priests that should have been stationed farther out, moving in. Idiots! What were they doing? Like lightening, a clawed arm shot out and grabbed up one of the men. Screaming and thrashing in the demon's grip, the priest tried to invoke the power of his god. Another of those nerve grinding laughs burst from the demon.

"Irhona's cronies always did make tasty treats," it said and slid its forked tongue up the priest's face. The man's prayers turned to screams as the skin bubbled and melted where demon's poison touched him. The demon took one clawed finger and dug it slowly through the man's middle as he continued to thrash. The screams slowly died into a bubbling gasp. Rekho closed his eyes to avoid having to watch the torture. Finally there was silence and Rekho looked back to the demon. It had bitten the man in half and devoured the upper portion, throwing the rest to the dirt.

Rekho thrust the vial forward and raised his voice, doing his best to infuse it with authority. "You will obey my order, Zar'leith!"

The demon opened its mouth. It screamed in defiance at Rekho but could do nothing against him. "What is it you command, Mage?" it spat at him through clenched teeth that still held bits of human flesh. Rekho swallowed back the gorge that rose in his throat.

"I command you to guard the magic in this place. Soon someone will come to try and retrieve the stone here that houses the magic of dragons. You will not let them."

The demon screamed again and reached out toward Rekho. A chain wrapped around the arm. Rekho looked to his right, eyes wide with surprise. Scar had invoked the power of his god and sent his weapon at the beast who now roared with pain as electricity snaked all along the metal barbs. Not missing a beat, Rekho continued, "Or you will answer to *my* wrath."

The Zar'leith pulled its arm back but reached out with another to grab the other priest that had moved in too close. The man screamed, having seen his fate played out with his brethren. The demon wasted no time with this one and bit down on the man's torso. The screams instantly stopped. The demon hurled the rest of the body through the trees.

"As you command," it said, reluctantly. Turning its back on the priests and Rekho, it curled itself around the place where the pulsing magic rested.

Rekho let out a long breath. Never taking his eyes from the beast, he gathered his tools, stuffed them in his pack and backed quickly away. His stomach was knotted and he shook badly. Once a safe enough distance had been put between him and the demon, he turned and moved quickly from the area.

He ran into the tall priest, he had begun referring to in his own mind as 'Captain.' The man's eyes were wild with fear and his other priests stood behind him, looking ready to sprint at a moment's notice. The Chosen, all except for Scar, were visibly rattled but they held themselves together admirably. Captain approached him.

"I lost two of my priests!"

"Casualties were inevitable." Rekho shrugged. "Demons enter our plane hungry and have to be fed."

"Wh-what? You used my men as…as…FOOD? How will you explain that to the Elder?"

"You were ordered to keep your men back, no matter what." Rekho leveled his gaze on the man. "How will *you* explain your failure to the Elder?"

SEVENTEEN

The sensation of flying through the air was exhilarating. Like a bird in flight, Thom soared through the skies, wind rushing all around him, creating a roar that blocked out all other sound. His eyes were clenched tight. Although he liked the feeling, he didn't care to look around. All too soon, the roaring subsided and he could hear a voice, someone talking to him. Shaking his head to dislodge the unwanted intrusion, he found that to be a mistake. A sharp pain shot through his temple and radiated right behind his eyes.

The voice became more insistent. What was it saying? He couldn't hear it through this pain. Bringing his hands to his head, his limbs felt heavy as lead. After flying and feeling light as air, it was strange how heavy his body actually was. Words were becoming distinct as the voice became clearer.

"Thom! Thom, can you hear me? Wake up, Thom!"

He didn't want to, but the voice was so compelling, so sweet. Like tiny tinkling bells it sang through his head, making the pain subside. He wished it would keep talking until all the pain was gone.

"Wake up, Thom. I'm here. It's Mey." A hand closed over his and gently moved it from his head. There was another hand smoothing his brow and gently wiping all the pain away as the voice pacified. "Shhh. It's Mey, I'm right here with you. Thom? Can you open your eyes?"

He tried to answer but it came out in an unintelligible groan. Turning his head toward the voice, he tried to open his eyes again.

It was her! Mey was with him and he wanted desperately to look at her. She was a dragon. He had seen it from the pit right before he left Yndar.

Determined to open his eyes, he concentrated on them. They felt heavy and he had difficulty making them do what he willed. He managed to open one to a slit. Dull light assailed him. Everything was a blur at first, he tried again to say her name but it only came out in another groan. He looked for her.

"Here. Right here, Thom." Her voice was like cool water and it rushed over him, soothing. He managed to find her and tried to focus. When she came into view he sighed. She was certainly *not* a dragon, but something covered her face. She reached up and removed whatever was covering her eyes.

"Mey," he finally managed the word. He was rewarded with the most brilliant smile she had to offer. She was different, but decidedly not a dragon, as he had imagined he had seen. Her eyes and hair. Changed. But to Thom, it only added to her beauty. He reached to touch the hair that had fallen over one shoulder, wondering at its deep purple hue. The color of the mane on the dragon he saw from the pit.

"Thom." She breathed his name, drawing his attention from her hair to her face. *Oh, her eyes*. She took his outstretched hand and brought it close to her face.

Clearing his throat, which was parched, he managed again to say, "Mey." He wanted to ask about her hair, her eyes, but his throat constricted and he coughed instead.

"Water," she said and pulled away from him. Back in seconds, she lifted a cup to his mouth for him to drink. He gratefully downed a large gulp. "Not too much. Slowly."

He watched her as she set the cup aside and moved back to him.

He reached again for her face and trailed a finger from her brow to her temple. "Your eyes," he managed.

She merely nodded.

Moving his hand to her hair again, he lightly ran his fingers through a silky strand.

She made no move to stop him. Looking back at her eyes, they were closed and tears squeezed from the corners.

"Don't cry."

"I thought you were lost to me."

Easing up on one elbow he said, “But you found me.” A smiled curled his lips. Then a new thought, “How long was I out?”

“Four days. The first two spent on the road bringing you here. We’re in Sorga; the temple of Sirrah.”

Lifting himself even further, Thom struggled into a seated position. Mey quickly lent her assistance. Muscles that had not been used in days screamed at him. He grimaced at their protest and stretched them anyway. She was watching him closely.

“I wandered the edge of the spiritual plane.”

Her eyes widened, but she said nothing.

“I met a dragon. His name is Yndar, and—“

“A dragon!” Her interruption was like a child too excited to wait for the Yule gifts and it made him smile.

“Yes. We spoke of how the world is coming along since his departure. He has been stuck on that plane for hundreds of years.”

“Did he give you any clue as to how we are going to call them back?”

He was thoughtful. “No,” he finally answered, “but we did discuss…other…matters.” A pain shot through his head and he gripped it with both hands.

Mey quickly moved closer to his side, making him lie back. Being this close to her was unnerving. *She smells like honeysuckle*, he thought as he gazed at her. Damn, he’d never be able to concentrate, he couldn’t take his eyes from her. He let out a long breath.

Every muscle in his body protested as he moved down slowly. Fluffing up the pillows behind him so he could stay elevated, Mey worked around him in a dizzying swirl of sweet smells and intoxicating colors. He had to close his eyes to steady himself.

He looked up to find her staring at him. Those beautiful, haunting eyes, one shining liquid silver, the other sparkling emerald green. How enchanting. She looked at something in her hand. He followed her gaze.

Holding out the mask that, until now, she had been loath to even touch, she said, “I…I put it on.”

Thom reached out to take it, but she pulled back. “I saw myself covered in scales. Everything in the room, save you, your magical elements and these two tapestries disappeared.” She hesitated before the next revelation. “I think I was seeing the truth of the past. The pictures showed dragons healing people and making things whole. My uncle said something on the road – 'a dragons' voice can give or take life at a whim'."

He was silent, instinctively knowing she had to come to terms with this on her own.

"I am dragon-kin, Thom. It's who I am. I thought I was losing myself, but I'm not. I'm finding out who I've always been." Tears glistened in her eyes, lending them an otherworldly shine. *Gods, she's beautiful.* Although she sat there, vulnerable with her tears, she was strong, shoulders squared, determination in the way she held herself and finality in her voice.

I love you. He wanted to say it so badly, but the words stuck in his throat. Was he ready to say it? Was she ready to hear it? For the sake of this quest and his uncertainty, maybe he should keep it to himself a little longer. His heart beat hard against his chest. So he opted for, "You're so beautiful."

She shook her head slightly and the purple strands in her hair gleamed under the soft candlelight. It was still dark outside, he noted.

"I…I don't know what to say."

"I'm sorry. I shouldn't have…"

"No." She moved in and laid a silencing finger upon his lips. "You just took me by surprise."

Keeping his eyes on her, he pulled her in and lightly brushed his lips to hers. They were as soft as he remembered. She sucked in a deep breath, but didn't move away. If it were possible, her eyes brightened even more. Putting his hands on either side of her lovely face, he brought her closer and again kissed her, this time more forcefully. *Sweet gods, I would lose myself to her*, he thought.

For long moments, but not nearly long enough, he held on to her for dear life, until the sound of someone clearing their throat broke the magic weaving itself around the two of them, shutting them off to anything but one another.

Mey pulled back and glanced quickly in the direction of the noise. Color rose to her cheeks and she lowered her gaze.

Looking at the intruder, Thom saw Elerbee standing, shuffling his feet slightly, his own face reddened with embarrassment. An awkward moment of silence hung heavy in the air.

Elerbee spoke. "Well, nice to have you back. We've all been worried sick." He absently dislodged a few bits of clinging lint from the sleeve of his robe.

Thom smiled, shaking his head. Not *that* much had changed.

"Mey brought me back." Turning to her, he continued, "Her voice. A dragon's voice can give life, isn't that what you said?"

"Yes," she said softly, stepping away from him. He felt a sudden chill of loss at her absence from his side. "I put the mask on."

Elerbee's face lit up with interest and he moved with hurried steps to join them. "Really? What happened?"

As the two of them discussed what had happened when Mey had donned the mask, Thom lay back on the cot. He felt whole, however a bit weak. Mey glanced at him a couple of times, concern etched on her brow. He smiled to reassure her that he was fine.

Durlag and Bob joined the reunion shortly after the priest, who had kept diligent watch over him, came to check on Thom's condition. Surprised to find him awake, the excited priest left the room to inform the others of Thom's status.

Thom smiled through all the "Glad you're back with us!" and "Welcome back." comments, slaps on the back and questions.

His silence was noted, however. They had been listening to Mey's account of how she had put on the mask and what she saw once she had done so, but now Bob looked at him questioningly.

"What did *you* see, Thom?" Bob asked him. "While you wandered the spiritual plane?"

Thom looked at him, but was quiet while he put his thoughts together. Before he could answer, Mey piped up.

"Tell them about the dragon. I'd like to hear more, as well."

"Dragon?" Bob's normally composed features, broke into surprise, something Thom had almost been convinced couldn't happen.

"Ah, yes." He smiled again. "Yndar. When I came to the spiritual plane, Yndar was there to greet me. Apparently it has been his home since the dragons were banished. His fate had him trapped between the two worlds. He was battling a force of Gnor in the Barren Lands. Their bites covered his body and his spirit fled to the realm where he now resides – it stayed because almost in the same instant, the Keeper tore the Idylic and fled the world. He was stuck."

He shrugged his shoulders. That was really all he gleaned from the dragon, except some very useful information about Gnor, who were nasty creatures to have to tangle with.

"Does he watch over what is transpiring on this plane?" Bob asked.

"No, he was not aware of any of our plight. I filled him in on what was happening thus far."

Thom grimaced as he adjusted his position. Mey quickly moved to him, helping him to sit up a bit further on the small cot. He'd have to get these damned muscles working and fast. They should have been halfway across the Barren Lands by now. The voices of his friends broke through his thoughts.

"Where's me flask, girl?" He heard Durlag asking Mey. She had his flask? The dwarf could no more whisper than he could stop growing a beard, no matter how he tried.

"Mey, tell me more about what happened when you donned the mask," Elerbee broke in.

A veil of silence laid itself over the small group and all eyes went to her. She squirmed a bit under their intense pressure. Truth be told, Thom was more than a little curious himself.

Looking down at the mask she still held in her hands, Mey swallowed. Moving her gaze to the tapestries that hung on the walls, she said, "Those were different. I didn't notice before, but they're not the same without the mask."

"How so?" Elerbee asked. "You mean the pictures?"

"The pictures, the words, the whole thing." Moving toward the large swaths of fabric hanging next to the door, she reached out and touched the cloth. Letting her hand slide slowly down, Mey turned and spoke over her shoulder. "There were words here. Words that told me what to do…sort of. I don't really remember them now…" she trailed, fingers still caressing the threads woven through the tapestry.

Going on as if no one else were in the room, Mey looked at the other wall hangings. "These weren't even here. They were gone, like they didn't even matter. There were only these two. I wonder why. What significance does the other one hold?"

"Use the mask," the voice broke into her thoughts. She turned to stare. Thom had said it.

"Mask," she echoed the word. "I was told to use the mask before." The memory came back like a hammer blow. "When I first came in, I stood by the table." She moved there. "A voice whispered to me. For the life of me, it sounded just like Garrin." She looked directly to Thom. Expecting to find disbelief reflecting back at her, all she saw was acceptance. "Is that possible?"

He shook his head slightly, raising his shoulders to indicate his uncertainty.

"Ye said there were two tapestries, girl." Durlag put in. "So, put the mask back on, tell us what the other one's about. But first, give me flask back."

It made sense. She looked down at her hands, still clutching the gold-covered cloth. Absently she reached down into her boot and retrieved the dwarf's flask and tossed it to him. Durlag let out a hoot of excitement. He had been a couple of days without his drink; never a good thing.

Thom watched as she slowly raised the mask to her face and tied it gently behind her head. She drew in a long, deep breath as she looked around. All the others watched as well, waiting for something, anything to happen. Mey stepped away from the table, holding her arms up in front of her face, staring so strangely at them.

"What?" he asked. "What is it?"

"You can't see this?" She held a hand out towards him. "Scales, claws. Am I the only one who sees it?"

"Apparently. Although…" Thom's thoughts trailed back to his last moments on the spiritual plane. He had seen *something*, it had been her but also a dragon. Shaking his head – he'd have to discuss that with her later – he said, "Never mind. What about the tapestry?"

****

Looking at the tapestry, its construction radiant compared to the other, Mey stepped toward it. This one, too, depicted dragons of all sorts woven throughout. There was one large dragon that took up the entire center portion. It was a glorious creature. Beauty and awesome power mingled in one being.

Mey felt drawn to it. When she reached out to caress the fabric, she found her hands were shaking. Peering closely, she saw that the dragon was curled comfortably around a pedestal upon which sat an open book.

The open pages faced outward and there were words there. All around the dragon and pedestal, there were small figures. Having never seen creatures such as these, she could not identify them. Some were flying, some were peeking out from hiding places. All of them were different; dark skin, pale skin, white hair, no hair, sharp, pointed ears, blunt, rounded ears, some had antennae and some had flowers or leaves streaming through their hair. But all of them were looking upward to the open book.

As she looked upon this image, she spoke aloud, relaying what she saw to the others.

"Can you read the words written in the book?" Elerbee asked.

"It looks like jibberish. I don't think it's actually…wait!" The words swam and spun, coming together into something she started to recognize. She gasped. "It's changing!"

"Adapting to the language she knows." She heard Bob say. The voices behind her continued, but she ignored them and concentrated on the words.

"It's elven," she whispered, more to herself than to anyone in particular. Damn. Her elven was really rusty, not having used it much in thirty years. Taking in a deep breath and letting it out slowly, she thought back to all the lessons her father had insisted on. There were times he would speak nothing but elven, forcing her to learn the ancient language.

"Uncle," she beckoned him.

Approaching her, his brow dipped deeper in confusion. "Meylaran? What is it?"

"It's in elven, uncle. I can read it but I don't think I can translate it all." She felt ashamed to admit that she had dishonored part of her heritage by not retaining the language skills of her father's people. And they were her people, no matter how far she tried to run, the elven people were in her blood, in her soul. This feeling surprised her. She had never felt sentimental to what she always thought of as her father's race, not her own.

The words rang with beauty as they flowed from her lips, the elven language had a mystical quality that Mey found comforting. As she recited, Bob translated for the others:

The truth to see,
To clear the lie,
Sheets of gold wrap the eyes.
Land of fey
'Neath constant sun's ray,
Find the key to prevent the fall
And cease destruction of us all.

"Land of fey," Thom echoed.

Mey turned to him. "Where?"

"The Faery Isles." His eyes met hers. "We have to cross the Barren Lands."

No one spoke. The Barren Lands would be a challenge. A complete expanse of nothing but hard, cracked earth and dust. Only one tribe of nomads lived there and they roamed with the changing seasons to follow food and water as it appeared and disappeared at a whim. The lands were unforgiving and hard; the people even more so. Not an exciting prospect to cross them.

"How long will it take?" Elerbee asked.

"Two weeks, less if we're lucky enough to cross where the oases have appeared," Bob told him.

"Aye, but if we're lucky enough to find the oasis, we also find ourselves facing the nomads," Durlag put in.

"True."

"We have to wait until Thom heals enough to travel anyway," Mey pointed out.

"I can have the priests work on strengthening my muscles. I can be ready to leave at any time." Thom stretched his legs and grimaced at the pain that shot through them.

She had to distract them for another night at least. There was something Mey intended to take care of before she left this forsaken town. Eyes narrowing as she pictured the priest with the marked face, she felt the heat tugging at her. She had to make something up quickly; she had no intention of letting anyone know what she meant to do.

"I wanted to commune with the priests before we leave," she said. "There are burdens I would relieve myself of."

"I suppose staying another day is not out of the question," Elerbee agreed. "I can inform the Temple Head that we will require his hospitality one more night."

"Yes," Thom said, looking at Mey, "I suppose I could use another night's rest, regardless."

She could see his doubt. He no more believed her desire to talk to the priests than he believed the world would fall from its place in the heavens. Avoiding his accusing stare, she made an excuse to leave. Staying and lying further to Thom was something she did not desire. Because she would lie; there was no way she was going to tell him her plans.

Finding a few priests gathered in the gardens, she asked a few well-worded questions to gather the information she needed. The other sects of priests in the city had been imposing taxes. They claimed they were following orders straight from the Provicaries themselves, though the Sirrahn priests had not heard of such taxes.

The Yenohan priests had bought up most of the properties in the northern parts of the city, while the Irhonan temple held most of the western end. Sirrah was quickly losing ground as a respected god in Sorga and the temple had already lost most of its followers to the other, more powerful sects.

Each of the temples had elected a Collector to make sure these so-called taxes were paid diligently by the people. Of course the taxes were too high and most could not pay. That's where the Collector's job came in. He would travel the city to demand payment from those who had not kept current. The tactics used by these Collectors had gotten increasingly cruel. The Collector Mey had seen was indeed affiliated with the temple of Yenoh.

His name was Maxus, not that she really cared to know but it would help her find him. After her visit to the woman whom she had seen, she knew all she needed to know of Maxus, the Collector. He was the worst sort of human; greedy, mean, unfeeling and soon, dead.

What he had taken from this woman was the last memento she had of her missing husband. A small stone set in silver she wore around her neck that he had given her just before he left to find work with the lumber merchants. They would travel to the forests just outside of Sorga's western edge. When the laborers had returned from their last trip, her husband was not with them. No one could answer her questions as to his whereabouts. He had simply vanished with no trace. She could barely afford to feed herself and the child without his income and now the Collector had taken the last thing she owned of any value.

Mey's throat tightened and she had trouble swallowing back the knot of anger that had risen as she listened to the woman tell how she had asked for leniency on her tax until she could learn what had become of her husband. Maxus had laughed at her. There was no leniency in the Yenohan territory he had told her, and then lewdly offered to keep her company in her husband's absence.

She knew everything she needed to know of this Collector except where he lived. That bit wouldn't be hard to ascertain with a few coins at the local tavern. Drink loosened men's lips and gold made certain the information was trustworthy. There were a lot of people with little trust for the gods who buried themselves in drink these days, and Mey easily found what she sought.

EIGHTEEN

From the shadows of an alleyway, Mey watched the Collector enter his home. Light erupted through the windows as he made his way from room to room inside the two-storied building. She would bet everything his bedroom was on the upper floor and that he slept with the door locked tightly. A Collector's job would leave anyone with a lingering feeling of insecurity, especially one of a dishonest sort.

She pulled the hood of her cloak tighter about her face as a man and woman, laughing and stumbling, passed not ten paces from her. They never knew she was there.

Patience was something a thief learned early. More often than not, Mey had to lie in wait in order to appropriate items she'd been paid to acquire. Whether awaiting the perfect moment to slip stealthily around previously locked doors or hunkering down until Garrin had met her at a designated point, she'd long ago grown accustomed to passing time. Plus, this wait gave her time to run through her plan once more.

Mey contemplated the best way to ensure servants wouldn't be a problem. If any stayed in the house, they could become a hindrance or alert the town guard and complicate everything. She had rope and a small bit of sleeping potion. Using those would be effective for incapacitating rather than killing them.

Kill them all, Makagesh whispered.

"You'll have your blood soon enough," she told him, steeling herself against his influence. The sentient dragon was relentless when he could smell a kill so close.

Sighing, Mey looked to the sky. She couldn't read the time by its stars; they had remained stationary for two weeks now. Gritting her teeth against her frustration, she sank deeper into the shadows as footsteps sounded down the block.

Night watchmen marched past, eyes ahead, not so much as glancing her direction. A smile touched her lips as she considered how easy this was going to be. Focusing again on the large house, she mulled over the beginning of her plan.

Search the bottom floor for remaining servants. Their rooms would be near the back of the house, around the kitchen. Once she secured the lower portion, she would make her way to the top floor. Judging from where the Collector lingered the longest, she felt certain his bedroom was the one on the far right. She would still secure all the rooms at the back of the house first, those she couldn't observe from her position on the street.

Makagesh broke her thoughts again. *I bet he squeals like a pig.* Laughter floated like tendrils through her mind.

"We do this my way."

Of course, he purred. *You certainly know what is best. Your plan is flawless, my dear.*

She rolled her eyes. "Flattery is useless. If you keep insisting on bothering me, I can make sure your participation is limited to cutting rope."

She heard his low growl of defiance, but he fell silent. Thankfully. His intrusive mental bombardments, gruesome and filled with thoughts of blood and torture, were bothersome and blurred her focus. Although, she had to admit he had some good ideas on making sure the Collector feared her before she took his life. She wanted the man to feel fear; that total loss of control he so skillfully instilled in the people from whom he pilfered.

Her thoughts drifted back to the countless times she had been in this same scenario. Garrin had been by her side then. His presence always lent a feeling of security. Unconditional trust had grown between them. She had never trusted anyone like that before. She had been convinced she never would again. But when she battled the spirits of Dharst with Thom, that same feeling emerged with surprising strength.

With Thom, she never thought of what the next move would be; never tense or constantly looking over her shoulder to protect her own back. He was there, she was certain, protecting it for her, just as she would shield him. He would definitely not approve of what she did now, but he would accept her decision. Her chest tightened at the notion.

Astonished she would actually care what he thought, she breathed out a long sigh. He made her want to lose control of every part of her soul and hand it over willingly. He was an excellent kisser and his hands were always gentle, even when they were firmly holding her.

Her breath caught. *Come on, Mey, get yourself back in the job at hand.* It was so easy to be consumed with Thom. And since Makagesh could see everything that passed through her mind, she would do well to keep *those* thoughts to herself.

No one had left the house for more than two hours, the last light extinguished over an hour ago. Pushing herself away from the wall, Mey followed the shadows from the buildings as she slid out of the alley and into the street. Sprinting across to the small yard of the Collector's house, she slipped around the side, making her way to the back.

Unlocking the door quickly, she snaked inside the tiny, darkened room where flour, potatoes and grain were stored. Mey paused, breathing in the natural smells and taking in the unique sounds of the house. *Each place has its own distinctive aura and a good thief will familiarize himself with it before commencing.* She could hear Garrin's voice as plain as if he were in front of her.

She continued on, keeping low throughout the first level of the house. A bit ostentatious, she noted and it made her blood boil to think of where the money actually came from. The servant's room was just where she thought, off the back of the kitchen; a small space only containing a bed and washstand. The rooms at the temple were in better repair than this rat's nest. It only strengthened the hatred she felt for the master of the house.

One man stayed here and he slept soundly, soft snores emanating from the lump of covers on the bed. She scanned the room. No windows and only one door. Moving in on the man, she pulled a vial from a pouch at her belt, uncorked it and let two drops fall just beneath his nostrils. He would sleep through the end of the world, no doubt. Backing out as silent as the night itself, Mey worked at the lock on the door for good measure. Satisfied, she made her way to the stairs leading to the second level.

Running her gloved hand over the wood railing as she ascended the lavish staircase, she cleared her mind. Alone. Silent as a whisper. A serpent poised and ready to strike. She couldn't allow her conscious to interfere at this point. Almost as if she were two separate beings, she disconnected the part that would have reservations and let the hard, unfeeling side emerge with each step she took. Makagesh chuckled in delight as her mind shifted into this heartless, cruel predator and his excitement built, almost beyond containment, in her head.

She had killed before. Never pointlessly, but she found it distasteful, not something she relished as Makagesh undoubtedly did.

Would she kill him? Her resolve wavered; she wanted the man dead, her anger demanded no less. But was it necessary? Maybe just striking fear into the core of his soul would be enough.

Drawing up a vivid memory of Maxus, the Collector, snatching the woman's last connection to her missing husband from her neck, she stopped on the landing to observe her surroundings and reassured herself she was doing the right thing.

Two doors to her left, three to her right with one set at the very end of the hallway. Stepping left to the farthest door, she slipped her glove off and laid a hand against the cool wood of the door. Breathing in, she concentrated on any smells or sounds in this room. Nothing. Mey repeated this process as she moved down the hall toward the Collector's bedchamber. Tedious but necessary, she couldn't leave any rooms unchecked behind her though she felt confident of her target's location.

Makagesh was losing patience. Images of bloody flesh, slashed by the sharp edge of a dagger flashed through her head. A smile curled her lips upward. This hardened side *did* find satisfaction in the task at hand. Moving as quickly as she dared but still satisfying the need to have nothing threatening at her back, Mey moved to the last door.

Flattening her hand to the panel, she pressed her cheek against the grooved wood, and listened. Breathing emanated from the other side. The pungent stench of sweat assaulted her nose; the faint rustling of cloth as the man shifted in sleep touched her ears. Focusing her attention on the door, she ran her hands lightly around the frame, looking for any tiny imperfections indicating a trap. Her nimble fingers passed over a small hole in the wood, which could be easily mistaken as a flaw in workmanship.

Stopping abruptly, Mey leaned in to examine the minute opening. Moving her eyes down the frame, she found five more of the same likeness, all in a row.

"Clever," she murmured.

The mechanism to trigger the trap would be either in the door itself as it opened or in the floor. Crouching to examine the floorboards first, she looked for anything out of place. There were no loose panels or movable sections of wood. As she prepared to move up the door, her keen eyes caught a slight glimmer. Leaning closer, the glimmer proved to be a thin tripwire stretched from one end of the door to the other, just at shin height.

Shaking her head, she pulled out a small razor-sharp blade. With a steady hand, Mey touched the sharp edge to the tripwire and in one flick of the wrist, cut it, leaning back in case it triggered the trap. When nothing happened, she let out a breath.

Ever cautious and thinking it had been much too easy, she continued her slow, intense scrutiny of the door. As her eyes roved over the handle, she found a small protrusion. A tiny lever, no more than a half-inch jutted out near the handle, clearly meant to be depressed when someone attempted to open the door. A breathless chuckle escaped her.

This man definitely didn't feel safe.

Moving back a step, she took the tip of a dagger and, quick as lightning, pushed the lever and pulled her arm back to her side, never losing grip on the weapon. Sure enough, six small darts—poisonous, no doubt—shot across the doorway, and thudded into the frame on the other side.

Waiting to see if the small noise had wakened her prey, Mey again leaned in close and placed an ear against the door. There was no change in the sounds beyond. She could still hear the breathing and the rustle of cloth as the man tossed and turned in sleep. Carefully avoiding the small darts, she turned the handle slowly. Opening the door a few inches, she slid her body into the room, closing it soundlessly behind her.

Her eyes adjusted to the darkness and found Maxus just where she expected him; sleeping on the large, lush bed, wrapped in fine silken sheets.

Creeping on the balls of her feet, she noted her surroundings. In only seconds, she knew the layout and contents of the space. Looking down, a sneer found its way to her face. She watched his tortured sleep. Covered in sweat, brow twisted, Maxus moved his head. She wasn't sure how long she stood there watching; long enough to conjure up the image again in her mind of him snatching the woman's necklace away as she begged for his mercy.

She bent very close to his ear, her voice full of hate, and whispered "Wake up." Had she not been totally detached, she might have been surprised it came from her at all.

Instantly, his eyes flew open, his body froze and she saw his throat work to swallow. He turned his head until their faces were mere inches apart. His eyes widened at first, his tension ebbing slowly. Knowing what she did about him, Mey figured he didn't feel so threatened by a woman in his bedchamber; a lesson he would learn too late this night.

"Wh-who…" he tried, but his voice caught in his throat.

"…am I?" she finished for him. "We'll get to that soon enough." Standing upright, Mey moved back a step. "Now, I want you to sit up."

He arose slowly, nodding once; his trembling hand wiping sweat from his brow. His gaze flicked to the nightstand and back to her. There was a small dagger there, she had noted earlier. Surely he wasn't stupid enough to go for it, but as he glanced back at her, he began to lunge for the weapon. In the blink of an eye, two daggers thudded into the headboard of the bed inches from the Collector's head, pulling him up short.

"I wouldn't," Mey warned.

Looking back, he squinted hard trying to see past the shadows to her face hidden beneath the hood of her cloak. He raised his hands in surrender.

"Maxus," she began once he was fully upright. "You're probably asking yourself right about now what this could possibly be about. And if you're thinking it is related to your duties as a Collector, you would be right." She lowered her voice to a whisper. "But you would be wrong as to your first guess at *why*."

He cleared his throat. "Seems you have me at a disadvantage. You know me. However, I've not had the pleasure of knowing you."

"All in due time."

Cut him. Make him bleed. The words floated through her head. She pushed Makagesh to the side for the time being; not gone; for she certainly agreed with his sentiment to make this foul being bleed. But first, she wanted answers.

Producing the jeweled dagger from her belt, Mey lounged in a chair across from the bed. Watching the Collector, she was satisfied that his gaze never left her. He watched every move she made.

"I'd like to see your collections from the day."

A smile broke his face. "A robbery? Is that what this is all about?"

Mey paused and looked directly at the man. "More a robbery reversal." Going back to her bored examination of the dagger, she continued, "You see, I intend to give the money back to the people. Now, if you would be so kind, where are the collections?"

His eyes cut briefly to the left, then quickly snapped back to her.

Chuckling, she rose slowly. Did he think her that stupid? It was so obvious he was purposefully misleading her. My, but he did have a low opinion of women. She sauntered to where he sat on the edge of his bed, leaned close to him, but not quite close enough for him to see through the shadows that hid her face.

"Lie to me again, Collector, and I will cut your throat." The dagger sang as it flashed to his neck. The voice in her mind was full of delight. *Yes! The throat! Slit his throat!* "Or cooperate, and there could be much less mess." She was still wavering on the idea of killing the man.

He swallowed audibly, the knot in his throat bobbing against the blade she held there. Makagesh laughed with anticipation. "In th-the study," he stuttered.

"Lead the way," she said casually and prodded him with the tip of the blade.

Maxus stood slowly and carefully, making no sudden movements before obeying her command. She followed him down to the first floor and into a room off the main chamber. Leather-bound ledgers lined the shelves. The large oakwood desk was carved with intricate patterns of crawling vines encircling the outside edge. Silver filigree wound through the pattern.

Mey grimaced at the excessiveness.

He continued on behind the desk to the bookshelf. Glancing over a shoulder at her, he quickly pulled a ledger halfway out and the bottom of the shelf popped open. Out of the false wall, the Collector took a medium-sized chest and, with a heft, placed it on the desk.

"Open it."

From his wrist, he produced a key attached by a bit of cord. He unlocked the chest and threw the lid back.

Mey exhaled slowly. *That's a lot of gold and gems*. There were various trinkets thrown in the mix as well, made from all manner of precious metals. On top sat a thin silver chain with a small silver circle set in ivory. Within the ivory center, two overlapping hearts were carved in elaborate detail. The words of the woman came back to her: *It's the last connection I have to my husband.* Grinding her teeth, she narrowed her eyes as she felt a familiar heat starting in her middle.

"Tell me something." She pushed the dagger into the soft flesh of his neck. "What part of this is *your* take?"

He hesitated, probably wondering if a lie at this point was worth his life. "Half," he finally said.

A muscle in her jaw ticked as the heat started to bubble through her.

"Why is the temple taxing the people so harshly?"

"On edict from the Elder. Every temple is to ask the people for a tithe."

"A tithe, yes." The dagger slid down to his chest where it pressed mercilessly. "*This*, however"—she gestured with her free hand—"is robbery."

"I have only done my job," the Collector said, wincing as the dagger pressed deeper.

Mey ignored him. Grabbing his hand with massive strength that only came with the heat she forced it atop the ornate desk.

"Now, what is the sentence for robbery?"

She moved her eyes toward his face to watch the reaction. Makagesh roared with delight.

Raising an eyebrow, she watched sweat break out on his forehead. Her face still hidden beneath the cloak, she smiled and a quiet chuckle escaped her. She had no need to glance back at the dagger; it moved of its own volition.

"Loss of a finger isn't it?" she asked.

Maxus was visibly shaken. He nodded once. He opened his mouth to speak but the words seemed stuck. He cleared his throat and whispered, "Yes."

"Hmmm. A finger for each offense." She laughed. "I daresay you don't have enough fingers." She clucked her tongue in mock disappointment.

In the next instant, the Collector's face blanched white, his mouth opened in an "O". After a moment of shock, the scream came. Mey placed a hand over his mouth.

"Shhh," she cooed. Heat filled her now and it felt good. Elation rolled from Makagesh and sped through every vein in her body.

"Would you like to spare your other fingers?" she asked. Her voice had hardened into a timbre foreign to her own ears.

A tear slid down the Collector's cheek. He nodded vigorously beneath the hand clasping his mouth.

"I want answers. Every time you are, in any way, less than truthful with me, I take another. Understand?" Moving her hand so that he could speak, she tilted her head to one side. The dagger never wavered as she moved it over the next digit.

"I understand." His voice was strangled with pain.

"Now, *why* has the Elder ordered this massive collection of taxes?"

"As p-payment," he said. "Th-the Elder has acquired m-massive debts as of late."

"Debts?" Mey was more than curious. What sort of debts would the Elder, head of every sect of priests in Cantor, possibly have? "What debts?"

"I don't know," the Collector sobbed.

Mey shook her head and clucked her tongue again. Another scream bubbled up from the man's throat. He swayed and fell to one knee. She held fast to his hand, though, keeping it securely in place on the desk, slick with the thick blood that seeped from each wound. Her mouth twisted up on one side.

"Care to try again?" She shifted the dagger to the next finger.

Maxus's breathing had become labored and his eyes rolled back.

"Stay with me," she told him. "Now, again. What debts has the Elder amassed?"

"H-he has hired a m-mage." His voice was so low, Mey had to lean close to hear.

A mage? That took her off guard. Priests and mages working in tandem? For what purpose? A hundred more questions flew through her head.

Makagesh's cry tore into her thoughts. *MORE!*

"Why?"

The Collector whimpered. But only hesitated for a second. Evidently, he decided to keep the rest of his hand intact. "To track and stop the Descendant," he blurted out in a strangled cry.

Completely taken off guard this time, Mey leaned back with an abrupt gasp. "What?"

"The Descendant…is supposed to…bring back the dragons." His head lolled from side to side and he sagged down to both knees, kneeling in front of the desk. "That cannot be allowed. Dragons will…kill…" His head fell forward.

Letting go of the man's hand, it fell to his side. She took a handful of hair, pulling his head up. *Still breathing*. Makagesh's disappointment left a foul taste in her mouth. He wanted more blood.

She slapped him hard. Twice. His sluggish eyes reflected obvious pain. Forcing him to look directly at her, she moved her other hand to the hood of her cloak and slid it back, fully revealing her face.

His eyes widened and he mouthed the question. "You?"

She closed her eyes and let the heat fully consume her. She felt the unmistakable strength as her dragon blood took over. When she opened her eyes again, Maxus let out a smothered cry. He began to sob uncontrollably, trying to shake his head but she still held tight to his hair.

"You have been punished for your thievery of the people in Sorga," she said. Grasping the delicate necklace from the chest, she held it up in front of his face. "But for this…" She leaned in so close her body was mere inches from his. "You should die."

She wanted to sink the dagger smoothly into his chest, watch his silent scream. The image of blood trickling from the corner of his lip and running in a rivulet down his throat as she plunged the blade deeper into his heart assailed her. Makagesh wanted her to kill him as well. She felt a wave of ecstasy as he howled in her mind.

The image repeated itself over and over as Makagesh's voice grew louder. *Do it! Kill him! He deserves it!* She wanted to. Wanted to turn herself over to the force of the sentient dragon.

Thom. His image hit her like a blow to the gut. She couldn't breathe. She squeezed her eyes shut and Thom's smiling face was there, etched on the backs of her lids. Acceptance in his eyes, he reached out to her. It felt right, even through the heat and barrage of hallucinations from Makagesh.

Thom felt right.

"No," she screamed at the dragon, shattering the images of death he had woven through her mind. Tears slid down her face and she screamed over and over, "No, no, no." Each time another binding strand snapped, freeing her from his hold.

Opening her eyes, she saw Maxus cringing before her. His sobs turned to whimpers.

"Tell them," she spat at him through clenched jaws. "Tell them they cannot stop me! I am here for the people of Cantor and I *will* bring justice."

He could only nod, cradling his wounded hand.

Hastily closing the lid of the chest, she hefted it with one arm and snatched the key from the Collector's wrist.

She needed to get back to the others. The servant wouldn't awaken for several hours, at least. But it wouldn't take long for Maxus to come to his senses and alert his masters to the fact that the Descendant stood in their midst.

The best bet was to make a swift departure—from the temple, from this town. Damn this perpetual darkness. It was harder to calculate the passing of time, but she figured at least a couple of hours had passed while she was with the Collector. The rest of her plan had to wait until she could clean herself up a bit.

Moving silently through the darkness, finding her way back to the temple of Sirrah, she snuck back to her small sleeping chamber without being seen.

Leaning her forehead against her door as it clicked closed, she felt herself connect once more to that side of her she had pushed away. A small knot of remorse made it hard for her to breath. Her senses still hyper-aware, the hairs on her neck prickled.

The atmosphere felt wrong.

Someone was here. Her eyes snapped open and she whirled around.

"Mey?" Thom's eyes were wide as he took in her blood-spattered appearance. He had been sitting on the edge of the small cot but stood as he spoke her name. His gaze landed on the chest, still in her arms, and his brow pulled together in a look of complete confusion.

NINETEEN

Stunned silence hung in the room for half a heartbeat. Coming to her senses, Mey moved, setting the chest on the cot and yanked her cloak free to toss over it.

Thom let out a strangled sound and burst into action. He quickly descended upon her, intense concern blazing in his eyes. "Mey! What happened? Where are you hurt? I'll get Elerbee." He grabbed her shoulders and held her at arms' length, scrutinizing her, evident worry in his voice.

What in the lower planes of Hell was he talking about?

"What do you mean, 'am I hurt'?" she said, twisting to break free of his grip.

"You're covered in blood!" he said, gesturing at her. "I'm getting Elerbee." Starting toward the door, Mey had to jump to catch him.

"Wait!"

He didn't even bother to turn. "I will *not* wait. You need healing."

"The blood's not mine."

He froze in his tracks. Everything slowed down and he turned back toward her. Skeptical but at least he was listening now.

Mey let out a long sigh. "None of it is mine. I'm not hurt."

"What? Who?"

Damn! Did he have to ask this now? "It doesn't matter right now, I can explain on the way. We have to get the others and leave as quickly as possible."

She started stuffing things into her pack. Halfway through, she noticed he hadn't moved.

"Now, Thom! We have to go!"

"I'm not going anywhere until you explain to me what is going on." He folded his arms across his chest.

Stunned, she tried to pull all the jumbled thoughts together. "Fine," she said. "But we talk while we pack. The rest I'll tell you on our way out of town."

"Agreed." He nodded once. "Now, whose blood is it?"

Did she have to make such a mess with the Collector? How was she going to avoid this one? She wasn't. The truth seemed the best option here, so she squared her shoulders and took a breath. "A Collector. For the Temple of Yenoh."

Thom's eyes moved to the cot where the chest lay, half exposed, under her cloak. *Oh, no, he thinks it was just a robbery. Quick, explain this!*

"I didn't steal it. I took it. *I mean…* I took it to give back to the people *he* stole it from." Seeing his skeptical look, she added, "And he's not dead."

"Stole? A Collector is *supposed* to collect tithes, it's what they do, Mey."

Tying the strings together at the top of her pack, she slung it over one shoulder as she recalled the way Maxus seized the necklace from the woman. The story the woman told about her husband and the Collector's lewd response to her concern for his whereabouts made bile rise in Mey's throat.

"No, it wasn't only a tithe." She felt heat rising through her middle but kept it down, refusing to let it spread. "His methods of collecting were tyrannical at best. He took more than he should!" Her voice rose but she didn't care. No doubt in her mind she had done the right thing.

She was so tired. Not just from tonight, but from all of it: Weeks sleeping on the ground, traveling through dangers no one should have to face, the constant tension of having to always be on her guard, mentally fighting with a sentient dragon hell-bent on having blood at the slightest shift in the wind. It wore her thin.

She dropped her head wearily into her hands as she sat heavily on the cot.

"Why don't you start from the beginning?" Thom urged.

Raising her eyes, she witnessed the acceptance she craved. His eyes widened and she caught the rapid flicker of surprise passing over his features.

"What?"

"Nothing."

He wasn't getting out of it that easily. She stared at him and repeated herself, more forcefully this time. "What?"

His hand came up and lightly touched her face. "Your eyes." A slow smile spread across his face, the undertone of sadness unmistakable. "Silver suits you."

She understood. They had transformed completely. This last unleashing of her dragon blood had caused it. Each time, her dragon nature consumed her a bit more. The worry and fear that she would fully lose herself surfaced for a moment. She couldn't think of that now, it would have to wait.

She broke his gaze and stared down at her hands. Blood caked the crevices and dried under her nails. *I look like I've slaughtered an army.* Her clothes, arms and hands were covered with sticky red stains. She felt the tightening as it dried on her face.

Loud banging on the door took away any words she would have spoken. They both jumped. Shouting in the hallway and more banging. Mey shook her head to clear her thoughts.

"Meylaran," a muffled voice, her uncle's, called insistently through the door. "Open the door."

She blinked and jumped into action. Two strides had her at the door. She opened it to Bob and Durlag, eyes wide with urgency. Elerbee stood a few paces behind them nervously shifting from foot to foot and picking at his robes.

"Here." Bob shoved her sword and bandolier into her hands. "We have to leave." He pushed past her as she stood there, dumbfounded.

"What's going on?" Thom asked.

Bob eyed him critically before answering. "They are searching the temples. Apparently the Descendant has been seen in the city." His eyes met hers, took in her appearance, eyebrows rising in silent question.

"Lass," Durlag said, worry coloring his words. "Are you hurt?"

"Hurt?" Mey repeated. Then remembering she was covered in the Collector's blood: "Oh, no. It's not mine."

A smile broke Durlag's serious visage. "Oh, well, then. That's me girl. Who was it? Some overzealous mage need puttin' in his place?" He threw a wink in Thom's direction.

Completely ignoring the dwarf's obvious attempts at levity, Thom directed his questions at Bob.

"What are they saying?"

"That someone is hiding the Descendant. They suspect the Sirrahn temple because they are sympathizers to the dragons. Elerbee is staying with the temple leaders to talk to the guards." Bob acknowledged Elerbee, lurking in the corner, with a nod.

"We have to go *now*." Already, Mey was buckling on her sword belt and bandolier. She grabbed her cloak from the bed, stopping short when she saw the chest. Vaguely aware of the conversation around her, she opened the lid, took the necklace from the top, and slid it into her pouch.

"…underground," Bob was saying. "We will use the network of tunnels beneath the city. Elerbee will meet us outside the walls."

"Hrumph," Durlag snorted, sneering at the priest. "Probably can't stand the thought of having to step your precious, lily-white foot into the sewers."

"I'll have you know-" Elerbee began, but Thom interrupted the tirade before it began.

"Do we know which way to go?"

Elerbee shot a glare at Durlag before he said, "Here is a map from the temple archives. It'll get you outside the west gate of the city."

They were all moving, pulling Mey along as they headed for the door.

"Wait." She planted her feet. "There's something I have to do first."

"Meylaran, we really do not have time for this." Bob was ushering the others on.

"Then go without me," she said, stubbornly standing her ground. "I *have* to do this, uncle."

Bob opened his mouth to scold her again, when Durlag came to her defense.

"Nonsense. Whatever ye have to do, we'll all go. Can't have ye wanderin' the streets alone after what's gone on." He looked up at Bob and with unusual sternness toward the elf, he added, "They're lookin' fer her. I won't leave her and neither should ye. She's yer kin!"

Precious seconds passed. "Alright," Bob finally conceded, nodding. "We will all go."

Looking to Elerbee, she asked, "Will you ensure these belongings are returned to their rightful owners? That the money is distributed among the people?"

"Of course," he answered immediately. "You have my word."

The four of them left the room, Bob leading. Mey glanced once over her shoulder, and saw Elerbee, chest tucked tightly under one arm, watching them leave.

Down the hall toward the back of the temple was access to the tunnels below the town that served as a sewer system. The grating on the floor was already open for them when they arrived

A foul smell assaulted her nose the moment she lowered herself into the dank passageway. Thinking about where the smell originated would definitely have her losing the contents of her stomach. She'd actually had to sleep in worse places over the years; she just had to let her senses adjust.

One by one, they lowered themselves down, Durlag crashing down unceremoniously, with as much noise as possible.

"We're headed to the street that runs beside the temple on the western side," Mey told them. "I could see it from my window."

"Do you care to tell us why we are making this little detour?" Thom asked her.

Mey met his gaze squarely. "I saw the Collector bully a woman on the street. He took this" - she pulled the necklace from a pouch at her hip - "from her. I intend to return it."

They all looked at her but it was Durlag who spoke up.

"Um, lass, I find it hard to believe that ye survived as a thief on the streets if you be givin' *back* things ye've taken."

She shot him a sour look. "I tracked the woman down. She told me her husband has been missing for weeks. She has run out of money to buy food for her babe and was uncertain how she would pay another month's rent." She paused to swallow the hate bubbling up through her core and into her throat.

"A Collector had taken the last memento of her husband. A necklace he gave to her. She'd considered selling it but didn't want to lose this last part of him." Narrowing her eyes, Mey continued. "He took it from her. Snatched it from her neck, claiming it was to pay her *tithe* to the priests who keep the town safe. She tried to explain but he only suggested that perhaps *he* could return at night to keep her company."

She forced the last words through clenched teeth, not realizing she had balled her hands so tightly the knuckles were turning white. Thom took her hands and eased them open with his touch.

Sparing a concerned glance at Thom's ministrations, Bob pulled a rolled parchment from his pack. "Light?" he whispered to no one in particular.

Reluctantly, Thom released her hands and whispered words to produce a soft light above them. Looking over the crude drawing, they were able to pinpoint their current location and trace the path they needed to take to find the street Mey referred to.

They made their way along the narrow, slick stones. With Durlag in the middle of the line, Bob leading, that left Mey and Thom trailing behind. Thom used their position to his advantage to question her further about what happened with the Collector.

"Who was he and how did you find him?" Thom asked.

"Maxus, Collector for the Temple of Yenoh. I started asking around as to his identity. The clearly distinguishable strawberry mark across his cheek made him easy enough to find."

"This is where you disappeared to when you claimed you wanted to commune with the priests?"

Ducking her head to hide the guilt she knew would be plain on her face, she nodded.

Then the words came tumbling out. She couldn't stop them; it was like a release of all the anger, fear, and loathing she had kept inside.

"He stole from them! If they couldn't pay, he would *take* their most precious possessions. It meant nothing to him to push his own advances on her; he didn't care! He kept *half* of what he collected, so he took more to fatten his own pockets. Robbery, that's what it—"

"Slow down." Thom put his hands up. "Tell me, slowly." His voice softened.

Mey knew Durlag and Bob were listening, although they kept their gazes ahead and feet moving forward, the underlying urgency to leave the city behind like an itch they could not quite reach.

"I found his home, intent on taking back what he'd frightened and terrorized the people into giving. I had a plan, but Makagesh was so persistent in his longing for blood, that-"

"Makagesh?"

"The dagger." Her hand automatically reached for the handle at her hip. Realization dawned - she had not told Thom about the sentient weapon. The only person she'd spoken to about it was her uncle.

It was out now. Might as well confess that, too.

"The dagger I picked up in Seaside. It's inhabited by a dragon. A dragon with an insatiable appetite for blood."

His steps faltered. "A sentient weapon?" he whispered, eyes glazed, talking more to himself than to her. "That explains a lot." He turned his attention back to her. "Please, go on."

Rushing through the next events, she relayed the rest of the story. "I cut off two of his fingers as punishment for robbing the people. I took his collections from today and came back to the temple."

The group fell into silence as they maneuvered the twists and slopes of the sewer tunnels. Mey wasn't sure why she felt so strongly about correcting this one small wrong in the world, only that she *must*. This wouldn't be the end, though. She had a whole world full of people counting on her.

****

He loved her.

It had been on the tip of his tongue to tell her, but it would be a mistake.

Watching Mey, Thom questioned if she felt as strongly. He, on the other hand, had been doomed the moment he laid eyes on her.

There was no denying how he felt; he *did* love her. Her beauty had drawn him in at first but now, everything about her was desirable to him. She was tough, graceful in battle, headstrong, and goodness shone from her soul, whether she was willing to admit it or not.

Damn it all, he was supposed to protect her, not lose sight of what was most important.

Knowing her intent to return the woman's necklace and all the gold in the Collector's chest made his heart swell with pride. She was truly beginning to put the people of Cantor before herself, just as dragons had always done throughout history.

But the physical changes scared him more than he would let her know. What was the purpose of it happening so rapidly? He pushed the thought to the back of his mind; he would ask the Circle when next he contacted them.

He had given up trying to orient himself in these tunnels in comparison with the city above. He was careful to breathe through his mouth. Thom was sure if he let the odor linger n his nostrils he would spend the whole trip throwing up, the smell was so nauseating. Had Elerbee been there, he could have created a barrier for them against the elements. *Where was the damned priest when you needed him? He always seemed to be there at the most inappropriate moments.*

"Halt," came Mey's whisper.

Above them was a large grate.

"Boost me up, so I can see," she told her uncle. He lifted her easily, standing strong as she balanced her feet perfectly on his shoulders, working the grating to the side. Sticking her head out of the opening, she looked around.

Ducking back in, she said, "This is it." She jumped down, landing silently on her feet.

Thom watched her face as she withdrew the necklace from the pouch. Her eyes softened as she looked upon the delicate necklace. Then, determination hardened the silver into iron.

Durlag was first out, as it took all of them to lift him up and push him through the opening.

Declining Bob's offer of assistance, Thom took a small stone from a pouch and whispered words of a spell that lifted him upward and through the opening in the street.

"Might've been useful for these old bones to have that spell," Durlag remarked snidely.

Thom laughed once. "Only works for the caster." He shrugged. "Sorry."

"Hrumph."

Bob pulled himself out next. Thom turned to help Mey from the hole to find her standing, not even winded, directly behind him. She grinned and with a wink, moved to the head of the group.

"There." She pointed. "I'll go first and make sure there are no guards. I'll signal if it's clear."

The others moved to the darkened alley between two of the tall apartment houses, while Mey slid silently into the shadows hugging the buildings. Immediately Thom lost sight of her form. He strained to hear her movements but the only noise was the wind blowing mournfully down the alleyway.

Concentrating on his breathing, Thom tried to slow his heartbeat, which thudded in his ears. His eyes darted constantly all around, unable to see more than a few paces ahead of him. He felt exposed, knowing there were people after them. *Stay calm. You can silence the area if necessary.* That would only work if they weren't listening for a signal, but he was ready if any guards surfaced.

A high-pitched whistle broke his thoughts. If he hadn't been ready for a signal, the noise would have blended flawlessly with the wind around him. Taking a deep breath, he followed the others into the street.

They made it without detection to the narrow building. Mey knelt in front of the door, hands moving so quickly the door was creaking open before Thom realized what she was doing. Under normal circumstances, he would have protested the need to break into a stranger's home, but normal had fled his vocabulary from the instant he had met her.

They slipped inside the darkened room. Thom the only one at a disadvantage with his human sight. Doubtless, the others saw everything in stark detail.

He heard whispers, a gasp and the whimper of a baby. Light flared, revealing the cramped living space in which they stood. Table and chairs, cooking stove and washing bin all graced the one room. As his eyes adjusted, Thom saw a woman holding a small babe close to her breast in the only doorway other than the exit. She blinked away sleep, confused as she took in the small band of adventurers that had taken over her home.

"We met earlier, remember?" Mey's voice was soothing. "I asked about the Collector."

The woman nodded and pulled her child closer.

"I have something for you."

Reaching into the pouch at her waist, Mey produced the necklace. It glinted in the light thrown from the small lamp. She held it out where the woman could clearly see.

A sharp intake of breath filled the woman's lungs and a small noise escaped her lips. Tears sprung to her eyes as she looked, unbelievingly, at Mey.

"How…?" she said, her voice strangled, too overcome to finish the thought.

"It's yours, isn't it? It was wrongfully taken from you. I'm here to return it." Holding the delicate jewelry out further, she said, "Take it. It's alright."

The woman reached a shaking hand and Mey gingerly laid the necklace in her upturned palm.

"Thank you," she whispered. She lifted her tearstained face to Mey. "But who are you that you would care?"

Mey smiled tenderly at the woman, then said, "My name is Meylaran." She reached out and smoothed a hand over the babe's head. "People call me the Descendant. Most importantly, I am your justice; yours and all people on Cantor."

Thom coughed to dislodge the lump forming in his throat.

Bob spoke up. "We need to go, *ta'wae*."

Mey nodded. "Right."

They left as quietly as they had come. Thom *did* silence the dwarf's movements this time. Quiet was not Durlag's strongest attribute. They made it back to the opening without incident and lowered themselves down to continue on to meet Elerbee outside the city.

As they passed through the sewer tunnels, Thom thought about little else but Mey. He needed to talk to her again, alone. First they needed to reach the path that led them outside and free from the stench of these damned passageways.

Elerbee awaited them when they emerged into the open; the lightened sky a magnificent mixture of colors ranging from red to yellow, just before the sun peeks through.

Squinting at the unexpected brightness, Thom brought a hand to his forehead to shield his eyes. The stars had faded. Wasn't continual light the second sign? Would there be sunset tonight or would it blaze on continually for who knew how long? They had no time to lose. When it happened, he wasn't sure how long it would last, but the darkness had lingered for two weeks.

Wrinkling his nose at the stench that clung to the rest of the group, Elerbee said, "We have to get away from the city. This way." He moved as far ahead of them as he could without them losing sight of him. *Hopefully*, Thom thought, *leading us somewhere we can bathe.*

TWENTY

Running a hand over his weary eyes, he scrubbed at the growth of beard spreading wildly across his face. This past month on the road yielded not one chance for proper hygiene. At least Elerbee had been able to find them a place to bathe. Clear and cool, the water fell in a cascade over the tall rocks above as the Range River wound its way along the border of Sorga. Thom let everyone else take a turn while he contacted the Mage's Circle.

The sun sat high in the center of the sky, following them, shining brightly, warming the air. Thom was convinced this was the second sign. The prophecy warned three signs would lead to the destruction of everything if they did not restore the balance between good and evil; the dragons.

Now, he reflected on the events of the past day.

As soon as they were safely away from the city, Thom had taken the opportunity to question Mey further on the events that took place with the Collector.

"So, that's it? You took his collections, maimed him in the process and left?"

"Well, no. I asked him why the temple taxed the people so vastly. He told me the priests had amassed large debts trying to pay off a mage they hired to stop me."

Thom's head snapped up. He stopped abruptly in his tracks. Everyone else had stopped as well and turned back, wary eyes on Mey and Thom. "*A mage?*"

"That's what I said."

"Did he tell you anything more? Give you a name? Indicate where this mage might be located?"

"No. I was so angry and Makagesh was pushing me to kill him…" Her voice trailed off and she cringed. "Thom?"

He had paced away from her but something in her voice made him turn back when she spoke his name.

"I…I, uh..." Taking a deep breath, she continued. Was she expecting he would be angry with her? "I revealed to him who I was. He knows I'm the Descendant."

Horror? Fear? Shock, or maybe pride? Which was it that crossed his face as she said those words? Perhaps all. He did not speak.

"I also told him he should let his masters know they would not stop me; that I would bring justice for the people of Cantor." Biting her lower lip, she watched him. As he felt heat spread up his neck and into his face, she held her breath, doubtless waiting for him to explode.

Instead, he turned away from her; his shoulders slumped. He felt all eyes boring into his back as he stood there. When he turned to face her, he was composed. She breathed a sigh.

Sadness overcame him as he stared into her haunting, silver eyes. He smiled as he stepped closer to her.

"It's who you are, Mey. A burden a lesser person could not bear, but you – you embrace it." His voice dropped to a whisper.

No one said a word, but glanced at one another, turned, and continued on their path. Elerbee's gaze lingered, reflecting the same sadness Thom felt. Losing her, that's what it was like. She was detaching herself from him and becoming part of something bigger.

She was never mine. He had to stay focused.

The mages deciphered the mask to be enchanted with a True Seeing spell. And the information the Circle had given him about the magical presence on the Faery Isles confirmed their destination.

The land was changing, the creatures living there were dying in droves and just recently, detection of a demon.

Demons had to be summoned. Only mages, very powerful ones, could summon denizens of the dark world. It fit with the information Mey had revealed about the priests amassing debts to pay a mage. The Circle was investigating who it could be. There was only one missing mage they knew of, however, that had enough power to summon a demon.

And one of his biggest fears had been confirmed by the Magister. The physical changes Mey had experienced were likely permanent and there would be more. He didn't allow his thoughts to linger on the prospect too long. What it meant, for him and for her, was something he'd gotten good at pushing away and so, he buried it under the mounting pressures of what lay ahead.

Thom shook his head. He didn't want to think about any of it. He just wanted to get across the Barren Lands. Durlag had traveled the border, but never entered. Bob had been through them before, so he knew how unforgiving the land was. He claimed he had never met the nomads wandering the desert land, but he was so evasive on the subject, Thom wasn't certain he believed *that* story. None of the others had ever been in the desert land, and not one of them had ever stepped foot on any of the small islands that composed the Faery Isles.

He sighed. A long, cleansing breath that pushed all his thoughts out to scatter in the wind and land where they may. He took in another lungful of air and plunged straight down into the water. It felt good, the feeling of weightlessness, and the rushing of the cool water over his skin as he rose again to break the surface. Savoring the last few moments of his bath, eyes closed against reality, he sensed he wasn't alone. He opened his eyes and turned.

Bob stood at the bank of the river. A tall, imposing figure, his green eyes pierced through Thom making him feel the elf scrutinized his deepest thoughts.

"What did your mages have to say?"

The voice took him off guard; it always did. One expected a hard, forceful sound from such an intense presence. But it was musical, floating through the air, catching the wind and instantly putting one at ease.

Thom made his way to the shore, climbing out and dressing quickly before the chill in the wind could set him shivering. All the while, Bob's posture never relaxed. He was always alert, tensed, and ready for anything from any direction.

Thom regarded him another moment before he answered.

“The mask is not part of dragon heritage. It is simply a Mask of True Seeing. It allows the wearer to see through illusion or to decipher the truths of the past ages.”

Bob nodded once. “And this mage working with the priests?”

Ah, that was the true reason for this unexpected visit.

“Only speculations at present.”

“Such as?”

So, he supposed the same, Thom realized.

“I want the truth,” Bob whispered.

Thom grew silent as he rolled the information around in his head, trying to figure out the best way to tell the elven fighter what the Circle suspected. Lying would offend Bob and for the life of him, Thom wanted his respect.

“There is only one mage unaccounted for who would have the power to call a demon of this magnitude.”

Understanding shrouded his bright eyes and dimmed them just a little. It was like a light had been doused in the world that could never be relit. “Of course,” Bob finally said.

“They’re not certain,” Thom said quickly.

The other merely glanced at him and let his gaze travel just over Thom’s shoulder.

Turning to see what had caught the elf’s attention, he saw Mey approaching, bandolier in hand. Her steps were swift until she lifted her head and spotted the two men.

“Sometimes,” Bob said, looking sharply at Thom, “there are destinies that are not meant to intertwine.”

He opened his mouth to reply, but managed only to stand, gaping at Bob’s back as the elf walked away abruptly.

“What was that all about?” Mey set her weapons down gently beside the water and began rummaging through her pack.

“Nothing.”

The thud of booted feet and cursing caused them both to look up as Durlag made his way through the scrub that grew thickly between the trees.

“Damned weeds,” the dwarf said. “How’s a body supposed to find the durned water?” Just then, he broke through the tree line and pulled up short when he spotted the other two. He smiled a wide, toothy grin.

"Well, looks like ye had the same idea, lass. Weapons do ye no good if ye don't treat 'em right."

He turned his attention to Thom.

"Ye talk to them other pointy hats, lad? What's the word?" He began unbuckling the leather straps that held his heavy axe on his back.

Thom pinched the bridge of his nose and sighed. "They don't wear pointy hats."

"Whatever." Durlag waved a hand at him, fell heavily back on his haunches next to Mey as she chuckled under her breath. "Did they have anything useful to say or not?"

"Oh! The mask." Thom pulled it from one of the pouches tied to his belt, still on the ground. Handing it back to Mey, he continued, "It has a True Seeing spell placed on it. When you wear it, illusion is stripped away and you can only see an object's, or a person's, true origins. It will also reveal whatever truth you need to see from the past."

She hesitated and made no move to take it. "You keep it."

He nodded, understanding her reluctance. "All right."

"What about the Faery Isles?" Mey asked. "Is it certain that is our destination?"

"Yes. The magical energy there has become very powerful." He didn't want to say the next part, but the sooner they prepared themselves, the better. "A demon has been detected."

"Demon?" Elerbee's voice broke in. Thom and Durlag jumped at the sound; Mey merely glanced at him, clearly the only one who'd heard his approach.

"From what can be deciphered, it is a Zar'leith demon. Reptilian, poisonous, and very powerful."

Elerbee uttered a prayer under his breath. "How is it defeated?"

"It relies on speed and poison to defend itself." Thom described the beast and its tactics from what he had read in texts. Never had he faced a demon. The older mages told stories of encounters with various denizens, usually minor ones, in their travels. Thom assumed the stories were mostly to frighten the younger mages in training away from the practice of summoning.

No one spoke at the end of his account. Each was thinking of the danger they faced, no doubt. Mey and Durlag cleaned their weapons mechanically, going through the motions, but not really paying attention to detail in their work. Elerbee's eyes were closed in silent prayer.

Durlag cleared his throat.

"We still have to make it across the blasted desert."

"My uncle would be the best one to tell us what to expect. He's the only one who's crossed the Barren Lands."

"He can fill us in on the road," Thom said. "Right now, we need to find shelter; a place to rest."

Elerbee spoke up. "I saw a series of caves back by the waterfall."

"Good," Thom and Mey said in unison. Thom smiled at her and she laughed, eyes dancing, hypnotizing.

Squinting up at the sun, which had not moved for hours from its position, Thom heard the echo of Bob's last words to him: *"There are destinies that are not meant to intertwine."*

****

Blood drained from his face. Rekho felt icy fingers of dread wrap around his body, one by one. *They know it's me*, he thought with growing defeat.

From what he'd overheard of the conversation, only the mage and his brother had any idea. His lips twisted into a sneer at the thought of Oboderen. Everything Rekho was not, the elven warrior seemed to know everything, made all the right choices and outshone his sibling at every chance.

It had always been so. Even when their mother had sunk deep into madness, Rekho found it harder to be a comfort to her while Oboderen spent nearly every waking moment catering to her, assuring she want for nothing.

He wasn't surprised Meylaran had asked him to go along. Her beloved "Bob": The uncle who never judged and always loved. Rekho supposed he probably would have been a better father as well.

His hands balled into fists. He wouldn't let this get to him, he couldn't. And so he shoved the thoughts of family, duty and fathering down the black chasm that had eaten his compassion.

If the dragons returned, the whole world would be lost, himself included. Wasn't that the reason for all this? Hesitating briefly, searching for an answer to that nagging question, he moved to his work table. Preparing more farthen crystals so he could be assured to view the small group as they faced the Zar'leith, his eye caught the form huddled in the back of the room.

Quickly looking away, he shuddered. That one was always watching him, his gaze boring holes right through Rekho, like he was stripping the skin from his bones. He couldn't wait to be rid of him, but for now, this was his only link to Meylaran. The bond her elven heritage provided with those closest to her was useful to him. It made it easier to follow her and always allowed access to her, which would be all but impossible without that bond. Rekho hated relying on the pathetic creature so much but since he had broken his own bond with her, it was his only choice at present.

Still, he used every moment he could to torment the foul human. Nothing said he had to be nice to it to use it.

"You are fast losing your usefulness," he said offhandedly. "You know, she cares more for the human mage who follows her around like a pup. I could simply snatch *him* up and be done with you."

Silence. Rekho smiled to himself. He enjoyed toying with the man. Although he had not spoken one word since he was taken, even when his gag was removed to eat and drink, Rekho felt he wanted to. So, he prodded him, poking hot sticks into his wounds with every word he spoke.

"She will hate you for it."

Those soft words froze him in place. The voice was weak, but the impact couldn't have been stronger. For some reason, it only invoked anger. Anger that overtook his reason and made him forget he wanted to avoid looking at the man. He whirled around and leveled his gaze on the wretched being. Blood pulsing furiously through his veins, heart pounding with the force of his ire, he moved a few steps closer.

"What did you say to me?"

The human shrank slightly as Rekho spat the words. But he did not back down from the hatred flowing out of every pore of the mage's body.

"She will hate you for it," he repeated slowly, forming the words more carefully as if enunciating them for an incompetent child.

Feeling his body start to shake with the enormity of the rage coursing through him, Rekho took another step toward the human.

"How dare you?" Rekho screamed. "She will *thank* me! All of this is to save her life. Don't you understand that?"

He felt close to falling over into that dark chasm, but he stopped just short of plunging headfirst into blackness. Halting his steps, taking a deep breath, he desperately tried to cling to his composure. As many times as he had endeavored to get into this man's head and intimidate him, it only took a few words to turn the tables.

It was fear, Rekho realized, not anger that had just overtaken him. Fear that the words this one spoke were true. He growled low in his chest and turned back to his work table.

Stop it! He told himself. *What will any of that matter if the world is destroyed?*

Gripping the edge of the sturdy table, his fingers ached with the effort to anchor and channel his emotions. He closed his eyes and evened his breathing; deep, cleansing breaths that pushed his doubt away with each exhale. This was the right way, the *only* way.

Composing his face and assuring himself his path was the only answer, he took the small silver bowl from the table and turned again to the human crowded in the filthy corner. A smile returned to his face and his steps were determined.

Rekho set the small bowl at the man's feet. Without meeting his eyes, he gripped the binding on the man's wrists and yanked him forward. Tiny wounds, all in various degrees of healing, lined his arms. Rekho produced a small blade and made another cut, just above the left wrist. He felt the man tense and a glance at his clenched jaw gave him the satisfaction of knowing the man recognized pain.

Still holding the prisoner's arm, Rekho held the bowl up to catch the trickle of blood that ran from the cut. He only needed a few drops, but it gave him a sense of power to drain as much as he wanted. He was still in control here and he intended to let the wretch know it. Dropping his arms, he glared at the man and returned to his table.

Taking a rather large crystal he placed it inside the bowl and whispered a spell that took him directly to Mey and the group of miscreants she surrounded herself with. Encased on every side by sand, it solidified what he suspected. They had already entered the Barren Lands. He vaguely recalled his brother having lived in the area for a time. Oboderen would get them safely to the border, no doubt. That aching prod of jealousy returned for a moment before he brushed it away.

Calculating their travel speed he assumed it would only take about a week for them to reach the tribes who made the shores of the Anarhet Sea their home. Of course, the sun shone continuously, which could pose a problem for the group while in the middle of the vast desert.

The oasis that sustained the nomads living throughout the merciless land, shifted constantly, effectively keeping the tribes living within the Barren Lands on the move. It was a question of when, not if, the group would run into them.

As Rekho viewed the scene playing out before him, a large, hulking figure entered through the opening to the makeshift laboratory and made its way to the work table. Scar stood silently until Rekho acknowledged him.

"Well, what is it?" he asked irritably.

"The Elder would like a word." The gravelly voice hardly rose above a whisper.

A long, exasperated sigh escaped the mage, but he nodded curtly at the priest. Rekho had decided to keep Scar in his small entourage and the priest had been agreeable. He didn't speak unless he had something of import to convey and he stayed to himself, not interested in the mage's affairs whatsoever. And he had saved Rekho's life.

"He's on his way."

Damn! He could have said that to begin with.

"Do you know what he wants?"

The priest only shrugged and moved to the side, giving the mage space to pass. As he did, Rekho noted the contemptible look Scar gave the man on the floor. The human only stared back. Interesting, Rekho thought. He had assumed Scar held no feelings one way or the other about anything.

Just as Rekho made his way to the door, the Elder threw the cloth hanging over the opening to the side and stepped in, his silken robes whispering softly. The man was bold. And his very presence annoyed the mage.

"I have a wounded priest in Sorga who tells me the Descendant assured him she could not be stopped and inevitably would bring justice to the people of Cantor." The Elder moved languidly past Rekho and a shiver crawled up the mage's spine. "Care to explain?"

Swallowing his revulsion at being in such close proximity to this man, Rekho thought quickly.

"I am working to discourage her faith in her heritage every chance I get."

The Elder raised an eyebrow. "Not exactly working out as you planned?"

"I am certain the demon will accomplish what I called it to do."

"But there *is* a chance they will overcome that obstacle as well." The Elder crossed the room and leaned in close to the prisoner, who did not blink as his gaze connected with the priest's.

"Th-that will not happen," Rekho stammered. He hadn't considered the possibility of them making it past the demon. How could he be so foolish? He lashed himself silently for failing to plan further. He had never been so careless.

Rising slowly and turning to face the mage, the Elder smiled reassuringly. "Of course not. After all, we have put our extreme trust in you at your word you would not allow her to open the pathway allowing the dragons to reenter this world." He stepped in closer to Rekho before the smile faded. "And we have paid you handsomely on that assurance."

Moving past the mage, the Elder headed back to the opening from whence he had entered. Stopping just before he stepped out into the maze of tunnels in the Caverns, he turned back.

"Perhaps I should handle this one myself, Rekho? I mean, if it's become too much for you to handle."

"No," Rekho quickly answered. This was his responsibility. He had a part in securing the prophecy coming to fruition and he would make sure he righted that wrong. "You have my word it will not come to be, Elder."

The Elder nodded once, shot a glance at Scar, then exited.

Breathing deeply to control the anger coursing into his hands, causing them to twitch uncontrollably, Rekho turned back to his work table. The image still played just above the silver bowl. The group was entering a camp of some sort. Nomads, no doubt. Yes, his brother had connections there, just as he thought.

He watched the scene before him. These people revered Bob – that much was obvious when he entered the biggest tent and spoke with what looked to be the leaders of the tribe. They welcomed him with hugs and gifts. Rekho's lip twisted into a sneer as he watched the group being accommodated within the camp.

"Do you think they will defeat the Zar'leith?" Scar's raspy voice broke through his fuming jealousy.

"None of them have ever encountered a denizen of the dark plane. How could they possibly know how to defeat it?"

"They have all shown considerable skill and courage along their quest."

"Are you suggesting I do not know what I am talking about?" Rekho's ire burned hot and threatened to lash out. Considerable effort kept it simmering just below the surface. Scar was one of the few he could trust. None of the priests believed he could accomplish what he said he could. They reveled in watching his slow downfall, he was certain.

"The mage is well-read. Perhaps he knows the weaknesses of demons. If they get close enough, and pierce the creature's heart, they will banish it back to his own plane."

"Impossible!" Rekho bellowed. "They will never get that close."

"There are several good marksmen with them. The elf is deadly accurate with a bow. The girl throws a dagger with such perfection you'd be dead before you realized she had even drawn a weapon."

Scar moved in closer. He was right. They were all very good with their weapons. They would have never gotten this far if they were not.

Rekho was distracted trying to wrap his thoughts around what he would do if they actually made it past his big surprise. The Heartstone of the Idylic the demon protected would lead her to the next destination and eventually right to him. His breath came in short, forced gasps as he imagined her finding him. It could not happen; he could not let it!

Frantically, he doused the image and paced around the table.

Scar had made his way to the man in the corner. As he stood close to the human, he smiled. To Rekho, he said, "There is one way you could *ensure* the dragons stay far from this world."

Rekho stopped, looking at the big man. A thick, corded scar running almost in a complete circle around his neck bobbed as the man swallowed.

"Well?"

"Kill her."

Those words in Scar's whispery rasp sent chills of…what was it he felt? The emotion was foreign to him. Almost familiar, but he couldn't put a word to it to describe it. Something buried deep in the far reaches of his mind nagged at him to protect her. But that didn't make sense.

The dark chasm opened wider even as he shook his head to deny it. Why was he denying it? The darkness was so warm and comforting; it beckoned to him.

Words echoed out of the deepening hole: "Kill her, kill her…"

He found himself nodding now. Yes. That was his purpose, the darkness confirmed it. It was so easy to see that.

As he stepped over the edge and let the soothing shadow envelope him, he saw one last confusing image in his mind: a beautiful woman, sobbing, calling his name, reaching for him as if to catch him before he slipped away into that chasm of madness.

TWENTY-ONE

The Nomads saw them safely to the borders of their land and secured a promise of further help from the population of the small port city of Nordis. It turned out that revealing Mey's true heritage to the Nomads helped tremendously.

The city, if it could be called such, consisted of a dock, a few buildings representing only the essentials; a baker, a tailor and cobbler (both housed in the same building), a blacksmith, homes and most importantly, a tavern.

It was at this tavern the five of them waited for word of their request to commission a boat to travel to the Faery Islands. Passing on the fish stew with its film of grease layering the top, Mey opted for bread, cheese and ale.

"Do you think we'll find anyone willing to take us?" She turned to Thom, who sat next to her with his own meager meal.

"If we offer enough, it's possible. The Mage's Circle has told me this region has been experiencing some trouble with strange creatures further out to sea."

"What sort of creatures?"

Just then the serving girl approached to set another round of drinks in front of them. She eyed them curiously. "You the ones lookin' for tha' boat?"

"Yes." Thom nodded, but gave no more information.

"Lon," she pointed to a man walking up to the long bar, and greeting the owner. "He's your best chance on gettin' out ta sea."

Thom placed a coin on her tray. "Thank you."

She winked at him and flounced off with a sway in her step that had Mey scowling at her retreating form.

"Let's talk to him, then," she said to draw the attention back to the task at hand. She pushed past the rest of them.

Approaching the man at the bar, she noticed his blonde hair was almost white. And just like most of the folks in the town, his clothes were well-worn and patched in several places. Calloused hands clasped the mug before him.

"Lon?" she asked as she settled next to him.

He glanced her direction, trying to see past the hood she wore pulled close around her face to conceal her eyes as much as she could. His curiosity got the best of him.

"Yeah. Who're you?"

"Name's Mey." Looking over her shoulder, she watched the rest of her friends settling back at their table. She tilted her chin in that direction. "My friends and I are looking for an escort across the Anarhet."

"Lots o' skiffs for rent dockside. I don't get out to sea much anymore."

"Hmm. I was told you were the best seaman of the lot. Suppose I was mistaken." She made a move to stand and leave, managing to drop a purse full of coins right at his feet. "Oh, sorry. Excuse me."

She picked up the bulging pouch, holding it up for a few seconds before stuffing it into the front of her tunic. She turned to leave.

"Uh, you said an escort?" The old sailor now leaned in a bit closer. "Where about you folks lookin' to go?"

"Oh, well," Mey seated herself again. "Our destination is among the Faery Isles. Island of Inispry, specifically." She eyed his reaction to her words, noting the look of shock that crossed his hardened features.

"Why would you want to go there?"

"Our business is our own. That is our destination; we'll pay generously."

"It's not an easy trip. How much you payin'?"

"Fifty gold before we leave and one hundred once we're safely off the island."

He hesitated, looked up as if searching the ceiling for his answer, then shrugged. "I don't have a large boat. Midsize. Only two sleeping cabins. And I don't carry a large crew. Just my two sons and myself. We'll take the smaller quarters."

Smiling in the shadows of her hood, Mey nodded. "How soon can we leave?"

"Be ready at daw-" Cutting off before he actually said the word dawn, he amended his statement, since they hadn't seen a dawn in over a week now. "Ten hours." He drank down the rest of his ale in one gulp, put his mug down. Taking another long look at her and glancing at her friends still at the nearby table, he nodded and left the building.

Proud of herself, Mey sauntered back to the group, smiling.

"We leave in ten hours," she announced.

They bathed and rested in preparation for the trip. It had been some time since she had slept in an actual bed, and although the ratty cot in a room small enough to be a closet could hardly be called a bed, it was as comfortable as a large feather-stuffed mattress. She woke refreshed and ready to set sail.

They found Lon and his boys waiting at the dock next to a decent-sized boat, with the name *Dragon's Glory* in peeling white letters pained on the side. Mey smiled with surprise.

"Has to be a good sign, right?" Thom said as he passed her.

The deck was large enough to move around without bumping into each other. The space they would be sleeping in was a bit cramped and they would be sleeping on the floor, but it would do.

Mey handed over a small purse with the fifty gold coins while Elerbee and Thom fortified the ship the best they could with magic and divine prayer; ensuring they would stay afloat in bad weather, strengthening the wood to withstand blows, and that the wind would always be in their favor. Lon's sons eyed them suspiciously but once they had money in hand, their attention turned to their own work.

The trip would take at least five days, six if they ran into bad weather. Lon told them things were more dangerous the closer they got to the island. Once out at sea, the journey became almost relaxing, but Mey knew better than to let her guard down. Bob spent most of his time at the bow of the vessel, scanning the horizon. If danger came in the form of another ship, they would know well ahead of time. Durlag was with the boys most days, who sat rapt as they listened to the dwarf's tales of adventure and monsters, which got more and more amazing as he sipped from that flask.

Never having been out to sea, even living in a port town for many years, Mey found she enjoyed the feeling of freedom that washed through her as the wind blew through her hair and took her breath away. The rocking of the ship cradled her to sleep and lulled her into a comfort that was startling. They slept nearly shoulder to shoulder in their cramped quarters and more than once she woke to find herself cushioned against Thom, his arms gently encircling her.

His face dominated her sleeping hours as well as her waking. He sought her out as she leaned against the railing of the ship, letting the wind take her thoughts and scatter them like leaves. The sudden touch on her cheek made her jump and she jerked her eyes open.

"You look so peaceful," Thom said, smiling at her.

She let out a breath, releasing the tension from the shock.

"Don't sneak up on me like that," she admonished. But his smile was catching and she couldn't help but smile in return.

"Only a couple of more days, Lon says."

She nodded. "You never did tell us what types of monsters are lurking in the sea around these islands."

"We should be prepared for anything, but the Circle received reports that normal sea creatures were mutating into huge, aggressive monsters attacking any ships that ventured into the waters they inhabit. One in particular, what appeared to be an octopus as large as the vessel itself, rose up and used its massive arms to pull the ship under, sparing none on board. The other ships in the fleet turned and fled as fast as they could."

"I have to stop this," she whispered. People were dying as the balance of evil overtook the good. She couldn't let it happen any longer. She was the key and as much as it frightened her, there was an irresistible need to set it right.

He pulled her close and she rested her head against his shoulder. This was the only place she felt truly comforted and safe; with him.

Elerbee's prayer for good weather kept with them and Inispry came into sight less than two days later, or what would be two days at best guess. The sun continued to shine relentlessly. Lon's discomfort with the entire situation was obvious the closer they got.

Once out at sea, where they couldn't turn back, Mey had revealed her face to Lon and his sons. They were nervous and she wasn't sure if they believed she was descended from dragons but ever since that moment, the sailor and his sons avoided her if they could. She could feel them looking at her but would quickly look away when she turned to them. She took it in stride. At least they agreed to continue the journey to its finish; money was a motivator even in the most extreme situations.

As the boat approached the shore, they watched as fish and all manner of swimming creatures attacked the hull but were thwarted by the armor spell Thom fortified the wood with. Odd to watch the smaller ones assault the large boat. They were surrounded as Lon dropped the anchor a short distance out.

"You'll have to use the smaller boats to get to shore." Eyeing the sea life encircling them, he added, "As soon as you're off, we'll sail around to wait on far side of the island."

Mey knew his trust in magic was tenuous but so far he had seen it prove itself by keeping the creatures at bay.

Four smaller boats with oars lined the ship on its port side. Dividing themselves between two of them - Mey, Thom and Durlag in one, Bob and Elerbee in the other – the three fishermen lowered them into the water. Immediately, fish with unusually large mouths and small razor-like teeth swam at them. Mey braced herself for what should have been a jarring impact but the creatures hit a wall of resistance. Elerbee's divine shield extended between the two small boats and encased them.

Maneuvering their small vessels to the shore, they dragged them up as far out of the water as they could and gathered around one another.

"The magic of the Idylic will be strong and it should be unmistakable," Thom was saying.

"What about the demon?"

"Humpf, that foul beastie's never met a dwarf, I'm bettin'!" Durlag heaved his large axe around into both hands.

Mey shivered as a breeze blew, leaving her with the distinctive feeling of fear. A small gasp caught in her throat. One moment she was fine, the next icy stabs of panic crawled up her spine.

"Mey?" Elerbee noted her reaction before anyone. He laid a

hand on her arm. "You're freezing!"

"I'm…oh." As soon as it had overcome her, the fear was gone and another feeling washed through her. "So sad…"

Uncontrollable tears stung her eyes and rolled down her face. She had never felt so sad, it was a hundred times more hopeless than anything she had experienced. She had to move, had to do something to try to escape this feeling. Her first instinct was to head into the foliage further up the shore.

She walked quickly and blindly, not bothering to note her surroundings, only sensing that she had entered trees and scrub. There was a faint, bothersome noise behind her. Tears blurred her vision and she stumbled many times. Finally she went down hard on one knee. Breath coming hard and fast, she choked on the sobs that were coming uncontrollably. The end of existence, hopeless loss of everything dear to her; the emotion was relentless. She heard the faint noise again. Was that her name? Someone was calling her name?

There was movement next to her, in the leaves, behind the fallen log she had tripped over. Suddenly the movement was all around her, tiny lights moving so rapidly there was only a blur of color. Lowering her head and closing her eyes to quell the dizziness, she thought she heard her name again, closer this time.

Confusion and curiosity hit her out of the blue and mixed with the fear and sadness that was already threatening her sanity. What in the name of the gods was going on here? Was this an attack? Mey hardened her jaw and determined to pull herself together. She looked up slowly, taking deep breaths.

She froze. A tiny creature stood right in front of her. It glowed a soft blue and the wings lining its back fluttered sporadically. Two long antenna curled up from its oval head. The eyes were large and set close together. Insect-like legs lined it's small, thin body but at the end of each leg, there were three slender fingers. The tail end of its body was larger, and a very sharp spike gleamed at the tip of the bulbous back. It leaned in to her. Curiosity washed over her in a thick wave as a tiny hand reached out and gently touched one of the fingers of her hand that was unmoving on the ground before her.

A burst of color moved all around her and she blinked. A dozen more of the small beings perched on the ground and the fallen log.

Mey's stomach lurched at the swirl of emotions flooding through her, compeling her to close her eyes again and lower her head. Forcing her breath to slow, she steadied herself and dared another look.

"Sprites," she said in wonder.

"Mey?" Thom's deeper voice behind her threw another wave of fear and the small creatures scattered and hid.

"It's alright," she directed to the sprites. "I'm okay," she told Thom. "Did you see them? They are wondrous! I've never seen anything like them." The fear started to subside. "Come out again. No one here will hurt you."

A small glowing head poked up from beneath a blanket of fallen leaves, the eyes wide and unblinking.

"He won't hurt you," she told it. Reaching out again, Mey offered her hand, the sprite touched her finger lightly. Wave after wave of fear crashed through her and thudded in her chest. "They are frightened of you."

"It's speaking with you?"

"No, not speaking. *Feeling*. It feels afraid."

Mey heard the others slowly approach and felt the fear of the sprite increase. So much so, she thought her heart would leap from her chest.

"They are my friends," she told it. "Nothing to be afraid of. We're not here to harm you."

Her heart calmed quickly and the sprite stepped closer, inch by inch. The curiosity overtaking the fear gradually. Large eyes took in each of them in turn. Sadness returned through all the other emotions.

"Why are you sad?" she whispered to the small creature. It flitted its wings and rose, leveling itself with her face. Looking away, then back again, it moved off.

"I think we're supposed to follow it." Elerbee said.

Dozens of the tiny beings rose from the leaves, the fallen logs, and from behind bushes to surround the group. Their quick movements were almost impossible for the eye to follow. They glowed with a faint blue light which reminded Mey of the glow that emanated from Elerbee's divine shield.

A sputtering noise accompanied by grumbling made her turn. Durlag swatted at the small flying sprites as they pulled at his whiskers while darting about his head.

"Durned gnats, is all ye are!" he muttered, trying to dislodge the knot two had managed to tie in his long beard. "Just ye wait, bugs! If I get me hands on a fly swatter…HEY!" He took off after one who had managed to lug the flask from the dwarf's belt.

Mey laughed as a feeling of glee passed through her. It felt good, even if it was mostly influenced by the playful sprites.

She matched her pace with Thom and they headed further into the island's dense forest. The good feelings faded as they traveled and the profound sadness and helpless feelings returned. A faint smell of rot stung her nose. Her steps faltered and she turned to look at her uncle. When their eyes met, she knew he could feel it too. This land was dying.

The trees were twisted and sagging, leaves fallen in piles at their bases. The decaying foliage was blackened and a foul, slick substance oozed from the bark of the trees. The smell was almost unbearable. It was death and rot and evil permeating through every fiber of this place. A sob choked her as she stopped and felt the stabbing panic that was bombarding her.

The sprite hovered at shoulder height, its eyes pleading with her. It dashed behind her, unwilling to go any further.

"Uncle…"

"Evil is taking this land," Bob said without having to hear her question.

Forcing each foot in front of the other, Mey moved slowly, careful not to touch the viscous slime that coated the limbs of the trees. At first she mistook the tug in her chest as her own sorrow for the destruction she was seeing. But as it grew stronger, she realized it was coming from outside her, almost as if fingers had grasped through her flesh and taken hold of her bones and were pulling her forward. It wasn't painful; powerful, uncomfortable if she stopped, it propelled her. Mey had never felt anything like it.

"Wait." Thom laid a restraining hand on her shoulder. "The demon." He turned to Elerbee. "We need a shield. As much as you've got."

"I can do better than that." Elerbee smiled. "I can boost each of you just enough to make your strikes slightly more powerful. As well as the shield."

Elerbee closed his eyes, lips moving as he prayed. Mey felt her energy increase starting at the top of her head and quickly flowing through to the tips of her toes. Thom was already moving forward with a plan.

"Bob, you and Mey should move around behind it. You'll have the best chance of surprising it. Durlag…"

"I'm no sneak. I'll take the beastie face to face."

"Right. Elerbee, you and I can flank it on either side. I've a few far-reaching spells. You concentrate on keeping us alive."

"Thom, I have to…" The tug was getting stronger. "I have to go." A familiar heat simmered in her middle, not quite bubbling over.

"The Heartstone." Bob looked at Thom. A silent communication passed between them, and Thom nodded.

"Mey, stay close to your uncle."

"I have to…go…"

She had to walk. Had to keep going. It was the only way to keep the heat from exploding. She still felt the wary fear on the edges, but the pull was her central thought.

Instinct had her crouching after a few minutes, searching for shadows, dark spots, anywhere she could hide. She was only mildly aware of her uncle beside her. A gurgling snarl ripped the silence that had shrouded them thus far and a sulfuric smell stung her nostrils, making her eyes water. Hand flying to cover her nose and mouth, Mey gagged.

Flattening herself against the ground, she peered through a tangle of dried limbs that had once been a small bush. Colors. Hundreds of them. There were beautiful hues of blue, green, purple, and red - some she had never seen before in her life. They swirled together and swam through tiny veins that lined the enormous wings attached to the long, serpentine body. The next thing she saw were arms, humanoid, lots of them. At least six. Swallowing back excruciating fear that knotted her throat, Mey let her gaze sweep up the slick, red body. She recoiled, bumping into her uncle, and stopping her from retreating any further. Only one eye sat in the middle of the face. Another growl erupted from the long snout as bubbling saliva dripped from the small, razor-like teeth.

Her heart started pounding in her ears, her breath coming fast. An indescribable fear overwhelmed her. Never before had she felt so strong a terror. Her uncle's steadying hand was on her shoulder, keeping her from standing and revealing herself. Looking to her left, she nearly gagged again. There, on the ground was what appeared to be the bottom half of a man. The clothes denoted it to be a person, but it was missing shoes, and the feet were mostly skeletal, bits of flesh clinging to the bone.

The pounding grew louder and Mey was certain her heart would beat right out of her chest. Surely the monster heard, it was so loud. Her uncle had nocked an arrow and aimed it at the towering beast.

"Ah, what a mixture of treats," the monster's many voices all spoke in unison.

Oh, gods, it speaks, Mey thought. If she hadn't been on the ground already, she was certain she would have fallen to her knees at the sound. It turned her flesh clammy and her insides felt like liquid.

"I smell you. Humans, dwarves, elves…and…," his head whipped left to right. "What do we have here?" There was a sick glee in its voices as they cackled together. "Dragon!"

The pounding in her ears grew to an almost unbearable level. In her urgent need for comfort, she automatically sought out Thom. The look on his face was full of pain. He was struggling, obviously, with staying put or running away as fast as he could. His chest was heaving with the effort of breathing, teeth clenched; she would find no comfort there.

Seeking out the others in her company in a sweeping gaze told her they were each battling with their own fear. Letting her eyes glide past the demon once more, something caught her attention. Instantly, the glowing pulse held her and drew her.

All tension melted and ran out of her body. It was obvious now that the pounding she heard was not her own heart alone but her life-beat mixed with the magical life of this object. This was it! What she had come for; it called her and pulled her. Overwhelming need to put her hands on it and posses it propelled her into movement. Pushing back up into a crouch, Mey glanced at her uncle. A vein ticked in his jaw, giving away his struggle with his own fear. Without thinking, she stood.

"I am dragon!" she bellowed above the roar in her ears.

The demon turned its full attention to her and Mey's stomach churned at the grin that spread across its disgusting face. It opened its maw and screamed at her.

The sound was excruciating. Her ears felt as if they would burst and she covered them quickly with her hands. Before she knew it, she had opened her own mouth, letting her own scream mingle with the many voices of the demon.

The Zar'leith threw its head back. Not sure, but the scream it hand unleashed seemed to Mey to be weakening. Another voice broke her concentration. A dwarven battle-cry. From her peripheral sight, Durlag charged straight in at the monster. Then everything exploded into action at once.

There were bright bursts of light glowing magical auras surrounding everything. Arrows flew past her head, striking the demon one after another with lightning speed. Fire exploded throughout Mey's body. In one leap she thrust herself upward toward the limb of a bare tree. She would lose her cover, but she had to keep the demon distracted from her friends.

A huge clawed hand reached for her as she flew up, missing her by mere inches. More arrows shot past her and thudded into the arm, the demon crying out in rage.

Gripping the bone handle of Makagesh, she pulled the dagger from her belt. A surge of power flowed from him into her hand and up her arm to combine with her own dragon spirit. The hand holding the blade was both familiar and alien to her at the same time. A smattering of soft scales covered the hand, more akin to a claw than anything else. That thought only registered for a moment.

Leaping from limb to limb of the skeletal trees around the clearing, Mey found her way behind the demon as it twisted, trying to follow her movement. The bombardment of magic and mortal weapons, however, divided its attention. Another scream ripped from its lips, definitely weaker this time.

The heart.

It was only a whisper on the wind, but the words were distinct. Pausing briefly, the voice registering somewhere in her memory as one she knew.

Yes, aim for its heart. Accessing the mental bond with her uncle, she relayed that information quickly to him. A volley of arrows flew into the Zar'leith's chest. Most bounced off the thick, slimy skin of the creature, but one hit home. It was not buried deeply enough to pierce the evil core of the demon, but Mey found herself flying into action.

She moved through the limbs, positioning herself in plain view of the arrow, she drew back her arm, poised to throw, as the Zar'leith raised his own to grasp the protruding arrow. She was quicker.

Makagesh spun toward the fletched end of the arrow, spiraling as it soared through the sulfuric air surrounding the beast. The thick, bulky handle of the dagger hit with a force that shoved the arrow deeper into the demon's chest.

The scream that bellowed from the Zar'leith was a thousand decibels louder than any sound Mey had ever heard. Her bones threatened to snap and her head felt as if it would fold in upon itself with the force of the noise. Massive arms reached for her; she had nowhere to go, even if she could move. She was frozen, perched on the brittle limb of a dead tree. The hands flailing at her stopped, suddenly hitting a force surrounding her, electricity snapping and popping at the contact. She looked down. Elerbee, on his knees, blood trickling from one ear and nostrils, held out his arms to her, divine power flowing in a solid stream to surround and protect her.

The Zar'leith teetered several times, its scream forcing them all to retreat as far as they could. As the beast crashed to the floor of the forest, Mey jumped from her perch to use her body to shield Elerbee, who was on all fours, struggling to stay upright. She gathered him into her arms, bending her body to cover his. He felt limp and lifeless in her grip. The thrashing body of the demon smashed to the ground, shaking the world around them. There were several more convulsive movements as the demon clung to existence. Mey didn't watch, she focused on her friend, speaking softly to him, assuring him they had beaten the demon and accomplished their goal. He was still breathing; she could feel his chest moving against her.

Quiet settled around them. No more movement or noise emanated from the direction of where the demon fell. Mey's head cleared and she could again hear the pulsing of the magic from the stone the demon had tried to keep from her. Elerbee moved beneath her and she scrambled back to give him room.

Tears ran down his cheeks, blood trickled from his nose and ears, but his color was good and he nodded at her.

"I'm alright."

Her eyes locked on his. She felt the connecting bond that stretched between them like a pathway into one another's minds and thoughts. A beautiful warm light flowed from him.

Mey turned to face the glowing, pulsating stone. It pulled at her like a magnet drawing metal. She couldn't stop it any longer and she moved slowly toward it. Kneeling before a small tangle of branches and bones, she peered into the pile.

The glow reached out and surrounded her, seeping into every pore on her body. Her hands moved out to push back the debris. A stone, the size of her hand, rested on a bed of dead leaves. Cradling both hands around it, she scooped it up. The moment she touched it, a barrage of images assailed her.

A woman, so lovely she brought tears to Mey's eyes stood with arms outstretched, her soft lavender-hued hair blowing around her face in an invisible wind. She knew this woman. But how? She had never met her.

"Mother." It was a whisper, barely audible even to her own ears.

The woman smiled. Mey sighed, feeling the love surround and enfold her. The image faded and others took its place. Garrin's face flitted through her mind several times, glimpses of a town, burned with small bodies strewn about the street. Dwarves? She was not familiar with any of the blackened structures that stood in varying states of destruction, and then the vision sped through another landscape. A thick, lush forest, huge oakwood trees dominating the background. A quick image of what looked to be the opening of a cave flashed before her. Then she was blinking the tears out of her eyes, the visions gone, but the blurred figures of her friends surrounding her.

Strong, supporting hands grasped her arms. Arms covered in the iridescent purple scales she had noticed earlier, running down and over her hands. Mey stared at the hands holding her, past the glowing stone she held, following them upward to look directly into Thom's clear, ice-blue eyes.

TWENTY-TWO

Stumbling their way across the island terrain, Mey and the group found Lon's boat waiting just where he said he'd be. She had never seen a more welcome sight. Still gripping the Heartstone in one hand, she climbed up the rope ladder Lon threw down to them awkwardly with one hand.

In a daze, she let Thom lead her to the small sleeping quarters. She cried, laughed, and confessed a myriad of transgressions. He sat silently, listening, letting her break apart and comforting her when she thought all was lost. All the while, the boat headed toward Rach-Ordin, the port city into the Rachnor Pass. Mey was convinced they should head into these dwarven cities, although she would not confess why. How could she tell Durlag what she had seen? All those dead and dying, their city burning around them. Another barrage of tears flooded her eyes and Thom held her as she let the sobs take her. The Heartstone was wreaking havoc on her emotionally.

"Your vision, when you first held the stone, what was it?" he asked.

Mey only shook her head.

"But you kept saying you saw them, all dead."

"I don't remember."

Taking her face in his hands, making her look at him, he asked again.

"What did you see, Mey?"

She wanted to tell him; no, *needed* to tell him. She so badly needed to confide the overwhelming feelings and visions. She knew she could trust him but there was a nagging logic that would always hold her back from giving him everything. That part of her was convinced as soon as she did, he would disappear forever. Ignoring what she considered her better judgment, she let it all out.

"I saw my mother." Tears gathered in her eyes once more. How was there still more? Her eyes felt raw and fevered from the constant flow. "I've never seen her before, but I knew her instantly. She was so beautiful and there was so much love." Wrapping her arms around herself, Mey closed her eyes trying to hold all those wonderful feelings in.

"Did she speak to you?" he asked gently.

Shaking her head, letting the tears pour over her cheeks, Mey looked at him.

"No. But I'm sure what I saw was her telling me where to go next. Dwarves. Lots of them. Lying dead in the streets, while a city burned around them. Oh, Thom, how could I tell Durlag what I had seen? I don't even know what it means!"

He put his arms around her and pulled her closer, but kept silent.

"Then there was a forest. I've never seen so many oakwood trees. It was full of them. Is there a forest of oakwoods?"

"In Nott. Mages were being sent to help with a new settlement there before I left. They were harvesting the trees."

"Are there caves there?" She lifted her face, looking at him.

"Why?"

She shrugged. "I can't be sure, but the last thing I saw looked like an opening to a cave."

"Mey…"

Something in his voice alerted her. He knew something he wasn't telling her.

"Maybe I should contact the Circle again," he said. "Perhaps they can confirm the things you're telling me. If they can sense a magical presence in the dwarven cities or even in the Forest of Nott, we would have a better direction."

Mey was nodding. "Yes. They could pinpoint the areas we need to go in the places I saw."

They sat a few more moments, not saying anything, just holding on to one another. She wanted so much to stay this way forever and forget all this dragon business. But as she moved her arms, she caught sight of the shimmering purple scales that had surfaced on her arms, stopping just before her fingers on the tops of her hands.

He caught her hand as she pulled it away. How was he not repulsed to touch her? He moved his hand up her arm, stroking the rough scales, amazement in his eyes. She watched his face. Not once did he flinch away from the changes her body was going through. He thought her eyes beautiful, he'd told her. And now, he caressed her skin as if it were the softest silk.

Admittedly, it felt nice to have someone accept her totally and wholly for who she was and what she was becoming. But an alarm somewhere inside screamed these were dangerous waters she and Thom were treading. With every effort in her will, she forced herself to pull away.

His brow pulled together in confusion as he looked at her. Laying a hand against his cheek, she felt the stinging tears again.

"We should get back to the others."

"What are you afraid of?" he whispered back.

She took a deep breath, intending to tell him all she was afraid of; the look in his eyes, losing her heart to him, not having control of what was happening to her, feeling her soul ripped to pieces at the injustice she saw around her, dying, living. But she simply said, "Nothing."

A knock on the door interrupted anything more he would have said.

"Meylaran?" Her uncle's voice on the other side.

Reluctantly, she moved to open the door. Bob's concerned face greeted her.

"Is everything all right?" He glanced over her shoulder to Thom.

"Yes, uncle. I was just overwhelmed with the power from the Heartstone. There were visions. Telling me where to go next, I think."

"Perhaps we should go up and talk to everyone." Thom had come up behind her.

Mey nodded and moved past her uncle and up the few steps to the open deck of the ship. Breathing in the fresh air, the closeness of the cabin and the fears Thom made her think of fell away.

They found a spot on deck to settle in and Mey told them everything, starting with the image of her mother and how she believed the visions following were from her mother, telling her what to do next. She told them of the image of dwarves and a city burning. It was hard, but she forced herself to look Durlag in the eye the entire time she retold that vision. If she could have, she would have taken all the pain she saw in his eyes and etched into his face and endured it for him. He was estranged from his clan but that didn't mean he didn't still care for them. Loyalty to one's clan was deeply ingrained in dwarven tradition. And not knowing *what* dwarven city she had seen gave no comfort at all.

She told them of the Forest of Nott, close to the new settlement. And finally, the cave within that forest.

The plan of action from there was to have Thom contact the Mage's Circle to see if they could pinpoint any specific locations for them and proceed to the Rachnor Pass. The Pass would lead them into the dwarven cities: Ordin, Chal and Stord. Which city their journey would take them to depended on the Mage's Circle. If the Circle couldn't help them, they would just have to visit each through the Pass.

****

Thom used the captain's room for his transport spell. Setting out his stones, the last of those needed for communicating with the Circle, he prepared himself for this meeting. He'd come a long way from the novice scholar they'd sent out to find the Descendant. Being close to evil and even closer to death had changed him. It was still his most important task to get Mey to the Idylic so that she could summon the dormant dragons. But, he knew also that he couldn't ignore his own thoughts and feelings. He was more than a pawn for the Circle to move about at their whim.

Mey taught him that. Being around her, protecting her, watching her change, it all added to his growing surety that he was meant to devote himself to her. Is that why the Circle sent him? Had it been known from the beginning? He was pushed from the time he could read to study and learn all he could of the dead race of dragons. Only it wasn't dead, he had eventually discovered. At that point, he was encouraged to follow his theories and learn more about them. It was always dragons.

Slowing his breathing, he let the words of the spell speed silently through his mind, calling up the image of the Mage's Tower. Magic energized him and the euphoric energy filled his body. The familiar walls formed and voices faded in and out as the spell concluded. When he opened his eyes, they were gathered around him.

After imparting the information of what Mey had seen when she took possession of the Heartstone, the Circle sat quietly. The Magister broke the silence.

"Thom, we have felt the growing magical energies in the locations you have indicated. Especially in the Forest of Nott."

"Is there a cave system there, Magister?"

"Oh, yes. The entrance to the Caverns of Time is in the heart of the forest."

Thom felt his pulse increase. It made sense that the Caverns of Time would be their ultimate destination. Where else would the dragons go but to a place where existence meant nothing and everything. A place where time stood still and split in every direction simultaneously. A place that could rip a person to shreds the moment he set foot in it. Quite possibly the most dangerous place on Cantor.

"Thom," the Magister's voice made him look at the man. "The priests are sending out every force they have to find you. Elerbee's sect has been in contact with us and we will do what we can from here. The danger to the Descendant has increased and will only keep increasing the closer you get."

"Yes, I understand."

"And you enter dwarven territory," a female member spoke up. "She will not be welcomed warmly there."

"Each dwarven city and its clans have a small degree of magic. However," the Magister tilted his head as if listening, "Chal is curiously devoid of any magical energy whatsoever."

Nodding, Thom thought of Durlag's stories of the land where his clan resided. Stord was his home, but the three cities worked together to survive. If one was cut off, the others would surely suffer.

"We will head for Chal, then."

"You must hurry. Two of the signs have already come to pass. The third looms close and will be upon us soon," a female voice reverberated throughout.

The walls shimmered once. The spell was weakening. The Magister stood and walked to the center of the Circle where Thom sat. Bones creaked as he knelt, and Thom had the urge to reach out and help him as he lowered himself agonizingly to the floor. It would have been useless since the image was just that; an image. Thom watched in wonder as the old man positioned himself just inches from where he sat.

"This will aid you." The Magister placed something on the floor, bent his head reverently and spoke soft words. Thom didn't recognize the spell but the power of it nearly took his breath away.

"You can call upon the energy of the Circle to infuse you if you should have need. What you do for us, for the world, is of the highest commendation, Thom."

Speechless, he let his head bow to the old man. They were gifting him with the Power of the Circle. Never in this generation had it been given. The histories' last record of it was over a thousand years old. He felt a cool wind blow gently across his face and he looked up. The Magister's hand was out as if laid upon his shoulder. There was sadness in his eyes, but hope as well. His voice was a whisper when he spoke.

"She *does* love you. But her love for the people and her duty to protect them is stronger. It grows each day. She needs you more now than ever. Protect her, Thom. Lead her to her destiny."

A hard knot formed in his throat and he swallowed several times trying to force it down. He could only nod his agreement. The Magister's image faded, shimmered and fell away in wisps of foggy color.

For a long time, Thom sat, attempting to calm his pulse and slow his breathing back to normal. Finally, he looked down and carefully picked up the black stone. He brought it close to his face, examining the silver and blue veins running through it.

Their course of action was set. They must head for Chal. The complete absence of magical energy indicated something amiss. Thom didn't want to imagine the next leg of that journey.

The Caverns of Time. The very core of magic in the world, the Caverns could shield the dragons from any force on Cantor. No one knew what became of the Idylic itself, but Thom was convinced they would find it within the Caverns.

Coming to this conclusion, he rose to inform the others. They would have to step up their protection of Mey. She was in more danger now and the dwarves would not accept her heritage gently. Preparations needed to be made to hide the physical changes distinctive as dragon-born. Magical disguise would be all but useless around dwarves, who naturally repelled most simple magic.

Emerging from the lower deck, Thom squinted in the brightness of the sun. How much longer would this last? There was no answer, but he knew they must make the most of the time they had.

He found his friends and the crew engaged in the normal activity of the ship. Elerbee stood at the ship's bow, coaxing the wind and waves to work in unison, speeding their travel. Mey was with him, face to the sky, wind streaming through her amaranthine hair, a tiny smile on her lips.

As if she sensed him, she turned, expectant. His breath caught. How could anyone find her anything less than magnificent? The changes only made her more so and lent to her beauty. She couldn't see it, but it's all he saw when he looked upon her. He moved toward her, restraining the urge to reach out and touch her.

"What did they say?" she asked.

"There is a magical void in Chal. We should target that city. There's been no other magical changes the Circle can detect."

Elerbee glanced over his shoulder. "And the cave?"

He hesitated, drawing full attention from them both. Taking a deep breath, Thom went on.

"The Caverns of Time are located in the heart of the Forest of Nott."

"The Caverns of Time!"

Thom swiveled around to see Bob. Durlag approached a few paces behind. Bob knew the Caverns, that much was evident by the look on his face.

"Yes," Thom said.

"We cannot go there. Any who enter are doomed to death. Time is unforgiving and cares not for the fate of the world."

"But it is where the Heartstone is leading us," Mey put in.

"Maybe it is not. Maybe it is tricking you!" His words were pleading and it was the most emotion Thom had ever seen the elf exhibit.

"My mother showed –"

"Your mother would never put you in danger," Bob interrupted.

"Stop!" Thom forced his way between the two. To Bob, he said, "We need to remember our goal. We get Mey to the Idylic so she can call the dragons and right the world." Turning to Mey, his voice losing its sharp edge, he said, "Your destiny is within the Caverns, but first, we must see to the dwarven city."

"Aye," Durlag spoke for the first time. "Me brothers and sisters may need us. I may be a shame to them, but I have a chance to change that. Concentrate on one thing at a time, lass." He put a soothing hand on Mey's arm. "We'll get ye where ye need to be."

No more explosive arguments presented during the rest of the trip. Thom chalked up Bob's worry to an overly concerned uncle. He didn't want to see his niece hurt any more than the rest of them, but she was the closest thing to a daughter Bob had ever had, so his overprotective flare was understandable.

The ship made landfall on the banks of Rachnor, the land that housed the dwarven cities. They paid Lon and his sons, bid them a safe trip home and continued on toward the Rachnor Pass, a path cut between the mountains that would lead them past each city.

Durlag chattered along the way, keeping Mey engaged in stories of his youth and his father and of the dragon that eventually "went wrong" and kept the city of Stord captive. Thom noticed the closer they got to the first city, Ordin, the more frequent the swills on his beloved, ornate flask became. At first it made his stories more colorful, full of grandiose adventure. Then, as he stumbled along, mumbling more to himself than anyone else, he became more introverted.

Mey glanced back, worry in her eyes.

Thom nodded, acknowledging her concern. The demons Durlag prepared to face were much stronger than any they had encountered thus far and if the dwarf needed to indulge a bit more to keep his courage, so be it.

Mountains rose on either side as they progressed. At one point, Thom couldn't resist stopping to examine a stone that caught his eye. It was very similar to onyxiad, the stone used for electrical spells. It had the same black hue but it was very brittle, almost falling apart in his hands.

"Shylyte," Durlag told him.

"What is it used for?"

"Hmph, not good for nothin' but getting' in a body's way when trying to tunnel through good rock."

Thom pocketed several larger pieces anyway. It would be interesting to study when he got back to Val. He stopped in his tracks. *Back to Val*. He wasn't sure he'd make it back.

As the Pass narrowed, the mountains grew taller and a strong, constant wind gusted through. The path channeled the wind, making it stronger.

"Ordin harnesses the wind and uses it to irrigate their crops and drain waste out of the city," Durlag said. "It gets worse afore it gets better." He chuckled as a particularly strong gust blew through and sent him skittering right into Bob's back, taking them both down.

Bob untangled himself as Durlag lay on the ground chuckling and muttering about some fool dwarf who thought he could trap lightening and use the wind to send it through the city creating light without candles and other tomfoolery.

"Maybe we should take a rest?" Elerbee suggested.

The consensus was that, indeed, they should give Durlag time to sober himself before they moved on. Soon, the dwarf's snores were echoing off the stone walls around them.

Eventually Thom was nodding off as well. Mey and Elerbee had already fallen asleep. He and Bob held out longer, trying to keep a watch, but fatigue won the fight and they both drifted to sleep as well.

The world shook violently. Something was coming and he had to protect her. Another shake, almost rattling his teeth. Why couldn't he see anything? Distantly, he could hear her calling for him.

"Thom, Thom."

Consciousness rushed in as he heard his name repeated over and over. Realization that someone was shaking him brought him closer to waking. He opened his eyes quickly. Mey's face was inches from his; better than any dream he could have wished to have. He smiled at her.

But she was not smiling in return. Something wasn't right. He sat up, trying to clear the fog of sleep from his head. As he came fully aware, he could hear Durlag's voice, raised and full of indignation.

"I tell ye again, we only want to pass through to Chal! I ain't no spy!"

There was only one other dwarf that Thom could see. His long beard was braided and decorated, he carried the largest war hammer Thom had ever seen, slung over one shoulder like it weighed nothing. He wore only breeches and a vest, showing his heavily muscled arms. The new dwarf barked something at Durlag in a gravely language Thom had never heard before.

Durlag growled low in his throat and before anyone knew it was coming, he pulled back his arm and let his fist fly. Straight into the nose of the other. A spell of defense automatically came to mind and he heard the others around him moving, presumably for their weapons.

Everyone poised to react. The two dwarves faced one another, Durlag scowling, the other shocked and bleeding freely from his nose.

Then the unfamiliar dwarf smiled, reached out and clapped Durlag on the shoulder. They spoke again in the strange language. Durlag offered over his flask and the dwarf drank in appreciation.

Thom's confusion was now complete. Looking around, he saw the others were just as mystified. What had just happened? Were they in danger? As if he read their minds, Durlag turned to answer the unspoken questions.

"Ye can't show any fear to these Ordinians. Kinda squirrely, ye see." He twirled a finger about his head to emphasize his meaning. "They understand drink, though. Like any good dwarf would!"

No one moved. Each still poised in defense.

"Put the weapons away, fools! They'll think we don't trust 'em," Durlag said.

Mey moved first, sheathing the daggers she held in each hand. Bob followed suit. Elerbee continued to whisper, however. Thom watched him move next to Mey and lightly touch her arm. The scales on her arms faded to a shade matching her skin tone. Disguise. The dwarves would be all but impervious to his magical attempts at covering her identity, but divine power would work to trick their clever minds into seeing just what Elerbee wanted them to see.

Thom nodded his quick approval.

Bob stepped forward to Durlag.

"Will they let us pass on to Chal?"

"Sure. We'll have to share drink with them first." He turned to the other dwarf and said something none of them understood. The dwarf nodded and took another long drink from the flask. "He'll lead us to Ordin."

****

'Sharing drink' with dwarves ended up meaning a full night's worth of reveling for Durlag and his newfound friends. And although night never actually came, Mey and the others opted to spend the hours coming up with and executing a better disguise for her. The divine magics Elerbee had placed on her were beginning to fade.

After spending hours drinking and defying all reason on how a person could possibly stay upright after so much ale, Durlag staggered into the small camp the group had put up hastily just beyond the main meeting hall where the dwarves spent much of their time drinking.

The dwarf had just enough sobriety left to tell them his new friend, Raf, had explained that this clan had not heard anything from Chal for weeks. They ventured to check on their neighbors but had been kept at bay by a mysterious force. Fear was virtually unknown to dwarves but each time they tried to enter the pass that lead into the city of Chal, a crippling fear would turn them back and not one of them wanted to try again.

"But I'll be damned if I let some silly magic…" his words trailed off into a loud snore as the hard dwarven spirits took him into slumber.

"Well, that probably cinches it. Chal is more than likely lost," Thom said as he threw a rough woolen blanket over the dwarf.

Mey stared into the small fire, watching the flames dance. She couldn't save them and the profound loss gripped her insides and twisted. She had failed her friend; a proud and trustworthy dwarf,

Durlag didn't deserve this pain. If she was so special, why couldn't she have saved them?

A comforting hand stroked her hair. Thom sat beside her, silently offering the reassurance she needed.

"He shouldn't go with us," she voiced her concern.

"You know that won't be an option for him. Mey, these are his people – I think he feels it's his duty to make sure they rest peacefully. No one here is under the false impression that we will find the city of Chal alive and bustling." He pulled her in and let her nestle into his arms. She should have felt reassured, but the weight of each of her friend's troubles felt heavy. *And this is only the beginning*, she thought. *The whole world is relying on me.*

After a few hours rest, the friends prepared to go on to the doomed city. A somber silence draped their travels and even Elerbee's normally inspiring presence had not helped ease the burden Mey felt.

They spent the better part of two days burying the dead of Chal. Durlag mourned as only a dwarf knew how; he drank. Elerbee gave rites to each and every soul; surely a painstaking process and Mey admired how much he gave of himself to serve the deserving people of the dwarven city. *I should be so giving of myself*, she vowed silently.

Durlag insisted he did not want to go further into Stord. He was not ready to face his own people. For now, it was enough to make sure his neighbors had the respectful burial they deserved. He was ready to move on and they all took his cue as he led the way out of Chal and onward toward their destination in the Caves of Endless Time.

TWENTY-THREE

The Forest of Nott. Squat trees with leaves larger than the average person covered the landscape as far as Mey could see. Something twisted low in her belly and she could hear Makagesh humming with delight. She knew, instinctively, she was supposed to be here. A buzz of excitement and fear mixed with adrenaline rushed through her veins.

As they made their way among the trees, Mey stayed close between Thom and her uncle. Not that they would have let her out of their sight, to begin with.

None of them had ever actually been to the Caverns of Time, though she had a feeling her uncle knew more about them than he was letting on. The Idylic was rumored to be in the Caverns and she recalled he had once seen the heart and soul of dragon existence when he was a quickling. That was over four hundred years ago. Maybe it had been in a different place.

When the dragons fled this world, they'd escaped through the Caverns. Lost in time, they mourned the fall of their homeland. She felt their pain profoundly here, just as she felt the pain and injustice of the people who still populated the land.

She reached up and wiped a tear from her cheek, wincing at the scratchy feel of her skin.

The scales on her hands and arms had roughened and the color had darkened to a deep, rich purple, matching the color streaking her hair. She still felt like a hideous monster but her worry about her appearance was fading. There were so many other things that occupied her mind.

The fact that she alone would be the one to save this world was a reality which weighed so heavily on her shoulders she'd begun to feel as if she walked with a permanent hunch. She curled her fists in defiance.

Suddenly, she couldn't breathe. Her feet felt as though stuck in quicksand, struggling to take a step and the harder she tried the weaker she felt. *The entire world is depending on me.*

"Mey?"

"Lass?"

"Meylaran?"

The voices were mingled and they all spoke at once, full of concern. She looked up to see all of her friends crowded around her. When had she fallen? She reached up with shaking hands. Thom grasped them and helped her stand.

"I need a moment…"

Thom led her to the shelter of a tree and helped her sit.

"We can't stay here." Bob said. "Something has been following us. I can hear it but I have yet to catch a glimpse."

"I can smell it," Mey confirmed. She inhaled and caught the faint fetid smell on the breeze. Instinct kicked in, and she knew they had to keep moving and get out of here. "I'm alright. Let's go."

Their pace quickened with urgency and an edge of fear at what could be tracking them.

"The Caverns are at the heart of the forest," Thom told them when they finally slowed. They had already been walking for hours, the trees and underbrush getting denser as they traveled. The sunlight had started fading that morning and their last glimpse of the sky was just before they entered the deeper forest. Stars like he had never seen were starting to emerge, but they were all different colors and were beginning to line up in the sky.

"We're on the right path. I can feel it," she assured him.

"Why don't we take a brief respite," Thom suggested. "Catch our breath." Grunts and nods greeted the suggestion.

"Mey, let's talk," he said abruptly.

Hesitating briefly to consider his intent, she nodded. They made their way through the trees and found a small clearing. Very little light shone through the cracks of the canopy of leaves that spanned across the opening. It was oddly beautiful watching the dust in the air float lazily through the light streamers. She felt Thom's hands rest on her shoulders, his breath heavy on her neck as he leaned in.

"I love you," he whispered in her ear.

Squeezing her eyes shut to keep the tears from falling and the anger from boiling forth, she only shook her head. The one thing she wanted in this world was to leave all this behind and run away with Thom. But that wasn't even an option; her destiny was to see the world righted. Her duty was to serve the people, not her own selfish desires.

"You can't."

"But I do. And I couldn't keep it to myself any longer."

"Thom," she said as she turned. "You do realize what is happening to me?"

"I don't care."

He pulled her closer and folded his arms around her tightly. It would be so easy to let herself go, let his love take her to a place where only the two of them existed. Without a doubt, she loved him, too. Deeply. *This isn't fair!* They could never have a life together. Even if he survived this, it was almost certain that she would not – not in mortal form.

Taking a deep breath, she froze. A wild smell filled her nostrils and sent her mind reeling. It wasn't right and it was close. Why hadn't she heard it?

Thom immediately sensed the change in her.

"What is it?"

Shaking her head, she said, "I don't know. Something is close. We have to get back—"

Her words were cut short as a feral scream sounded behind her. The blood in her veins turned icy and she felt the heat in her middle rise quickly in response. A low growl rumbled through her clenched teeth. Thom dropped his arms and reached for his pouches of gemstones.

Turning in time to see the two milky white eyes that stared at her from the trees, Mey let another growl erupt. She sent an urgent mental alarm to her uncle. A deep loathing for this creature flowed through her. She didn't know what it was but she knew it didn't belong in this world.

Slowly, it stepped from beyond the protection of the trees with another cat-like scream. Its focus locked on her. In a blink, she was holding a dagger in each hand. She could hear Thom chanting in a low voice behind her.

Makagesh's voice trickled through her consciousness: *Gnor.*

Gnor!? What was a mythical beast doing standing right in front of her? A mammoth creature, its shaggy hair covered only its head and chin. Muscles in its arms and legs rippled with each move it made. It reeked of evil.

The air in front of her shimmered slightly. Elerbee's shield. Good, her message got through to them. As soon as it sensed the magical shift around her, the Gnor leaped, hitting the shield that sparked and crackled at the intrusion. Short, barking sounds came from the Gnor's throat. Was it laughing?

An arrow streaked by her, flying straight at the beast's face. The Gnor dropped at the last second and the arrow sank into the tree behind it.

Turning, it charged for Mey.

Summoning strength from the dragon blood coursing through her veins, Mey fell into a crouch, daggers in hand. She threw as the creature bounded toward her. They stuck fast in its thick hide. Four more blades appeared, seemingly out of thin air, in her hands.

Three glowing bands materialized, encircling the Gnor and tightening quickly. Silently thanking the gods for the presence of a mage, Mey didn't miss a beat. She sprang easily to the nearest branch, vaulting over and landing behind the creature. As soon as her feet touched solid ground, she let all four daggers loose. Each one buried to the hilt in the Gnor's large back.

The monster screamed and thrashed at the binding circles, breaking two of them.

From the corner of her eye, Mey caught flashes of light in the vicinity of where Elerbee had stood moments before. Quickly drawing two more weapons from the bandolier across her chest, she skittered back a couple of feet. In the next beat of the deadly dance, Durlag charged in.

Only she had to check her shock, because it was Durlag but he was almost as large as the Gnor. He let out a massive yell as he brought his axe about to land a solid blow on the creature's shoulder.

More arrows flew in, exploding on impact with the monster. Mey smiled; Elerbee was certainly working his divine energy just where it was needed most.

She danced lightly around the partially entangled Gnor, placing herself opposite Durlag, who winked at her as he prepared another powerful swing of his axe. Mey planted her feet and put all her power behind the two daggers she aimed at the beast's face. One sank into the muscular neck, the other struck right on target, through the left eye of this unnatural beast.

The screams from the Gnor rose to an ear-splitting level as it thrashed against the last restraining band. Mey heard Thom's chanting grow louder. The air around where she last stood shimmered and twisted and moved into a cone of humming energy that hurtled toward the monster's chest, knocking it back into Durlag, whose curses were drowned out by the gruesome beast's dying cries.

Quiet settled on the small clearing. Smoke rose in wisps from the unmoving Gnor. Muffled sounds emanated from someplace on the Gnor's body, though she didn't perceive them to flow from his mouth. Her weapons back at the ready in the beat of a heart. Mey slowly approached the creature, wrinkling her nose at the sight of the huge, gaping hole in its chest. Another muffled sound made her tense as she watched unbelievably as the Gnor moved. How in Sirrah's name could it have survived that?

Then she saw the source of the movement. Durlag, trapped underneath the corpse, wriggled his head free.

"A little help?" he growled.

Mey tried not to smile, but the dwarf had returned to his normal size, his face red with the strain of trying to escape the heavy weight on top of him.

"Don't just stand there gawking, get yerself over here and move this stinking hulk off o' me!"

Mey and the others moved swiftly to free him. He cursed Thom the entire time.

"Coulda given a body some warning you were about to blow a hole through the nasty thing!"

"I'm sorry. I…I just…threw the first spell that came to mind." Thom shrugged.

"What in the ten hells was that thing?"

"Gnor," Bob said. "They have not been seen since the dragons left." His gaze landed on Mey.

"We have to keep moving," Mey said.

A sense of urgency compelled her. A scream in the distance confirmed her thoughts. They were being hunted. More of these things, surely but gods only knew what else. "We have to find that cave."

They made haste toward the center of the forest. Mey caught shadowy glimpses from the corner of her eye as they traveled.

Nerves on end, she jumped at every sound. She was leading them now, instinct and the Heartstone guiding her. The trees started to thin and the dirt path turned rocky. All around them now, the cries and screams of unknown beasts sounded. Oddly, no closer than before. Almost as if they were being herded and watched.

"The things inside that cave are just as bad as what we have already faced." Bob's soft voice floated on the slight breeze. "Or worse."

"I knew it!" She wheeled on him. "You've been here. You know what we face. Why would you keep that from us?"

Bringing his hands up in a sign of surrender, Bob's brow came together. "Meylaran? What are you talking about?"

"You just said we would face worse things inside the Caverns!" she accused.

"I…I do not know what you mean." He shook his head. "I did not speak."

Another voice in her ear sounded. "It was me."

She turned; no one. Then from another direction. "No, over here."

"Stop it!" she screamed at the voices. Bringing hands to her ears, she tried to block them out, twisting, trying to find who spoke.

A bright light. The voices started to fade as the light grew larger and came closer to her. Hands reached forth from the light. She backed away, but as she drew apart from the light, voices began whispering to her.

"What do you want?" she asked weakly.

The hands came closer. She no longer shrank from them, because they were keeping the voices away. They rested on her shoulders and a feeling of calm descended on her. She sighed and closed her eyes.

"Mey? Mey, can you hear me?"

"What happened?"

"A Confusion spell. A ward of some sort. We must be very close."

Opening her eyes cautiously, she looked at the hands still resting on her shoulders, following them to their source.

"Elerbee."

"Good thing I recognized it so quickly or we would have all been drawn in." He smiled reassuringly at her.

"We should check the area for more," Thom broke in.

"You'll be fine," Elerbee told her before moving away.

She nodded.

"That was a divine spell," he told Thom. "There has to be several priests here. It takes more than one, working together, to create that level of power."

Mey moved to the side of the path as Thom and Elerbee called up spells that would reveal both divine and arcane magics. She scanned her immediate surroundings for signs of physical traps. None found, she sniffed the air for any changes. Nothing had changed but her sense of urgency had increased.

Her hands went to the small pouch hanging at her hip where the Heartstone rested. It seemed to vibrate at her touch, as if it too felt an unexplained urgency. She felt tugged in a southward direction.

"Thom." Unable to resist the energy, she stumbled forward. "This way." She called the last over her shoulder as she gripped the stone and obeyed its insistence.

Mey led them down a winding path that took a sharp turn to the right, into a grove of thick trees. She took a deep breath, looking at the fracture in the rock, opening into darkness beyond. The others came up behind her.

"This is it."

Voices from inside the Cavern had them scattering to find concealment.

Two men emerged, both wearing vestments with the symbol of Yenoh. A plan formed quickly in Mey's mind and she imparted it to the others. Thom was next to her, shaking his head but she grabbed him by the arm and before he could protest further, pulled him out into the opening.

The two priests stopped short, surprised. Their stance changed quickly to one of defense.

"What are you doing, there?"

Smiling her sweetest smile, Mey sauntered forward, careful to pull the cloak around her face.

"We're lost. You see, we wandered off of the path a while back…" She moved her wrists slightly, allowing the concealed daggers there to release from their harness and slip into her hands.

The younger priest was accommodating.

"You should take this small animal trail," he began but the elder priest cut him off.

"This area is off limits to anyone but priests. You'll come with us and we will let the Elder decide what to do with you."

Mey's smile turned into a sneer and the cloak slipped, revealing her eyes. The men's shocked expressions froze on their faces. They didn't move, held fast by magic. She looked over her shoulder at Thom.

"There's no sense in killing them." He moved past her. "Here, help me get their robes."

They donned the oversized robes and moved the men's immobilized bodies into the brush where Bob was hiding. They tied them with rope and Bob stood guard in case the spell wore off before they could return. Mey and Thom made their way into the Caverns.

The air was cooler and the smell of rot mingled with beeswax candles and a sweeter smell she couldn't identify. The walls were smooth rock. There was a lingering sadness that permeated these walls; an ancient sorrow that awakened something familiar.

The first three rooms they passed were sleeping quarters, containing only a cot, a bucket, and a basin for washing. The fourth and fifth rooms, however, revealed more of what was really happening in this place.

One seemed to house a high official, with all the comforts of a ruler of great stature. Silk tapestries, plush floor coverings, cushions, comfortable chairs. But a little further down, the next chamber's entrance shimmered with a hazy cloth and when she reached for it, Thom grabbed her arm.

"No. It's magic. If you touch it, you'll lose your arm."

"But I don't sense anything."

"It's been concealed. Someone who knows what they're doing. I barely detected it, myself."

Thom pulled a green stone from his pouch, placed it between his palm and the wall and chanted softly. The words reminded her of breaking glass. The shimmer fell away from the cloth and he nodded. "Now we can enter."

Mey slowly moved the cloth aside enough to peek in and determine there was no one in the room. They both stepped through. Quickly scanning the contents, she noted a large table covered with books, vials, scrolls, and stones of all sort scattered from one end to the other. A dark stain in the far corner, possibly blood, had seeped into the stone of the floor and a small bowl sat next to it.

"This is a mage's laboratory," Thom whispered.

"So, the theory of a mage working with the priests is right," she whispered back.

"We'd best get the others. Let them know what we've found. We can discuss how to proceed from here."

He was ushering her out, when she caught sight of something. The bright blue paint stuck out from the other mundane things on the table.

"Thom, wait!" Yanking her arm from his grasp, she darted over and grabbed the hammered silver charm attached to a leather strap and shoved it in the front of her tunic.

They made their way back toward the opening of the cave.

"You know, I can't help but wonder where everyone is," Thom was saying. "There's obvious signs that people are inhabiting these caverns but the only sign of life we've seen are the two priests out front."

"Maybe they're worshiping. Don't priests gather at certain times to heap praise on the gods they've chosen? I remember Elerbee saying once…"

A loud grating sound of stone on stone stopped them in their tracks.

Glancing at one another, no words were needed to hasten them toward the opening where their friends waited.

The others had gathered with Bob to watch the two priests Thom had spellbound. Switching the robes back to the men, they quickly imparted the information of what they had discovered to the rest of the group.

"Well, what're we waitin' for!" Durlag hoisted his axe and

stood.

"We do not know how many people might be in there," Bob answered.

Durlag harumphed, but remained where he was.

"The chamber you said looked as if a high official resided there," Elerbee said thoughtfully, "was there a carving on the chair?"

"Just some weird symbols inside a circle," Mey said.

"Think. Was one of them like my own symbol? The one on my neck?"

"Yes, I think it was. But there were others, as well. A large 'X' with a circle around its middle and another with smaller circles set in the crevices."

"The Elder."

"Who?" Mey asked.

"He is somewhat akin to what the Magister is for the mages. Am I right?" Thom asked him.

"He is the head of all three orders of priests. I don't think I have ever heard of an Elder leaving his tower in all the years I have served."

"Well, he's here now. And with a mage," Thom continued as he wrapped his stolen robe around the frozen priest. "There was another room, protected by a powerful magical ward. A mage's laboratory."

"Oh," Mey said, remembering the necklace she had taken from the scattered mess on the table. She pulled it out to examine it more closely.

"What's that?" Durlag asked her.

"A charm. Hammered silver, made in Seaside by the baker's boy."

"How d'ye know that?"

"Because I bought it from him." She looked up at Thom. "This is Garrin's."

"I'm sure there are hundreds of charms with that design out there."

"Perhaps," she said. "But none with this blue paint. I painted this myself. 'To add some color to his dreary life.'" Mey's hand shook. "What would this be doing here?"

No one spoke. None of them had an answer.

"Let's get in there and see if we can't find out what's going on." Durlag insisted.

Mey tucked the charm in the pouch with the Heartstone. When she did, she felt and heard the comforting hum that had been leading her on for weeks now.

It's time to finish this.

TWENTY-FOUR

As they made their way down the tunnels, past the chambers at the front of the Caverns, twists and dips and rises had Mey wondering how they would ever find their way out.

But I won't be going out, she reminded herself. The sting of tears threatened several times as she kept moving, staring at her uncle's back as he led the way, swords drawn.

At one juncture, they stopped to get their bearings. Mey was relying on the Heartstone to lead her in the right direction. The pull she felt in her chest accelerated her urgency to continue the further in they traveled.

Thom, Elerbee and Durlag were already showing signs of confusion of time. Thom told a story of being back in Val, saying it had happened just yesterday. And Durlag and Elerbee insisted that tomorrow they would arrive at the Dharst Hills. The only thing those two had agreed on for the months they'd spent on the road.

"Uncle, why are we not affected?" she asked as they climbed a small rise.

"Elves are long lived and dragons nearly timeless. We are not bound by the same laws of time as humans, dwarves and lesser creatures."

Bob seemed distracted by something so she refrained from asking any more questions. She didn't have to, anyway. He turned abruptly, stopping mid-stride.

"Can you hear that?"

Pausing to take in the sounds around her, she did indeed hear a faint murmur of many voices.

"Chanting," she said.

"We're close." He moved to Elerbee and looked him right in the eye. "We need you to try to give yourself, Thom and Durlag protection from the time-twisting effects."

Elerbee nodded slowly, a bit confused, but he knelt to ask for his god's divine intervention. It didn't take long before he emanated the radiance of Sirrah, starting from the raised symbol in his neck and traveling down his arms into his hands.

He rose and laid a hand each on Thom and Durlag, the light moving into them as if being soaked through their skin. The light faded and all three looked around at their surroundings.

"Good?" Bob asked Elerbee.

"Yes." He looked to the other two who nodded in return.

"Follow me," Bob said. "Stay low and for all that is holy," he shot a pointed look at Durlag, "*be quiet.*"

Durlag glared and swigged on his flask before falling into position as the rear guard on their small group.

Crouching, they moved forward slowly, coming up to the lip of an opening. Light shimmered and danced at the entrance as people moved past the glow thrown from candles and torches.

As they crawled toward the opening and could see inside, Mey was surprised that there were not more people. It sounded like hundreds of voices when, in fact, there were only about thirty robed figures kneeling before a pool. A man at the far end of the room, stood alone before a figure who was bound on the ground.

What do you think they're doing? She sent the silent communication to them all. It was Elerbee's voice that came back to her.

It's a sacrificial ritual. And that, indeed, is the Elder.

"Who's that?" Durlag refused to communicate mentally, so his harsh whisper was a jolt.

Thom immediately threw a cloak of silence around them. They froze waiting to see if anyone had heard them over the chanting priests.

They all looked in the direction he pointed. Another man stood off to one side, his face partially turned and hidden in the shadows. He did not wear robes. His stature was slender and he stood with his arms folded across his chest.

Mey's attention only fell to this person briefly. The tug she had been feeling rose to an irresistible level pulling her gaze back to the Elder and the bound man. But it was not them that drew her attention.

The wall behind the Elder wavered with an unnatural haze. As much as she was loath to do it, she knew what she needed. She turned to Thom.

"I need the mask."

"What?"

"There's something behind that wall. I need the mask to show me."

"You're sure?" He scrutinized her face, his piercing eyes softening as he apparently was satisfied with what he saw there. She held out her hand. He took a moment to reach into the pack he carried over his shoulder. Retrieving a small box, he opened it and handed over the small mask.

Hastily tying the strings behind her head, she focused on the wall behind the Elder. The rock seemed to melt away and a tunnel, running back out of her line of sight appeared.

"A hidden path," she said aloud. Colored lights snaked close to the ground, leaping around the hidden entrance and she felt something beckoning her on. "That's the way to the Idylic. We have to find a way to get in there."

She took the mask from her face.

Looking at Thom, holding out the mask, she asked, "Can you immobilize the priests? Like you did outside?"

"I…I don't know how many would be affected."

"I can help with that," Elerbee put in.

"We can only assume this man in the corner is the mage the priests have paid to do their bidding." The thoughts were coming so fast now she had a hard time vocalizing it all. "Durlag, you and Bob can handle those that are left. Thom will deal with the mage…I have to get through that secret door."

"Maybe we should immobilize the mage first?" her uncle said.

"But we would be facing massive resistance from the priests at our back," she protested.

"I just think I should help Thom with the mage."

"Whatever. Durlag can handle the priests with Elerbee, right?" She looked at the dwarf, who smiled slyly.

"Yer talkin' to a Rockcrusher, dearie. Them dress-wearin'

priests are like flies." He then took a long, deep draw on the flask. "What're we waitin' for?"

"I'll have to lower the silence spell," Thom warned. They all fell silent.

Just as he made the last gestures that would break the cloak of silence, the man bound before the Elder moved to stand, drawing her attention.

A blow like that of a hammer hitting her solid in the chest nearly knocked her backward. It was only shock, however, and she took a step back.

Her gasp was sudden and very loud. "Garrin?"

His eyes locked on her. Everything around her exploded into movement, giving her no more time to ponder what on this world was happening. She heard Elerbee's and Thom's voices and Durlag's battle cry, but it was like a dream happening around her.

Someone shoved her from behind and yelled, "Get moving!" Blinking, she lost sight of Garrin when she looked up again. It couldn't have been him. She knew it was, though. Her heart told her it was him; it explained the necklace and the instances where she thought she had heard his voice.

The floor around one group of priests turned muddy and they sank, yelling out as they tried to move. Mey caught Elerbee's movement as she sprinted past. He waved his hand in the direction of the sinking priests and the floor became solid rock once more and the priest's yells became agonizing cries.

Thom held a large stone that guided a huge black mass through another group of priests. As it moved in, anything it contacted disappeared, leaving nothing at all behind it except a massive emptiness.

She cleared the small pool with a running leap, throwing a set of daggers as she flew over the water. They thudded into one of the three priests that had backed Garrin, still bound, against the wall. She landed lightly next to him, drawing Makagesh from her waist and Garrin's sword from the sheath at her hip.

"What took you so long?" he asked her, the familiar crooked smile beaming at her through a trail of caked blood that ran from his head down the length of his face. In one fluid movement, she slashed the ropes binding his hands and put the sword into them.

"Fight now, talk later."

Garrin spun away just as a massive spiked chain landed right where he was standing. An acrobat by trade, Garrin had taught himself to mingle those skills with his blade. Lunging forward, he sprung up and vaulted over the larger priest to land nimbly behind him. He lashed out with his sword, drawing a line of blood from the man's back.

Mey saw the priest's eyes were scarred by lines that formed an 'X' over each eye. She grimaced at his mangled face turning in time to watch as the mage in the corner threw a line of electricity that hit her uncle square in the chest and leapt out his back, the other line hitting Thom in the shoulder.

She growled and sprinted in the direction of the mage. The heat in her middle was coursing through her now, infusing her limbs with strength and lending to her speed.

Two priests intercepted her. They sprang at her, both swinging war hammers. She managed to twist out of the way of one blow, but another caught her on the shoulder with a force that made her drop the bone-handled dagger she held.

Pain shot up her arm but she could still move it. Grasping another dagger, she fell into a low crouch. Trying to divide her attention between this annoying interruption and her uncle and Thom, now up and moving, heading in the direction of the mage. Confident they would be fine, she focused solely on the two priests before her.

As one moved at her with his weapon raised again, the other started a chant. Can't let him get that spell out, she reasoned and her dagger flew at him. His hands came up to his throat, grasping at the small blade as his words became a gurgling sound and blood spilled from his lips. He fell to the ground.

She leaped, drawing another weapon and threw it, all in the same movement, down at the top of the priest's head even before he registered that she had moved. The blade stuck straight up from the top of his head as he, too, fell lifeless to the ground.

Looking for Thom and Bob, she found a scene that took her breath away. Her uncle lay in a twisted heap against the rocks, his legs and arms bent unnaturally. Blood ran in rivulets down one side of his face. Flashes of light and crackles of energy sparked next to him. Her shocked gaze moved to Thom and the mage throwing power-filled energy at one another, neither making progress as the energies met between them. She looked back to her uncle.

No. She mouthed the silent plea and she felt as though she was moving in slow motion as she willed her feet to move. She tried to connect with her uncle's mind as she ran. Her consciousness hit a wall each time. She sensed his bond was not broken but he was blocking her.

"Uncle!" she cried out. Thom's concentration broke for a split second as he looked to her.

"Mey, don't-" His words cut off suddenly in a gasp.

She slid to a stop, falling next to her uncle, ignoring the stinging scratches she inflicted on her knees.

His lips were moving, but she couldn't hear his words.

"Uncle Bob, stop. Stop speaking. You'll be fine." The words were lost in her sobs as she tried to wipe blood from his eyes. But his lips kept moving and his hand lifted. She bent close to him.

"Thom…" he whispered.

She turned. Thom was on the ground, hands clawing at his neck, lips tinged blue.

The heat coursing through her veins reached a searing boil. Clutching two daggers in her hands, she let a growl rumble in her throat and rip from her in a screeching yell as she bounded toward the figure standing over Thom.

As she did, the man looked up at her. She had thought she could not be shocked any more than when she realized Garrin was living and breathing and stood in the cave not ten feet from her. She was wrong.

All the blood in her body seemingly dropped to her feet leaving her numb as her breath came out in one great whoosh. Like the hammer blow she felt from the shock of seeing Garrin, this time it felt as though someone was pulling her in two and she felt the sting of the massive ragged wound.

The noise around of clashing swords and yells of fighting men died away instantly.

"Father?"

A flicker of recognition flitted in Rekho's eyes but died almost as quickly as it came. Instead he snarled at her and, still holding one hand out at Thom, lifted the other in her direction.

He didn't recognize her. She was changed, so different. She had to make him realize it was her.

"Father!" she screamed at him. "It's me! It's Meylaran. These are my friends! You have to stop! Uncle Bob," she pointed, "he needs our help!"

Rekho laughed. A crazed, frenzied laugh as he twisted the hand that was holding Thom in the choking spell. Thom's eyes rolled back in his head, his feet kicking as he tried to break free to draw breath.

"You're killing him!" she screeched at her father. "Stop!"

"A bug crushed in my way to destroying you," her father said. It wasn't the loving, soft voice she remembered. And spittle flew from his lips as he barked out another laugh.

He's going to kill him, she realized. *And then he intends to kill me.* She shook her head in disbelief even as she raised her daggers to ready a throw. She felt a powerful force overtake her body and her entire being went rigid. She could only move her eyes and she searched frantically around her as far as she could. Thom still clutched at his throat.

Please, she begged trying to speak to him with her mind, tears streaming down her cheeks. *Please stop.* It was a weak plea. She watched helplessly as Thom's legs kicked out once, then stilled. Rheko released his hold on the younger mage and Thom crumpled to the ground.

Her body began moving toward him and there was nothing she could do to stop it. As she came eye to eye with him she squeezed her eyes together, trying to will it all out of existence. This couldn't be happening. A sob ripped through the tenuous strands holding her heart together.

A soft noise made her eyes fly open. She saw Thom, and he drew a long breath, coughing at the effort it took. Her father didn't seem to notice. He was occupied with her.

"You have been a thorn in my side long enough!" He said. "I have tried over and over to give you a chance to quit this ridiculous notion of having dragons re-enter this world. You will NOT go further." His eyes were wild and crazed; this man before her was not her father. No longer the man whom she had loved and trusted with every fiber of her being. Not the man who had lulled her to sleep at night with stories of elven princesses.

Both of his hands were around her neck and he began to

squeeze. She felt the pressure that was quickly cutting off her airway and darkness began to rush into her vision. She felt a touch on her ankle and her muscles began to relax. With the last gasp of air she had, she managed to rasp, "I love you, Father." His eyes went wide. As he tried to speak, blood bubbled up through his lips. His grip on her neck loosened and his mouth moved, trying even now to defy the death that rushed to take him. He let go of her and she stumbled to the floor. He grabbed at the dagger sticking out from between his ribs.

In the next moment, her father lay in a heap on the rock floor. Her heart sank and her hands shook.

She flew at Thom and threw her arms around him as she sobbed. He drew a few more ragged breaths, then leaned away to look in her eyes.

"Your uncle."

Bob's breath came in short, hesitating bursts. Mey reached for his hand and took it in her own. His eyes moved to her as she leaned over him. With a will only an elf can posses, he found strength to utter the most beautiful words she had ever heard.

"Meylaran, *ah la'endra ute. Fur'ye.*"

His body relaxed as his life passed out into the world and his spirit mingled with the wind and infused with the tress, the plants and all living things; just as the elven people believed. She felt a part of him flow through her and embed itself into one of the pieces of her broken heart.

"I love you, too," she whispered, leaning close and softly kissing his forehead. "Forever."

"He gave everything for you to accomplish your journey." Thom said. He wrapped his arms around her and pulled her to him. She wept.

Lifting her head, she watched as Durlag and Elerbee approached, sorrow filled their eyes as they knelt next to Bob. Garrin stood near, watching her as she held on to Thom for dear life, fearful if she let go, she would fall into a black abyss that would swallow her whole.

"You still have to find the Idylic," Thom said to her quietly.

Elerbee said a prayer over her uncle's body. He looked to her and said, "You still have to finish this, Mey. Let his strength guide you now."

"My father..." she choked out.

"He wasn't your father any longer," Garrin spoke up. "He was consumed by evil, empty inside. That was not the man you told me of so often."

"Garrin." She broke from Thom to stand and approach him. She hugged him close. "What happened to you?"

"They made it look like I should have been dead. He ordered me brought to him. But he only used me to get to you."

There was more to that story; she saw it in his eyes, but she didn't push him. His pain was always his own, he didn't share.

She made vague introductions of the rest of the group that had gotten her safely to this point and explained her journey. He was fascinated by her dragon features but still had the same light-hearted outlook for things.

"I always knew you were special, kid."

She smiled slightly.

At the entrance to the secret tunnel, they stopped as Mey examined the opening. Taking a step through, the air instantly changed. It was charged and the urgency returned. The others followed her lead.

Sparks of colored lights floated down the path, always staying ahead of her, as if they were guiding her.

The pathway widened gradually, and a soft blue light glowed distantly beyond another pool of clear water. Peering in, she saw huge clusters of the sparkling farthen crystals Thom had used to weave the magic that let him contact the Mage's Circle. She heard his sharp intake of breath as he approached, not far behind her.

"I've never seen so many in one place."

"It's beautiful."

Just past the pool, the blue glow brightened and the lights danced wildly at the base of a set of stairs. They were crumbling but their shape was discernable. Mey felt the strong tug pulling her forward. Thom's hand slid into hers and he squeezed lightly.

They walked together toward the light, the rest following them, strangely quiet. Even Durlag remained hushed as they ascended the short flight.

Mey had to put her free hand up to shield her eyes. Light prismed and shimmered and created blinding bright bursts. Color swirled through the white starbursts and wind blew in great gusts across the open cavern. Crystal formations stuck out of the walls, the ceiling and the floor, throwing light endlessly around the room.

There was a shape in the center of the room. Mey squinted at the unmoving image and it came into view. A stone structure rising as tall as the cavern itself. As her eyes adjusted to the swirling lights around her, she could better focus on the effigy.

A glorious creature, rising regally from the stone base, the etched detail of the scales, wings, claws and face were faultless. No sculptor on Cantor could have created something so perfect.

Mey drew the Heartstone from her pouch. Looking from it to the statue, she saw the portion missing from the dragon's chest, where the heart should be situated. A low hum sounded and the shard in her hands began to vibrate slightly. The statue was calling to it, wanting to be rejoined with the absent part that would again make it whole.

Turning to face Thom and her friends, she knew what she had to do. She would never see them again, not as a person that could share laughter and feeling and love with them.

She touched Thom's cheek. Tears blurred his image briefly before they fell, unchecked down her face. "I love you. Don't ever forget."

"Mey." He choked on her name.

"No words," she said. She leaned in to him, their lips almost touching. "Just feel." She kissed him, letting everything she ever felt flow through her into him, infusing every pore and binding them together with tenderness, rapture, passion, hurt, pain, love. Everything they would never share in this life, she gave to him in the few moments they had left.

As she pulled away, she faced the others. The friends that had stood next to her, fought beside her and made sure she followed the right path. She said her goodbyes to each of them. She knew what she had to sacrifice to ensure humanity survived and gave goodness a chance to triumph the growing evil.

She turned to face the statue and took a faltering step forward, placing her foot carefully among the crystal stalagmites. Then another and another, until she stood before the towering structure. Her mouth was dry and her breath came fast. With her heart pounding in her ears, she found a foothold on the stone base and climbed to where she could reach the chest.

The stone fit perfectly as she placed it. A bright light shone around the cracks and molded it solidly in place. The hum rose to a deafening level and Mey held on desperately so the impact of power wouldn't knock her to the floor, where crystal stalagmites larger than a man shot up in lethal points.

She heard Thom call out to her. But lights so bright she thought for certain she'd gone blind erupted all around. A white-hot fire burned through her middle, spreading to her limbs and all the colors she could imagine and some she had never dreamed existed moved around her. Her body bowed forward involuntarily and her back burned as she felt something erupt through bone and skin. I'm dead, she thought.

As she arched back, her hands ripped from the stone structure, she knew she would land on one of the deadly crystal spikes. But her body floated securely above the floor, weightless.

She caught glimpses of color again but these were solid shapes. Moving so fast they were merely blurs in her vision. Gradually they slowed and she could see them clearly. Dragons. Graceful, elegant bodies slid lazily through the air around her. She turned all around but couldn't see her friends. Only the light and the dragons.

There was a brighter spot not far in the distance and she concentrated on it. Coming into focus, it was the most awesome creature she had ever seen. A brilliant golden dragon with eyes the color of clear, pink crystal. She felt her feet find solid purchase on the ground before it. Instinctively she bowed her head low.

"Meylaran." The voice was sweet music in her ears. "Stand."

She obeyed.

"You've opened the doorway for us."

"Yes. As I was meant to do. The world needs your presence to survive. The balance of evil has overcome all else and is consuming mankind."

"You are needed as well."

She shook her head, her heart heavy with pain and sorrow.

"I completed my task on this world. I accept that I must now move on."

The golden dragon was silent for a time.

"I see that you have, then. You have sacrificed much to become one of us. Behold your true self, Meylaran." The dragon gestured to a large shimmering oval and she stepped closer to it.

Raising her head, she stared into liquid silver eyes. The richest purple she had ever seen infused the scales covering her body and majestic wings flowed out from her back and fluttered once. How could this beautiful creature be her? When her hand reached out, the image's hand reached as well. Hard as it was for her to believe, *this* was her true form.

"Your mother sacrificed as well. You have inherited her generous nature."

"Thank you. Will you enter the world now? Will you make sure justice prevails?"

"We will. Will you join us?"

"I…I thought I would have to." There was no keeping her confusion hidden, he would read it in her thoughts even if she tried. Wasn't that her destiny? Wasn't the end of her journey to become a dragon and serve the people of Cantor?

"I can bestow upon you one gift for your magnanimous sacrifice." He smiled at her with such sincerity she found herself smiling back at him. "I know your deepest desire. I can see it in your heart. Would you have me grant it to you?"

"But what of my duty? Certainly I cannot have both."

"I am offering you both. If you speak it, it will be so."

There was no way she could be so lucky. Would they let her have her fondest wish so easily? There had to be strings attached. Her whole life had been giving up things she loved and cared for. No way could she have it all.

He was waiting for her answer. She had done what she was born to do. She had opened the doorway for the dragons. Why not take what he obviously thought she deserved for accomplishing that? She could feel her heart bursting with excitement at the prospect.

"I chose…" She closed her eyes and pictured Thom. In seconds she imagined an entire life with him, a home, children, all while keeping true to her dragon heritage and serving the people. Being able to walk among dragons and human-kind alike; it was her deepest desire and one she thought she would never have. A single tear slid down her scaled cheek.

The golden raised his wings wide and spread them around her.

"So be it."

ABOUT THE AUTHOR

Lela Robichaux is a contributing writer for local publications in her Northern Louisiana hometown. She has been a fan of writing and reading fantasy and science fiction since she was a teenager. She recently took a plunge and went back to school and graduated in 2015 with her Bachelor of Arts in English, where she was a member of the English honor society, Sigma Tau Delta and the History honor society, Phi Alpha Theta. She has served as a research assistant for one of her professors on the local history of prominent figures in her hometown. She loves spending time with friends, reading, writing and "nerding out" with her husband and son.

16738934R00145

Printed in Great Britain
by Amazon